When a Good Girl Falls for a Boss

When a Good Girl Falls for a Boss

B. Chanel

www.urbanbooks.net

Urban Books, LLC
300 Farmingdale Road, N.Y.-Route 109
Farmingdale, NY 11735

When a Good Girl Falls for a Boss

ISBN 13: 978-1-64556-698-4

First Trade Paperback Printing June 2025
Printed in the United States of America

10 9 8 7 6 5 4 3 2 1

Distributed by Kensington Publishing Corp.
Submit Orders to:
Customer Service
400 Hahn Road
Westminster, MD 21157-4627
Phone: 1-800-733-3000
Fax: 1-800-659-2436

The authorized representative in the EU for product safety and compliance
Is eucomply OU, Parnu mnt 139b-14, Apt 123
Tallinn, Berlin 11317, hello@eucompliancepartner.com

When a Good Girl Falls for a Boss

by

B. Chanel

Dedication

To my dad: I never thought I'd be doing this without you being here to witness everything your girl is becoming. You're supposed to be here celebrating with me, telling me how proud you are, but it's okay because I feel it. I feel you all around me. The fight in me came from you. From a distance, you molded me. You told me to breathe easy when something knocks the wind outta me, but what do I do when that something is you? I'm still waiting to breathe easy, Dad. I love you, and I miss you like crazy. Rest in peace, Clinton D. Hall, Sr.

Dominik Andreas: This one's for you, babe! Every day, I strive to be a better version of myself for you, and even when I fall short, you still look at me like I'm the greatest, and because of you, I am. You've been my saving grace, and for you, I am thankful. I love you, Pootie!!!

Acknowledgments

Ma: Girl!!!! Thank you for every time that you've taken my boy so I could write, sleep, whatever it took to accomplish this dream of mine. When I told you I wanted to write, you were so supportive, like that was the best thing you'd ever heard, and I can't tell you how much I appreciate you. IT'S UP, BABY! I love you, girl!

Onna: Best friend, you told me I could, and guess what? I did! Taking this step had my nerves shook, but you always told me that I got this. I couldn't imagine doing life without you in my corner, so get ready, because it's champagne time!

Parkssss: For every time we watched the clock hit 3 a.m., every idea, for all the stress I put you through writing this book, lawd, thank you. It's nothing but genuine love for you on my end, boo. Now let's get ready for round two. lolllll!

Latoya Nicole: I know I probably stress you all the way out, but I appreciate you for taking a chance on me and pushing me. You're more than a publisher to me. You're my friend, and I can't thank you enough.

Chapter One

Dreux McCoy

Driving through the streets of Dallas at two a.m. was always my go-to when I had a lot on my mind. Three months ago, I graduated from El Centro College with a degree in diagnostic medical sonography, and two weeks later, I found my best friend of fourteen years dead in her bathtub. The happiest time of my life was also the worst. Every night since I found her, I would wake up in cold sweats at one a.m., and by two, I was in my car cruising the streets, crying my eyes out. Some nights, I'd be so out of it I wouldn't even remember how I ended up in certain places. Like the night I woke up on a bench in Kiest Park.

My eyes were cloudy from the tears I was trying to keep from falling as I listened to "Missing You" from Set It Off for the millionth time, I'm sure. I missed my girl, and I'm not sure how I would be strong enough to move forward with her being gone. Pulling into the Denny's on Skillman, I sat in my car for fifteen minutes, gathering myself before I got out. I threw my hood on, stepped out of the car with my head down, and made my way inside.

"Welcome to Denny's. Will it be just one?" the chick at the counter asked.

All I could do was nod with my head still down.

"Would you like a table or a booth, ma'am?"

"I'll take a booth in the back." My reply was barely above a whisper.

Following her to my booth, I slid in and ordered a coffee, hoping that would make me feel a little better. When the server brought my coffee out, I pulled off my hoodie. When I looked up, my eyes locked with the most handsome man I'd ever seen. This man was everything a woman could wish for, standing at about 6 feet 3 inches, looking to be about 215 pounds. His sculpted, cocoa-colored body was nothing but pure muscle, covered in tattoos from his neck to his arms. He had juicy pink lips and hooded hazel eyes that would make a gay bitch reconsider. I think the way his hair was cut is called a drop fade, with the sexiest black curls and a part on the side. It instantly had my kitty dripping.

What the hell is going on?

He was dressed in all black from head to ankles. On his feet were a pair of red Retro 11s. My ass was staring hard as hell, and when I scanned back up his body, he licked his lips and winked at me. I felt my face getting hot, so I knew my cheeks were red as hell from blushing. The way he stared at me with those honey-tinted bedroom eyes made me feel so naked. Looking down, I pulled my phone out of my pocket and started scrolling through Facebook.

"Can I refill your coffee, ma'am?" the server asked me.

I was so caught up in my phone that I forgot I was even at Denny's. "Oh, no thank you. I'm okay. I'll take the check when you have a chance."

"Yes, ma'am."

Finishing up my coffee, I checked the time and realized it was after four in the morning. Pulling my hoodie back on, I made my way to the register to pay. As I was walking to my car, I heard a voice from behind me.

"Aye, li'l bit, hold on. Let me talk to you," the mystery voice called out.

When I slowly turned around, there he stood.

"My bad. I know this is probably awkward as hell for you, but you're beautiful. I'm sure you've heard that a million times, but I gotta know you. I can't, and I won't, leave this parking lot without your name and number." He was extremely confident.

"I'm sorry. I really appreciate that, but right now isn't a good time for me to be making new friends. I got a lot of shit going on, and I'm just not feeling it." As soon as I replied, I got in my car. *Damn,* I thought, *even when I look a fucking mess, I still got it.* Pulling off, I left him standing there looking pissed.

One month later

Lying in my bed, my mind drifted to my best friend, Ebony. Her funeral was a few months ago, and it was by far one of the hardest things I'd ever endured. I missed her like crazy, but I knew I couldn't live like this. I threw the covers off me, grabbed my phone, and headed to the bathroom to take a shower. I connected my iPhone to the surround-sound system and stripped out of my pajamas.

As I let the water fall over my body, Keke Wyatt was singing everything I was feeling. My mind drifted to the man from the diner. I hadn't seen him since that night, but there was something about him I just couldn't shake. It had been a month, and I still wondered what he was like, what made him laugh, and what he did for fun. Just thinking back on that night, I wanted him in the worst way, but my inner shy girl wouldn't let me be great. When he stepped to me, I didn't know what to do. Maybe I could have given him my number, but I didn't wanna seem easy, and for some reason, I figured he would find me if he wanted to.

While I was strolling down memory lane, my phone started to ring, and when I lifted it, I saw it was my sister, Ahdia.

"Heyyyyy, sis."

"Siiiiiis! What are you doing? I miss you," she screamed in my ear.

"I'm not doing a thing. Just finished showering, and I plan on cooking some breakfast before I head to work. What's up?" I asked, laughing. See, that's the thing with me and my sister. We could go days without talking, but when we did, the vibe was always the same.

"Shit, let me get dressed, and I'll be over. You know I love food. You and Mom have spoiled me something serious."

Her greedy ass was right. We always cooked for her.

"Come on, crazy-ass girl. It should be done by the time you get here."

This bitch didn't even say bye. Pulling the phone from my ear, I walked over to the fridge to see what I could whip together for her fat ass and decided on oatmeal, bacon, biscuits, and strawberries. As much as I wanted to throw down for breakfast, my mood wouldn't let me.

Fifteen minutes passed, so I picked up my phone to call my sister and see where she was. It shouldn't have taken her but five minutes to get here. Before I could push her contact name, Ahdia and her loud-ass mouth came waltzing through my front door.

"Dreuskiiiiiiiii! I'm here," she yelled through the hallway.

Like always, I cringed at the sound of her high-pitched voice. No matter how old we got, I would never get used to that shit.

"Dia, damn. Why you yelling like it ain't nine a.m.? Your mouth is loud enough to wake the dead. Shit."

"I don't know why you act like I ain't been loud all twenty-two years of my life. You and I both know that shit is never changing."

Unfortunately, she was right. I don't think she knew what an inside voice was. I took a seat at the island across from my sister and admired her beauty. Despite sharing the same parents, we were complete opposites. Her skin glowed the color of rich salted caramel, and her slim face housed a set of light gray eyes that could hypnotize even the strongest man. She had high cheekbones, a slender nose, and big, beautiful lips that she kept glossed. Since the day she was born, she was my baby, and I would protect her with my life.

"Dreux, you're doing that thing again." Dia shook her head and rolled her eyes.

"What am I doing, Ahdia? I haven't said a thing, nor have I moved." Looking at her like she was crazy, I waited for her to respond.

"You're staring at me with that stupid grin on your face."

Jumping off the stool, I walked around the table and grabbed her face in my hands. "That's because you're my little baby, and I never grow tired of this sweet face." All I could do was laugh as I squeezed her cheeks because I knew she hated that.

"Blahhhhh whatever. So, listen. It's time to get you out of your funk. I miss hanging out with you like we used to do before . . ." She let her voice trail off.

"It's okay. I know. I miss hanging out with you too. So what do you have in mind?"

"Wellllll, Parker put a bug in my ear about the grand opening of a club on Saturday night. I was thinking about sliding through to see whose man I could leave with." Sticking her tongue out, she started twerking in her chair.

Shit, here she goes. I will never understand why she don't want her own man. Hell.

"Okay, that's fine. I ain't been out in a long-ass time, so I need to find something to wear."

"Cool. I'm heading to the mall as soon as I leave here. My ass got a closet full of clothes, but I gotta make sure I'm the baddest bitch in the room. Yaaaaaassss!" Dia was turned up as if we were in the club already.

"Of course, I wouldn't expect anything less than. You know we shut shit down wherever we go. I have a short day at the clinic today, so when I close up shop, I'm gonna shoot to the Galleria and see what I can find."

"Ooooh, I didn't even think of going to the Galleria. I was gon' go to NorthPark, and if I didn't find anything, I was heading to Parks in Arlington. That's why you're the oldest." Laughing, Dia got up to leave.

"Yeah, let that be the reason. I'll see you later, boo." Handing over her belongings, I got up with her.

After kissing her cheeks and walking her to the door, I proceeded to clean up the mess we made during breakfast. I always enjoy having my sister over, because she was the breath of fresh air I needed when I constantly felt like I was suffocating.

Finishing up, I made my way to the bedroom so I could get dressed and take my ass to work. I walked into my closet, flipped through my many pairs of scrubs, and reminisced on how far I'd come. I'd sunk so low after Ebony's death that I just knew that I would eventually lose my job at Tiny Heartbeats, one of the best clinics in Texas. It was a fight to get where I was, and I was grateful to have made it. I decided on a pair of pink scrubs, since it was breast cancer awareness month, and my all-white Adidas originals. Walking into the bathroom, I pulled my shoulder-length curls into a bun at the nape of my neck and brushed my teeth. Taking the steps two at a time, I grabbed the keys to my custom-painted olive green Mercedes Benz C350 that my daddy bought for graduation, and I was out the door.

With my windows down and "Mo City Don" blazing through my speakers, I backed out of the driveway to my condo in Highland Park and jumped on 35, heading toward downtown Dallas. I hated the days that I worked from 12 p.m. to 5 p.m. because I caught traffic going to and from work, with people going to lunch in the afternoon and then home in the evening.

As I pulled into my job, Big Moe was getting my mind right, because even though I loved my job, some of these hoes sure could take me there. I picked up my lunch and my MK crossbody bag and made my way inside.

As soon as I entered the door, Nariyah, the receptionist, spoke. "Good afternoon, Dreux. How are you today?"

Here this bitch goes. She knows damn well I don't fuck with her.

"Hey, Nariyah. I'm good. You?" Even though I asked her, I really didn't give a damn.

"Me too, girl. You got a full schedule today, so I hope you got some rest and wasn't out creeping at two a.m." She chuckled, throwing shade.

This bitch knew that was a touchy subject for me, so I guess she thought shit was sweet. Leaning down so only she could hear me, I whispered in her ear, "Don't act like I won't take you outside and beat yo' ass like yo' ho-ass mama should have a long time ago. Play me close again, Nariyah. I can show you better than I can tell you. Now, you have a great day."

Leaving her sitting behind the counter, flustered, I headed to my office to prepare myself for my patient. I needed to take a few minutes to gather myself because I was still healing, and this raggedy bitch just really took me to a place I'd been fighting to escape from.

I grabbed the file off my desk, entered the ultrasound room, and waited for Ms. Johnson to come in. Ten minutes later, my first mommy of the afternoon waddled her way to the exam table. Ms. Johnson was one of my favorite patients. It was like a light came from her every time she came in for an ultrasound, because that's how bright her personality shined.

"Good afternoon, Ms. Johnson, How are you and the little one feeling today?" My ass was too excited.

"Oh, girl, I keep telling you to call me Peyton. Ms. Johnson makes me feel old, lord, but we're doing okay. I hope this munchkin is feeling up to showing itself today. I'm so ready to know what I'm having."

I could tell she was excited. "Well, let's just take a look. We'll start with the little heartbeat, and before you ask, yes, the gel is warm." I swear I loved my job and the bonds I made with all of my patients.

Squeezing the warm ultrasound gel on her small belly, I moved the transducer around until we finally heard the tiny heartbeat.

"Wow, Mom, one fifty-six. That's a strong heartbeat for such a tiny girl," I said, making sure I slipped the sex in there.

"A what? Did you say girl? I knew it. I can't wait to tell her daddy. I hate that he couldn't be here for this today, but I'm gonna look so good in that G-Wagon that he owes me now." Her laughter was catchy.

"Well, shoot, if that's what they're handing out for having babies, then I need to get on it." While wiping the gel from her stomach, I joined in on the laughter. After I printed her pictures, I gave her a huge hug and sent her on the way.

It seemed as though the hours flew by after Peyton left, and before I knew it, it was five. Wrapping up some last-minute scheduling, I gathered my things, locked my office, and headed out the door. When I made it to the front of the clinic, I made sure to deliver one final message to Nariyah. You know, just on some petty shit.

"Aye, buttercup, don't forget our little chat, okay?" Winking at her, I walked out of the door.

Jumping in my car, I took my ass straight home. After a day like today, I figured I could find something to wear to this party another time because I was beat.

Chapter Two

Kamron Vega

Lying in bed, staring at the ceiling, I started contemplating my life. I'd been terrorizing the streets of Dallas since I was eighteen, fucking bitches since I was thirteen, and now I was twenty-nine and tired of the shit. I was tired of having no one to share this big-ass California king with, tired of walking around in silence, no laughter in my mansion, and no sounds of tiny feet running across my marble floors. After a year in the pen, I knew it was time to do something different.

Throwing the blanket off, I got my ass out of the bed to handle my hygiene. I'd been home for almost three months, and the only person who knew was my moms, because I wanted to sit back in the shadows and watch how my business was moving. I decided that today would be the day I came out of hiding, and the first person I planned to pull up on was my right-hand man, Dash. He'd been my nigga since he moved here from Illinois, and I had yet to cross a muthafucka as solid as him. Dash was one of them niggas where, if shit started going south, I'd never have to worry about him rolling over on a G. As sappy as it may sound, I appreciated the fuck out of him.

I grabbed my Dove Men+Care body wash and walked into the bathroom to adjust the water so the temperature wasn't too hot or too cold. I shed the wife beater and shorts that I slept in and stepped into the shower. Standing under the waterfall-style shower head, I let the warm water cascade over my body. When I went to wash my dick, that muthafucka was harder than high school chemistry.

It had been years since I jacked off. Shit, I didn't even jack off in prison, but thinking about Dreux had my dick on brick, and I needed to bust a nut. I squeezed some body wash on my hand and started stroking my dick nice and slow. I closed my eyes, dropped my head back, and Dreux invaded my mind. The curve of her hips, the curl of her smile, and the way her eyes peered through my soul had my nut at the tip of my dick. I stroked my shit faster, and before I knew it, I shot a gallon of cum on the shower floor. Feeling relieved, I washed my piece off again, turned off the water, and stepped out of the shower. Wrapping my towel around my waist, I brushed my pearly whites while I was in there and headed into my closet to find something to jump into. Since this would be the first time the hood had seen me in over a year, I decided to come out dripping sauce.

I flipped on the light switch, and my closet wall slid open. My drawers popped out, giving me an eyeful to all the shit I missed being locked up. Thanks to my mans, my wardrobe was laced with the flyest shit of the year. Looking through the drawers and hangers, I settled on black Tom Ford trousers, a casual, solid black long-sleeve, with a black belt and all-black Tom Ford loafers—some shit that would let you know a boss was in your presence. I walked over to my jewelry case and grabbed my gold big-face Rolex along with two gold rope chains. I had two diamond earrings, one in each ear, that I never took off, not even in the pen, so I was good.

Checking myself out in the mirror, I brushed my hair down on the sides and ran my hand through my curls, debating on whether I was gon' cut this shit off or not. While I was locked up, my shit grew past my shoulders. I ain't trust them jailhouse barbers, so I kept it in a low ponytail, but as soon as I popped lock, I got my hair cut back to my signature drop fade. Stroking my beard, I gave myself a head nod, flashed a smile, and was on my way.

Walking through my bedroom, I picked up my phone and grabbed the keys to my blacked-out Audi R8. I hadn't touched my baby since I'd been home, but today was our time to get reacquainted. Backing out of my garage, I took the long drive down to the wrought iron gate that surrounded my mansion, and once it swung open, I made my way to Clean Cutz, my favorite barbershop. As much as I loved my house out in Rockwall, this hour-ass drive to Oak Cliff for a haircut got on my damn nerves, especially since Dallas had the worse fucking traffic on earth.

Pulling up in the hood, I could see people looking and pointing, knowing that the only muthafucka with this R8 was me. I ain't even gon' front. That shit stroked my ego a li'l bit. When I finally made it to the shop, I saw Dash's car out front, and as soon as I stepped out of the car and hit the locks, the kids from the neighborhood ran up to me. This was one thing I took pride in: giving back to the same streets that took so much from our youth.

"Mr. Vega. Man, where you been? The hood ain't been right without you sliding through." Tytus, one of the teenagers said.

"Aww, my man, I was outta pocket for a li'l minute, but I'm back. Y'all gon' be straight."

They nodded as they listened to me talk.

"We know. You never let us go hungry. You really like the hood Santa Claus to us, and we appreciate it fo'real fo'real." Tytus was excited as hell.

Hearing him say they appreciated what I did touched a nigga in a place I ain't felt in a long time. I reached into my pocket and pulled out a knot of money. They knew what time it was, because they started to form a circle around me. As I peeled off ten twenties for each kid that was out there, the shit really tugged at my heart because these kids didn't deserve this shit. If I could, I'd take all of them home with me. The young dudes dapped me up, and the little girls hugged me, thanking me for being what they needed in the hood.

After cooling it with the kids for another minute, I walked into the shop, and like I knew it would, the muthafucka went up.

"Ohhhhhh, what the fuck is this? Nigga, when did yo' ass pop lock?" Dash yelled when I walked in.

"Myyy nigga, fuck is up? I broke chain 'bout three months ago. I just been laying low with moms." Laughing, I pulled him into a brotherly hug. "I took a minute to sit back and see how my muthafuckin' business was running without me."

"Man, bro, you know as long as I have breath in my body, this shit gon'always be straight. We been doing this too long to let it go under." Dash got all passionate. Crazy thing was, I knew that. If nobody in this world had my back outside of my moms, Dash did. In the three months that I'd been kicking back, not once had shit fell off or even looked like it was going to. It's one thing to be locked up and hearing that your shit is still good, but to see it from the shadows was something different, and that let me know that I picked some thorough-ass niggas to ride with me.

"Yeah, fam. I'm already knowing. I didn't doubt for one second that you'd make sure shit stayed afloat. Aye, Iggy, lemme get next. I know you see this bullshit growing on my head." We all laughed.

"Ight my nigga, you got that. But don't make it a habit." Iggy, one of my soldiers, replied, smiling.

My nigga Donk was the coldest barber in Dallas, so muthafuckas stayed beating down the shop, tryna get in. Whenever I came through, he would make whoever was in the chair raise up, but I'm not that kind of nigga unless I need to be, so usually I'd wait. Not today, though. I had shit to do. After he finished the head he was cutting, I made my way over to the chair and dapped him up because, you know, germs.

"Chop, how it feel to be out the chain gang, bro?" Donk asked.

"Maaaaan to keep it a hunnid witchu, shit still feel unreal that I even got knocked. We been doing this shit for years, and ain't nobody ever fell victim to the system, now all of a sudden, they lock me up? Naw, some shit ain't right." That shit had been on my mind.

"I knew I wasn't the only one that felt like that. It's a muthafuckin rat in our shit, and I'on care what nobody says," Dash piped up.

"We'll talk." Leaving it at that, I turned to my barber. "Say, Donk, lemme get my signature cut and take the curls off, man. I'm rocking the waves from now on." My ass was over them damn curls.

Twenty minutes later, Donk was finally done cutting me up, and when he slapped that alcohol shit on the back of my neck, I almost beat his ass. Bitch-ass nigga had me feeling like Trey from *Don't Be a Menace.*

"Ight, bitch, you could have warned me shit, ol' playful-ass nigga." Laughing, I fanned my head.

"Aye, real shit, fam, we missed you in these streets, terrorizing niggas and shit. Whatever is going on in yo' camp, find it, eliminate it, move on." Donk was attempting to drop some knowledge.

"You already know how I do. 'Preciate the cut. No change." Dapping him up, I slid him a hundo.

"Dashir, meeting tomorrow at seven a.m." Nodding at Dash, I walked out the door.

"Say less."

Jumping back into my whip, I headed back to the house to get my mind right for tomorrow. The way I was feeling, it was gon' be some slow singing and flower bringing real soon. All this bullshit had a nigga forgetting how backed up I was. I fucked a few bitches here and there the first few I was home, but ever since the night I met Dreux, I ain't had a desire to fuck shit else. I wanted her in the worst way possible. Knowing I needed a release and quick, I pulled my phone out my pocket, calling up one of the shorties I had on standby.

"Hello." This thick li'l bitch Shakala answered.

"Aye, you tryna suck this dick or what?" I said, getting straight to it.

"You know the address," her thirsty ass replied and hung up.

See, that's why I fucked with her freaky ass. All she wanted to do was suck my dick and g'on on. She wasn't beat for no extra shit, so I always made sure to break her off when I came through. I pulled up to her crib in the Grove and jumped out, hitting the locks two times. Jogging up her steps, the door swung open before I could even knock.

"Damn, shorty. Was you waiting on me?" All I could do was laugh when I walked in.

"Nigga please. Who the fuck else is it? I heard when you locked yo' funky-ass doors." She rolled her eyes, but I didn't give a fuck.

I went and sat on her couch, thanking God that she wasn't a nasty-ass bitch. Without missing a beat, she slid down on her knees, freeing my dick at the same time.

Before I could even relax, she had all ten inches down her throat, eating it up.

"Fuckkkk, Kaa. Suck that shit." This muthafucka had my dick and balls in her mouth and *still* managed to lick the gooch. She pulled my shit out, and a trail of saliva came with it. Using those soft-ass hands, she double-handed my piece while sucking the head, and I almost lost it. This li'l bitch had me moaning like a female. When she ran her tongue up the thick vein underneath my dick, I grabbed her head and shoved my rod back down her neck. As soon as I heard her gag, I was done for. I pulled out and nutted all over her titties, preparing to get cussed at.

"Choppa, what the fuck? You always doing that dumb-ass shit when you know damn well I swallow." Shorty was pissed.

Laughing, I ain't say shit as I tucked my dick back in my drawers. Instead, I peeled off three Benjamins and tossed them on the coffee table.

"A'ight, shorty, I'll get up with you. Keep that mouth wet." That was the last thing I said as I walked out the door.

Whoo, shit, baby girl got some award-winning head, I thought to myself. Hopping back in my R8, I drove toward the house because after neck that fire, a nigga needed a nap.

Chapter Three

Ahdia McCoy

After kicking it with my sister, I headed to the mall to do my best shit—shop. My parents spoiled me and Dreux, so it was nothing to burn a hole in Daddy's black card. Everyone thought my daddy was just a bomb-ass lawyer, but he was really the plug. I don't know how he managed to remain low-key, but if it worked for him, then it worked for me.

I didn't give a damn how old "The Weekend" by SZA got, I was gon' blow every time with my no-singing ass. That was the type of time I was on. I didn't want a relationship that was mine. Hell, I was content fucking somebody else's man. No strings attached, bih. Most people thought, *she's a home-wrecking ho,* and shit they was just about right. The only thing was, I didn't let these niggas get caught up.

Pulling up to the Galleria, I threw my Model S Tesla in park, pulled down the visor, and looked myself over. I'm a pretty-ass bitch and I know it. I stand at 5 foot 8, nothing but legs, a good 175, with small breasts and a nice round ass. It isn't a stupid booty, but it's enough to make heads turn. Once I put on my Literally by Kylie Jenner lip gloss, I grabbed my bag and headed inside. It was something about shopping that put me in such a relaxed mood.

I adjusted the straps to my Louis Vuitton backpack and strolled to the True Religion store. Feeling my phone vibrate in my back pocket, I rolled my eyes when I saw who it was.

Bugaboo #1: Bae when you gon' stop playing and let me suck on that pussy?

Me: When you can afford something other than the dollar menu at McDonalds, nigga bye.

I was so busy texting this whack-ass nigga back that I wasn't paying attention to where I was walking. Before I knew it, I'd bumped into the whole fucking wall, or so I thought. Recovering, I looked up into the face of the most gorgeous man I'd ever seen. He was dark, like roasted coffee minus the creamer, with the prettiest set of perfectly aligned white teeth. Although he wore a mean mug, I couldn't help but notice how his eyes matched the color of his skin. Like I knew she would, Ms. Kitty was jumping in this thin-ass thong I was wearing.

"I'm so sorry. I wasn't paying attention to where I was going, obviously." Apologizing, I continued to look him over.

"Yeah, well, maybe you should get the fuck off the phone when you walking through a busy-ass mall. Keep you from running into muthafuckas," his rude ass retorted.

"Well, damn, it was an accident. Yo' fine ass ain't gotta be so rude, but I'll take your little advice. You have a nice day." I walked off, not giving him a chance to respond.

Damn, I thought to myself, *I didn't even look at his penis, but as fine and rude as he was, that shit gave off big dick energy.* As I walked around the True Religion store, thumbing through shit I knew I didn't need, I had a half mind to turn around and look for my future daddy bae. Settling on some super skinny distressed jeans and a velvet bomber jacket, I handed my shit to the cashier.

When I reached into my wallet to pull out my card, I felt somebody press their big dick against my ass. Imagine my surprise when I turned around and bumped right back into Mr. Rudeness.

"Here you go, ma. Put that shit on this." He smirked as he handed over his black card.

See, most bitches would have been like, "nah, I got it," but me? Shiiiid. You wanna pay for my stuff, then who the fuck was I to stop you? Grabbing my bag from the cashier, I brushed past whatever the fuck his name was, trying to get to my car as fast as I could because the way my libido was set up, I'd be fucking this man in the parking garage.

"Damn, you just gon' take the shit and leave? No thank you?" I heard him say from behind me.

Against my better judgment, I stopped and turned around. "Well, for one, I didn't ask you to pay for shit, so yes, I'm taking my bag and getting away from you."

"What the fuck did I do to you? Last I checked, you bumped into me, so if anybody reserves the right to be rude and shit, I do." Oh, he was mad.

"Okay, and? I bumped into you, I apologized, and I left. You decided to turn around and come find me. You decided to pay for my shit. Hell, I don't even know your fucking name. I stopped owing you anything right after I apologized, so if you don't mind, I'm leaving. Once again, you have a nice day." With that being said, I turned and headed back to my car.

"Dash," I heard him say, and as bad as I wanted to go back and tell him my name, I couldn't. He seemed to be a pretty decent guy, and the last thing I needed was for the ho in me to taint him. Did I really just think that? Like, I actually considered someone else's feelings. What the hell was the world coming to?

Getting in my car, I pulled out of the parking garage and merged onto 75 toward Princeton and my parents' house. I hit play on my phone, and "Single" by Killumantii feat. Omeretta started blasting through the speakers. This song described exactly why I couldn't fuck with these niggas. They wanted us to play faithful to their cheating asses but couldn't handle what they dished out. Fuck them.

After an hour of driving, I finally arrived at my parents' house in Princeton. I reminisced about life growing up and how we didn't always live in the biggest house on the block, but it was always decent. When Big Drew and Lolita first met, he was a dopeboy putting himself through law school. Mama was a gum-popping, hoop earring-wearing, loud-talking around the way girl. They couldn't stand each other from what they told us, but over time, a friendship formed, and Big Drew tamed the ratchet beast that lived inside of my mom. By the time they were really in love, my dad was in his third year of law school, and Lolita was pregnant with Dreux. He'd planned to marry my mom once he graduated from law school, but when they found out about the baby, he decided not to wait any longer. They flew out to Vegas with my uncle and aunt and eloped, making it a moment just for them and no one else. Five years later, my daddy was one of the most sought-after criminal defense lawyers in the state, and lo and behold, Lolo was baking another baby—me. Growing up, my parents' love story was one I'd only imagined to have one day, but all it took was one incident to change my mind, and it had been "fuck these niggas" ever since.

Shaking outta my thoughts, I put my hand over the palm reader and waited for the wrought iron gate to slide open. I chuckled to myself. My daddy really had this place locked down like Fort Knox, but I guess when you're big-time like him, you don't have a choice. Making my way up this long-ass driveway, I admired my childhood home. Big Drew built this mini castle when I was five, and I'd loved it ever since. It was a Mediterranean-style home that had to be about 10,000 square feet, made from concrete block, sitting on ten acres of land with floor-to-ceiling windows. Big Drew always said if a muthafucka could get past his security gate, then they must've wanted all the smoke, and he was gon' be the one to give it to them.

I used my handprint to enter the foyer, and like the big-mouth bitch I am, I hollered for my mama. "Lolooooo! Where you at?" I listened to my voice echo throughout the house.

"Ahdia, if you don't shut yo' ass up hollering in my house. What the fuck you want?

Gahdamn," she said as she came from the kitchen.

"Mommy, I can't come see my parents without wanting something?"

"Hell naw, Dia, because every time you come over you want something. So what is it this time?" she replied, serious as fuck.

Walking into the living room, I went and took a seat on the white sofa, preparing myself for what was about to come.

"I know damn well you ain't lost yo' shit like that. First the fuck of all, why do you still have shoes on in my house? Second, why the fuck do you have them on in my white-ass living room? You must be out your rabbit-ass mind," Lolo yelled from the doorway.

"Damn, Ma. Why you gotta handle me so rough? I forgot."

"Who the hell you raising yo' voice at? Dia, stop playing with me and go take them shoes off. Meet me in the kitchen. I just made lunch for your dad, and I know yo' chunky ass likes to eat."

I stood up and took my shoes off at the front door, since Lolo was around checking muthafuckas like she was a TSA, knowing damn well she ain't ever worked a day in her life. But hey, that's Moms. Strolling into the kitchen, I leaned against the island, facing my mom as she cut the hoagies she'd made. I let out a deep sigh, prompting her to put the knife down. She turned and look at me.

"What's wrong, sweet pea?" my mom asked in the gentlest voice, and the shit had me looking at her crazy, because not even five minutes ago, she was just cussing me the hell out. That's Black mamas for you, I guess.

"Ugh, Lolo, I ran into a man today, like literally ran into him, and I don't know what it was—hell, *is*—about him that left me so flustered."

"Flustered, huh? I wonder who this mystery man is to have *the* Ahdia McCoy feeling some kind of way. The last time you felt like this was when you were dating—"

"Ahhhh, okay, Mom, I don't even wanna hear that nigga's name in this house. It ain't full of nothing but bullshit and lies."

"All right now, your lips are getting a little loose over there. Now, my bad for bringing him up. So, does your mystery man have a name, or were you too turned on to even ask?" Her ass started giggling.

"I didn't ask, but he said his name was Dash, and Mom, I wanna know so much more about him, but you know how I am. You know my past—"

"Yeah, you been fucking and finessing ever since." Her ass interrupted me. "But at some point, Dia, you gotta let the past go because you never know what kind of blessing you're blocking, and baby, he might be it. That man could be the one to heal the broken parts of you, but you'll miss out on him because you're too hurt to see that all men really aren't the same."

"I know, Mom. I know, but how can I be open and vulnerable with him when I'm still holding on to the things that hurt me the most?"

"Did your hardheaded ass not hear shit I just said? What y'all young kids be saying? Let that hurt go, sis," she said, all loud and ghetto.

"Okayyyy, and on that note, I'm gonna head home. I love you, Ma." I leaned up from the counter and kissed her on the cheek. When she turned around, I slapped her on that ratchet-ass booty she had.

"Keep it tight," I shouted on my way out the door.

"I'ma beat yo ass next time," was the last thing I heard before the front door closed.

I loved my Lo and everything that came with her. Now all I needed to do was find a way to take her advice and move the hell on.

Chapter Four

Dreux

Saturday

Fuck! I swear it feels like I can never sleep in on the weekends.

Like, what's the point in having a Monday through Friday job if I was only gonna be awakened at the same time on my off days? Jumping out of bed, I threw on my housecoat and my pink slippers, then went to see who the hell was knocking on my door at eight a.m. Stomping down the stairs, I rolled my eyes as I checked the camera that hung on the wall in my foyer. My attitude instantly changed. I ran to the door and swung it open.

"Dadddyyyy, what are you doing here so early?" Moving out of the way, I let him inside as I questioned him.

"Well, a little bird told me that you're finally coming out of your 'in house' funk, and you're stepping out tonight. So, I decided to come by and drop something off."

"Yes, sir, I'm finally shaking back, and even though I'm kind of nervous, I'm more excited than anything." My ass was grinning from ear to ear as I responded.

"That's good, li'l bit. Here, take this. Go buy yourself something nice, and make sure you're the most stunning person in the room." He pulled out two stacks of money, each wrapped in a $10,000 band, as he spoke.

"Daddy, I do not need twenty thousand dollars for an outfit that I'm only wearing for one night out. You know you don't have to give me any money. That's why I work."

"Whatever you don't spend, put that shit in your bank account, and no, that's not why you work. You work because you want to. Hell, I pay every bill in this house and Ahdia's, too, but if you wanna take over, then be my guest." Big Drew laughed.

"Nah, no thanks. You got it, big homie. Thank you for the money, and as much as I would love for you to stay, I still need to go shopping."

"All right, baby girl, I'll get out your hair and let you go do the things the women in my life seem to love. Spending my money." He wrapped me in his arms and kissed my forehead.

Watching my daddy walk back to his car, I couldn't help but think of how thankful I was to have him, and I prayed that the man who was meant to love me had some of my dad's same traits.

I went upstairs to handle my hygiene because there was no way I'd be able to go back to sleep. Once I was up, I was up. Stepping into my closet, I picked out a dark denim pair of skinny leg Levi's with a cream-colored crop top and my favorite cream-colored Louboutins. I decided to wear my natural curls and a light beat because tonight, I was popping out in the worst way, honey. I snatched up my Louis Vuitton handbag, tossed my phone and the money Big Drew gave me inside, and headed through the kitchen to my garage.

Looking at all my babies, I jumped in my pearl white BMW X5, which was my favorite before I got the Benz. Sitting in these leather seats, memories of the shit Ebony and I used to get into started flooding my mind—sneaking out to kick it with the dudes from school, all the late nights coming from the club, cleaning throw-up from the side of car, and the times crazy-ass Eb got her rocks off in the backseat while I drove home. After all this time, I'd finally gotten to a place where I could miss my girl and not be flooded with tears.

I laughed out loud, let back my sunroof, and went straight to Nicki Minaj's *Queen* album, hitting shuffle. "Good Form" blasted through the speakers, and like the undercover ratchet that I am, I pulled over like got-damn Zo and started throwing ass on the side of the highway.

Laughing at myself, I got back in my car and finally made my way to the mall. Pulling up at NorthPark, I tried to park as close to the Gucci store as I could because who not about to walk all over the mall in these heels is me. Shit, I didn't know what the fuck I was thinking wearing these muthafuckas to the mall anyway.

Locking my doors, I strutted through the parking garage into Gucci. For thirty minutes, I flipped through rack after rack, not finding shit that I absolutely loved, until it hit me that I had the baddest Angel Brinks jumpsuit in my closet with the tags still on it. Leaving out of Gucci, I decided to shoot over to Nordstrom to find the perfect pair of shoes for the night.

As I walked through the store, picking up shoe after shoe, I couldn't help but think of Kam. From what Ahdia said, this was some big-ass grand opening, so I wondered if he would be there, if he would remember me, or if I was thinking too much into that brief encounter. He was so intriguing, from the way he walked to the way he talked and how his eyes roamed over my body. That man had me tingling all over, sparking shit in me that I hadn't felt in a while.

Chuckling to myself, I thought, *It's been so long, I damn near forgot what an orgasm is like. Shit, I'm starting to feel like my celibate-ass homegirl, Cocoa. I need somebody to touch me on the inside part and make me feel good real fucking soon.*

Lifting a blush-colored pair of Giuseppe Zanottis from the shelf, I knew this was the one. It was a simple three-strap stiletto, which would make it perfect for the Brink's Touch jumpsuit. I took the shoes to the register, so I could check out and head back home to take a nap before the night's festivities.

"Thank you for choosing Nordstrom. You found everything you were looking for, ma'am?" the over-friendly cashier asked.

"Yes, actually I did, thank you."

"That's just wonderful. Okay, let's see. Your total is $914.71," the clerk said, all excited as she bagged up my shoes.

I reached inside my bag and peeled off ten big faces and handed them to her eager ass. Muthafuckas bought shit here every day, I was sure, so I did not understand why she was acting like she'd never seen somebody with money before. After she handed me the change and my bag, I left the store, damn near running to my car because Lord knows I was beyond ready to lay down.

I made it back to the house in thirty minutes, thanks to lack of traffic, and I just about broke my neck in those dumb-ass heels tryna go through the grass. Once I made it inside, I stripped down at the door, took the stairs two at a time, and dove into my bed. I set my alarm for a three-hour nap, and before I knew it, I was out like a light.

Three hours later...

I didn't realize how tired I was until my alarm started blaring in my ear. Instantly rolling my eyes, I turned the stupid-ass thing off, and when I stretched my arms, my hand hit a body on the side of me. I jumped up and yanked the comforter back, only to be met by the eyes of my annoying-ass sister.

"Ahdia, what the fuck, bro? Why are you in my bed? You do know that breaking and entering is a crime, right?"

"That's what I've heard. Thank God I used my house key and didn't bust the window out," her smart ass retorted.

"Whatever. Get your ass out. Shit." I grabbed my robe and walked in the bathroom.

"No. I brought all my shit here so we can ride together. You know I hate driving in Dallas traffic, sis," she hollered from the bedroom.

I swear that girl worked my damn nerves. Like, who the fuck just shows up at somebody's house and goes to sleep? A damn creep, that's who.

Throwing my bonnet on, I adjusted the water to a nice hot temperature and got in. After a cool thirty minutes, I stepped out of the shower, but instead of grabbing my robe, I air-dried. Ahdia had the music going in the bedroom, playing old-school Mya featuring Sisqo, like she knew something about that. Vibing to the music, I reached under the cabinet and pulled out my makeup caboodle, preparing for a beat that was gon' be worse than anything Ike ever gave Tina. I prepped my face with my favorite NYX Hydra Touch Primer, then filled in my eyebrows. An hour later, I was finally done with my beat, and I must say I was in love with the Fenty by Rihanna foundation. It was lightweight and smooth, so I wouldn't have to worry about it sweating off. I had a glittery eyeshadow look going on, with a nude lip and winged eyeliner. I decided to straighten my hair, since I usually wore it in its curly state. After another two hours, I was wiggling my ass into my outfit for the night, a silver lace bodysuit with thin sleeves. The top half was sheer with glitter and jewels that only covered my breasts, and the bottom half was silver and jewels, starting from my waist and ending at my ankles.

"Ahdia, can you come and zip me up, please?" I yelled to my sister who was across the hall getting dressed as well.

When Ahdia came through the door, she looked like the whole dinner plate. She was matching my fly in a strapless gold sequin dress that came mid-thigh with a split up the side, showing off her Cleopatra tattoo. She had her curls in a half top bun with the bottom hanging loosely down her back.

"Oh, hell yeah, bitch. We did not come to play with these hoes," Ahdia exclaimed in that squeaky-ass voice of hers.

"Sure the fuck didn't, honey. I'm ready to go, so hurry up with this zipper and let's ride out."

After Ahdia zipped me up, I slid my feet into my PINK fur slippers, picked up my shoes, phone, and clutch from the bed, and then we headed out the door. We settled on taking my candy red 2018 BMW Coupe because there was no way we could be this fly and not bring out the baby Beemer. I hooked my phone up to the Bluetooth, and as soon as I heard Drake's voice, I instantly knew my night was about to be lit as fuck.

"Ayyyy, got Ms in the bank, like *yes indeed.*" I looked over at Ahdia twerking in the passenger seat. I was glad my li'l baby was finally legal to drink in the club with me because we were about to turn this club out tonight.

Pulling up to the grand opening of Luxe, I couldn't help but think that the owner of this club was *that* nigga, because the line was wrapped around the corner and damn near down the street. Normally, I wouldn't name-drop to cut the line or get me in anywhere for free, but tonight, I was breaking that rule. Wasn't no way in hell I was about to stand in this bullshit-ass line. I grabbed Ahdia, who grabbed Parker, and walked to the front of the line. I was glad I didn't put the money my dad gave me in the bank since I was about to use that to finesse the bouncer.

"Gahdamn, who the fuck is that in the jumpsuit? Li'l mama got more ass than Goodyear got tires," I heard as I walked by. I chuckled because niggas really didn't give a damn what came out of their mouths.

Walking toward the bouncer, I noticed he was eyeing me before I made it all the way to the front. So, me being me, I pulled out my best shit.

"I saw you checking me out on my way over here, so what's it gonna take a girl like me to get a guy like you to let me skip the line?" I whispered in his ear while caressing up and down his arm.

"Shit, you can start by letting me rub on that big, fat fanny, and we can go from there," he responded with a smirk on his face.

"Or I can slide you five hundred dollars, and I won't tell Big Drew that you tryna feel up on his daughter. How about that?" I asked, challenging him.

"Aww, shit. Why you try to play me like that? You know just like everybody else know that nobody wants those kind of problems, ma."

I peeped the look on his face after he said that; then lo and behold, he was letting us in the club. Right before I walked in, I slipped him the money and kept going.

Inside, I couldn't help but admire the setup. There were white lowlights illuminating the marble floor, with diamond chandeliers overhead, creating the perfect amount of lighting. I took in the dynamic of the club. There were black couches trimmed with gold on the first level, and white couches on the second level. The dance floor had yellow lighting to give it a gold look, setting the tone for the rest of the club. The vibe was real grown and sexy, with some old-school Lauryn Hill playing.

I felt Ahdia tugging on my arm, so I stopped walking to let her catch up.

"Hey, me and Parker gon' go to the bathroom. You rolling with us?" she whispered in my ear.

"Nah, I'ma head over to the bar. I need to start getting on my level shit."

We went our separate ways, them to the bathroom and me to the bar, where I ordered two shots of Avion and a rum punch. I took my shots while standing there and then headed to find a section for me and my girls After paying for our section and the bottles of Ace of Spades that Ahdia just *had* to have, the two whores finally came from the restroom.

We had a nice little vibe for about an hour, and when "Booty" by Black Youngsta came on, the club went up like I knew it would.

"Ayyy, that booty, that big ole booty, toot toot. That's my shit!" Ahdia started singing.

I couldn't help but laugh because this girl turned into a whole stripper when this song came on. Parker leaned and whispered something in her ear, and they turned to hit the dance floor. Grabbing my clutch off the table, I got up and followed behind them to go and shake a li'l ass myself.

As I was making my way through the crowd, I got a feeling that someone was watching me. I scanned the first level but didn't lock eyes with anybody, so I continued to look around the second level, and then it happened. There he was, staring at me, watching me look for him. When he flashed that smile, showing all thirty-two teeth and that sexy-ass grill, I knew right then I wasn't leaving tonight without him.

Chapter Five

Kamron

That same day

"Bro, are you that fucking stupid? I'm really not understanding how you keep fucking up the same shit. You got lucky the first fucking time because I let you make it, but this is the second time you done brought my money back short. So that means one of two things. Either you stealing from me, or you smoking an ass-load of cocaine. Which one is it, bitch?" I screamed on Qua dumb ass, who I had tied up in my torture chamber, better known as the Dungeon.

"Choppa, I swear on my life I ain't ever stole shit from you, and you know I ain't a muhfuckin' base head. I legit don't know what the fuck is going on. My team and I slang yo' product day in and day out, so why shit is coming up short ain't making sense to me either. I think somebody is tryna set me up to get knocked off," he pleaded.

"Maaaan, I'm not tryna hear that shit. You already know how I give it up. Shit, I was really extending you the courtesy to tell the truth, but since you can't, sit back and let me show you something."

I pushed a button on the remote in my hand, and a large screen came down from the ceiling and started playing a video. I looked over at Qua to make sure he was seeing the same shit that I was seeing. On the screen was him taking money from the duffle labeled *D-Town Dopeboyz*, while another foot soldier took my fucking product from another and stuffed it all into two backpacks. Watching this shit again had my blood boiling even more than it had the first time. I cut the video off and turned to look at Qua, who immediately started pleading his case again.

"Aye, dawg, shut the fuck up. Muhfuckin' Bill Cosby said the proof is in the pudding, and bitch, you Jell-O. Big Bo, get my shit, fam," I hollered to one of my guards.

Big Bo came from the back with two of my carbon steel machetes, a broken wooden bat, and one of them lighters you use to ignite a barbecue grill. Rubbing my hands like Birdman, I felt myself slipping into the dark place where all my demons lived, and my adrenaline started to rush. I took the machetes from Bo, sharpening them on the leather strap that hung from the table behind the chair Qua was tied to, and with no warning, I swung the first machete, cutting his right hand smooth off. Like the bitch he was, Qua started screaming as loud as he could, I guess thinking someone would hear him, but he knew better than that. I watched in amusement as blood started to spill from the severed limb, and when I noticed him about to pass out, I chopped off his left hand. I knew that would wake his ass up.

"Choppa, please. Just take me outta my misery. I can't even apologize because I know even that won't save me. Just please take me out," the little bitch cried, but that shit fell on deaf ears.

"Didn't I tell you to shut the fuck up? I'll kill yo' punk ass when I'm ready. You think I'ma let you take the easy way out? Shiiiiid, you funny, Bre Bre," I said, mimicking them memes off Facebook. I picked up the wooden bat and lit that bitch like we were about to have a Fourth of

July cookout. I put the flame against his forearm, and the smell of burning flesh invaded my nostrils and sent me into a state of euphoria. Deciding not to waste any more time on this muthafucka, I pulled my gun out of the holster and fired two shots to his dome.

"Aye, you know what to do. The club opens tonight, and this shit done set me back."

Leaving Bo to clean up that bullshit, I hopped in my R8 since it had become my everyday car, and made my way back to the house. Drake's new Scorpion album was on repeat as I cruised through the Dallas streets, admiring my city. This has been home all my life, and I couldn't see myself living anywhere other than here.

Absentmindedly, I wound up driving out to my t-lady's house. I hadn't seen her in almost two weeks, so a visit was well overdue. Pulling into her driveway, I shook my head at how simple my mama was. Growing up in the projects of Oak Cliff, I lost my pops to a bullet that wasn't meant for him when I was six years old. From that day on, I watched my lady work two jobs, day in and day out, just to make ends meet. I never went to bed hungry, and I always had clean clothes on my back. I was always taught to get it by any means, and that's what I did. I jumped off the porch and got to it at the age of fifteen. The day I sold my first bag, I vowed to move my mama out of the hood, and a year later, I did just that. I told her to pick any house, any price, and it was hers, no questions asked, so imagine my surprise when she chose a single-story, three-bedroom brick home. There was nothing particularly fancy about it, but it was what she loved, so I let it rock.

Carrying my unit for tonight, I moved the mailbox off the wall and grabbed the key that was hidden behind it. I tried to respect her privacy, so I had opted out of getting my own key to her spot. Normally, I wouldn't pop up without calling like this. Inserting the key into the slot, I knocked as I pushed the door open, and slipped inside as quietly as possible. As I walked past the living room in search of my ma, I saw her sleeping in the big recliner that she just had to have. I let out a small laugh and proceeded to my old bedroom to crash for a few hours.

Five hours later. Seven p.m.

"Scooter, wake up baby. Scooter."

I heard somebody calling. There was only one person that called me that. I slowly opened my eyes, and they landed on the most beautiful girl in the world, my mama.

"You must have been tired because that alarm of yours has been going off for the last hour."

"Nah, I wasn't tired Ma Dukes. I had some business to take care of before I came over, and I guess it knocked me on my ass." I laughed as I stretched.

She picked up one of the pillows from my bed and slapped me upside the head with it. "Boy, what I tell you about that damn cussing in my house like you grown? Hell. Next time you say some shit like that, I'ma knock your damn teeth out. Keep playing with me, Kamron," she snapped, getting on my ass.

Getting up out of the bed, I wrapped her little bitty ass up in my arms and kissed her on the top of her head. "I love you, Ma."

"Mhmm, I love you too. Now, go get yourself together. You got another big night ahead of you tonight." Pushing me off of her, she walked out of the room.

After about two hours, I was done handling my hygiene. I picked up my outfit for the night and took it out of the black Armani bag. Smiling, I approved of the burgundy three-piece suit with a black quarter-length button-up that my stylist chose for me. The slacks were tapered, and the vest had one black button to hold it together, giving off that grown and sexy look that I was going for. Once I was dressed, I paired the fit with my black velvet GA loafers, diamond cuff links inscribed with my initials, and then finished it off with my favorite Guilty by Gucci cologne.

I came down the steps, preparing to leave. My ma was waiting for me at the door, and just like every other grand opening, she had tears in her eyes. “Look at my handsome man. You look so much like your father it’s ridiculous. Now, I want you to enjoy yourself tonight. I’m so proud of you.” Squeezing my cheek, she hugged me.

“I know, Ma, I know. I do it all for you to see that smile you have on your face right now. I’m gonna get out of here. Lock up. I love you.” Kissing her forehead, I left.

Tonight, I was pulling out the chrome Rolls Royce Wraith. When you a boss-ass nigga like myself, ain’t no such thing as half stepping. I hit Dash on the jack as I coasted through traffic to make sure he was on his way because that muthafucka was always late.

I pulled around the back of the club to avoid the line of people that was standing at the front waiting on me to walk in. Dash met me at the back entrance, and I dapped him up before we got on the small elevator that took us up to the top VIP section.

Getting comfortable on the expensive-ass couches, I waved the bottle girl down and had her bring over a bottle of Dom Perignon for me, then a bottle of D’usse for Dash.

“Ohhh, shit, look out now. The muhfuckin’ Block Boyz are in the building. Kiest and Polk in this bitch,” DJ Bone shouted over the club as the spotlight shone in our section.

Looking down into the crowd, imagine my surprise when I spotted a brown-skinned cutie standing at the bar. "Aye, man, that's her. Remember the chick I told you that turned me down at Denny's last month?" I said to Dash, pointing down at Dreux, who just so happened to meet my gaze at the same time.

"Gahhhh damn, shorty fine as fuck, and that ass sitting up like two midgets on her back. I might need to shoot my shot," Dash's dumb ass replied.

"Say, man, relax all that. That's my wife you talm bout, G." We both laughed.

Picking up my glass of Ace of Spades, I sat back on the couch and reminisced on the brief but memorable encounter.

I rolled over, checked my phone, and it was almost two in the morning. Restless and hungry, I jumped out of the bed and threw on my black hoodie, jogging pants, a black fitted Chicago Bulls cap, and my all-red Retro 11s. Getting in my 2017 matte grey Aston Martin, I pulled out of my driveway and headed to my favorite restaurant, Denny's. I didn't give a fuck how much money I had, Denny's would always be my shit. As I coasted down the highway, Song Cry by Jay-Z started playing on the radio.

. . . on repeat, the CD of Big's 'Me and My Bitch,'
Watching Bonnie and Clyde, pretendin' to be that shit
Empty gun in ya hand, saying let me see that clip.

Listening to Jay-Z rap them lines, I was more than ready for a nice female by my side that I knew was down for me. When I pulled into the parking lot of

Denny's, it was after three a.m., but I noticed another car there too, so I figured it must be a late-night drunk. I reached under my seat, grabbed my strap, and headed into the building.

"Welcome to Denny's, sir. Will there be just one, and would you like a table or a booth?" the waitress asked.

"I'll take a booth in the back of this closed section, li'l mama," I replied. No doubt she knew who I was because as soon as I hit the door, she was on my dick like white on rice.

Being the nigga to see in these streets, I could tell when there were eyes on me. So naturally, I looked up from my phone into the eyes of the prettiest female I'd ever seen. I'd had my share of bad bitches, but she wasn't that. She was just what I said—pretty, genuinely pretty. I chuckled to myself when I winked at her and she put her head down.

Following the server to my booth, I declined the menu she tried to hand me. "I'm good on the menu, ma. Lemme get that lumberjack with my eggs over medium, and instead of that ham, lemme get extra bacon and sausage."

"You good with white toast and pancakes, sir?" the server asked.

"You know what? Keep the toast and lemme get French toast, no pancakes, oh, and two cups of orange juice."

"Yes, sir, I'll have that right out." She had lust dancing in her eyes.

When my order came out, I glanced at my watch, checking the time. I noticed it was damn near four a.m., and I really wasn't hungry anymore. Downing my last cup of orange juice, I saw the pretty girl from earlier checking out and leaving. Trying my best to hurry up and catch her, I pulled a big face out my pocket and threw it on the table.

As I was walking out the door, I let homegirl know I left the bread on the table, and I was out. I saw my future halfway to her car, so I hollered for her to stop. "Aye, li'l bit, hold on. Let me talk to you."

When she turned around, I swear I saw everything I'd ever wanted in her eyes, and up close, she was so much more than pretty. She was breathtaking.

"Me?" she questioned, making me laugh.

"Yeah, you, shorty. It's only us out here."

"Oh yeah, I guess you're right."

I peeped how nervous she was by the way she shuffled back and forth and tucked her hair behind her ears. This girl was so beautiful. She had to be about 5 foot 6, 160 pounds, with doe-shaped eyes, eyebrows that fit her face perfectly, and the prettiest set of pink lips I'd ever seen. Her hair was big and brown, with natural curls cascading down her back. Her skin—gah-damn her skin—looked to be as smooth as a baby's ass, and the natural glow that radiated from her rich chocolate skin had me ready to find out what was under that big-ass hoodie she was wearing.

"Umm," she said. I didn't realize I was staring until she said something.

"My bad. I know this is probably awkward as hell for you, but you're beautiful. I'm sure you've heard that a million times, but I got to know you. I can't and I won't leave this parking lot without your name and number."

"I'm sorry. I really appreciate that, but right now isn't a good time for me to be making new friends. I got a lot of shit going on, and I'm just not feeling it." She opened her car door to get in. "And my name is Dreux."

"Wait. What about your number, ma?" I asked.

"You're a well-connected man, so I'm sure you'll figure it out." With that, she was in her car, disappearing into the darkness.

Damn. She knew who I was, which didn't surprise me, but what did was the fact that she knew me, and she wasn't falling all over me like most of these hoes. I got in my car with thoughts of Miss Dreux invading my mind. An hour later, I was pulling into my driveway, tired as hell. I made my way upstairs to my bathroom and stripped out of my clothes. I jumped in the shower, handled my hygiene, then laid my ass down. As I stared at the ceiling, I rubbed the empty spot beside me, imagined Dreux laying there, and in no time, I was out like a light.

Snapping outta my flashback, I stood up to go and grab Dreux from the dance floor to bring her back to my section. As soon as I made it to the velvet rope, shots rang out.

Tat-tat-tat-tat! Tat-tat-tat-tat!

On instinct, I pulled my strap from my waist and started bussing back in the direction of whoever it was that had me fucked up, trying me on this night. Suddenly the shots ceased, allowing me enough time to grab my shit and get out. From my peripheral, I could see Dreux running toward the back exit, and the first thing that ran across my mind was, *Damn, she's running out of my life again.*

Chapter Six

Dashir Edwards

Growing up on the Southside of Chicago, my life wasn't always easy. I was raised by a single mother who did her best to give me the world but couldn't seem to shake the monkey that was on her back. The neighborhood I lived in gave you two options: use 'em or sell 'em, and I damn sure wasn't about to shoot up shit. By the time I was thirteen, I'd been initiated with the Stones and had a body under my belt. My life changed on my eighteenth birthday when I watched my best friend lose his life in front of the corner store. After that, I was done. I packed up everything I could fit in two duffle bags, and I moved to Dallas with my Grammy.

I was on my way home from the gym, smoking an L, when my nigga Choppa hit my line.

"What's up, bitch boy?"

"I got yo' bitch when I see you, muthafucka. Where yo' punk ass at?" Choppa was always talking shit.

"Shit, I'm on 635 headed to the crib. What it's looking like?"

"Like money. You heard from Bruce about that bread?" Nigga didn't play about his money.

"Man, that muthafucka been dodging me like I don't know where he be at. I'ma let him get comfortable, then I'ma sneak up on his ass."

"Dash, don't be fucking playing, bro. You start messing with these hoes and lose focus. This shit better be handled soon. That's real talk," Choppa yelled into the phone, then hung up.

I know this baby bitch didn't hang up in my face, I laughed to myself. Little did he know, I had deaded that shit with Bruce yesterday, literally. I just liked fucking with Choppa because he was sensitive about his shit.

Fifteen minutes later, I was pulling into my condo in North Richland Hills, and even though I was the only nigga in this white-ass cul de sac, I loved my spot. Parking my Ferrari 488 in the garage, I stepped out and stretched my legs. I don't know what the hell had possessed me to drive that muthafucka to the gym. I locked my doors, and as soon as I walked inside, the smell of bacon hit my nose, which only meant one thing: Kayla was here. She was a little baddie I met two years ago at a Labor Day picnic that the Block Boyz hosted. I wasn't looking for anything serious then, and I still wasn't. She kind of just stuck. I wouldn't call her my girl, but shit, here she was.

"Kay, how many times I gotta tell you not to pop up at my house, especially when I'm not here?"

Hearing my voice made her jump. "Shit, Dash! You scared me. I knew you would be at the gym today, so I wanted to do something sweet for you. What's better than a home-cooked meal after the gym?" she shot back.

"A fat-ass blunt, a shower, and a fucking nap, that's what. So, since I already smoked, I'm just tryna wash my dick and lay down."

"Damn, why can't you just appreciate *something* for once? All I wanted to do was feed you, fuck you, and g'on on about my day."

"Ight, man, if it means that much to you, bring me a plate, and after I eat, you can bless me with those juicy-ass lips."

Just like I knew she would, Kay sauntered her thick ass right to me and set the plate in front of me. I would be lying if I said this shit didn't look good. Li'l mama had cooked bacon, French toast, over medium eggs, and red potatoes for a nigga. While she cleaned the kitchen, I sat back and thought about how fresh I was jumping tonight. Choppa and I had finally opened our first business together. He was the face, and I was the silent partner, and tonight was our grand opening.

I finished my food without saying anything to Kay and made my way to the bathroom. I dropped clothes into the hamper in the closet, stepped in the shower, and let the water fall over my body. While I stood under the shower head with my eyes closed, I felt the cool air from the door being opened, so when I peeked with my left eye, there was Kayla in her birthday suit.

"You gon; stand there and stare, or you gon' get in?"

Joining me, she instantly invaded my space and rubbed her soft hands over my shoulders then down my abs. When she started stroking my dick, I let out a low moan, and in one fluid motion, she was on her knees, circling the head of my dick with her tongue. I ran my hands through her hair before placing them on the side of her head and guiding my piece to the back of her throat. She repeatedly sucked me in and pulled me out, letting her tongue lick my balls every time she hit the base. I fucked up when I looked down and saw her playing in her pussy, rubbing her juices over her clit. My nut began to rise, and I swear I felt that shit in the pit of my stomach, but before I could warn her, hot cum was raining down on her face and in her hair.

"Whooo, fuck! That shit damn near brought me to my knees, girl."

"You're about the nastiest person I've ever met. It must have been too hard to tell me you were about to nut so I could get out the way, huh?"

"Shit, you act like I planned to nut on yo' shit. You betta relax yo' throat before I put something back in it."

"Whatever. That was so fucking disrespectful, Dashir. Like I'm some ho."

"You are. Now get yo' ass out. I'm about to take a nap."

Standing there with her arms folded across her chest, she stared at me for a while as I washed myself off, but eventually she got the hint that there was no more conversation and stormed her mad ass out my house.

I'd been trying to shake this girl for the past six months, and it was like she just didn't get it. I screened her calls, cussed her ass out. Shit, I'd even shook the shit out of her, but this bitch really wasn't getting it. I would hate to off this crazy muthafucka, so she better get it together.

Turning the water off, I wrapped my towel around my waist, and when my head hit my California king mattress, I was out for the count.

"You know this shit is for the birds, right? Go pull the tapes, bro," I overheard Choppa saying to Meech, one of our security guards.

"Chop, you good here? This shit done stressed me the fuck out, and I ain't tryna hang around too much longer."

"Yeah, bro, Meech about to get the tapes so I can look at 'em tomorrow. Where you headed? Back to the house?"

"Nah, I think I'm about to hit the Denny's off Skillman. That's where all the hoes go after the club. I'ma check it out to see if there's anything worth taking home with me."

"Bro, yo' ass always looking for something to fuck on. Sit down, nigga. Damn." Choppa was laughing, but he was right.

"I'll sit down when I die. Until then, I'ma keep sticking and moving like I been doing. You down to ride or nah?"

"Yeah, that's cool. Lemme get these tapes from Meech, and I'll follow you over to the spot. I might bag me a li'l bitch tonight too." Now his ass wanted to fuck.

"That's a bet fa sho."

After Choppa got the shit, we made it to Denny's in fifteen minutes, and just like I expected, the parking lot was flooded with bad bitches and bad-built bitches. When we stepped out our whips, like always, all eyes were on us. Bitches were whispering to their homegirls when we walked by, but of course, there was always one muthafucka bold enough to try it.

"Aye, are you fucking crazy? Don't grab my dick if you ain't about to suck it, ol' bucket-head-ass bitch!" This broad really had me fucked up.

"Pull it out, daddy, and I just might."

"Mites is on a chicken's ass. Fuck out my way," I said, mushing her out my face.

Strolling into the restaurant, I had the li'l bitch at the register put us in a booth tucked off in the corner, so we could scope the scene. I had a phobia of sitting with my back to a crowd, and leave it to Choppa's playful ass to slide in the booth by the window. Shit, we was two big-ass, straight niggas, so I had no choice. Plus, if anything popped off, Chop was gon' bust, no questions asked.

The waitress came over to take our order, and while we waited, I heard the voice that had me ready to wring her neck and fuck her at the same time. I turned slightly to look over my shoulder, unprepared for the sight of her standing at the register. The little dress she was wearing had them cheeks on full display, and the top hung so low that if she moved wrong, titties would be on the Denny's menu. As she walked to her booth, that ass was clapping more than Grandma at Sunday service, and I was tuned in.

"Say, bro, I'll be back. I think I found my victim for the night, so hold it down while I go shoot my shot," I said as I stood up from the booth.

"Aww, shit, here yo' ass go. I hope she ain't a duck like the ho you brought to the smash house last week."

"Aye, bitch, you said you wasn't gon' bring that shit up again. How the fuck was I supposed to know she looked like that without makeup on?"

"Whatever, nigga. Bye."

I swear that muthafucka got on my nerves, but oh well, baby girl was about to change my whole mood. Making my way to her table, I noticed that she was sitting with the same chick that Choppa pointed out at the club. Seeing them together, they favored, so I assumed they were related some way. I watched shorty lean over the table and whisper to boo, so I guess she was letting her know that I was walking in their direction. Approaching their table, I caressed her back, and when she turned around, there was the fiery beauty I had met in the mall.

"Excuse you. You don't know me, so I would appreciate it if you kept your ha—oh, hell, it's you again. Dash, right? How can I help you?"

"Ohhh, bitch, you know him? I need one of them," the girl with her said, giggling.

"Unfortunately. This is the guy from the mall I told you about," Shorty replied as she rolled her eyes.

"Well, shit, you got a brother?"

Laughing, I replied, "Yeah, I do. Matter of fact, he here. Hold on." Pulling my phone out of my pocket, I sent Choppa a text.

Me: bruh, you'll never guess who my shorty here with.
Moneybagg Chop: aww shit, who?
Me: yo li'l mama from the club.
Moneybagg Chop: heard you.

I put my phone back in my pocket and sat down next to future bae, forcing her to slide over. Just to fuck with her, I laid my arm across her shoulders, pulled her into me, and held her tight when she tried to jerk away like I knew she would. Watching homegirl's eyes get big, I knew that only meant one thing: my bro was on his way over here. Shorty started grabbing her shit, letting us know she was going to the bathroom, and when I saw Choppa following behind her, I knew baby girl's time was up because what he wanted, he got.

"Now that she's out the way, what's up? How you been, gorgeous?"

"I was good before you came over and interrupted my dinner. What do you want, Dash?"

"You, but you making it real hard to get that. Can you at least tell me your name?"

"Ahdia, but to people close to me, it's just Dia."

"Ahdia, that's a beautiful name," I said, stroking her soft-ass cheek that was turning red underneath my touch.

"So I've heard. Do you know how to keep your hands to yourself?"

"Nah, I don't."

"Obviously." She rolled her eyes, and even that was sexy.

Shit, she had me feeling like a sap-ass nigga. I had to abort mission for a minute before I ended up asking her ass to marry me.

"Aye, chill right here. I'ma be right back." I ain't even wait for her to respond. I just hopped up and went back to my booth. I sat there for about five minutes, gaining my composure, then tossed a hundo on the table and got up to find baby girl. By the time I reached the table, I noticed that she got low on me, so I turned around and headed to the car. Choppa hit my line and said he was outta pocket for the night, which let me know that him and shorty had dipped off.

I spotted Ahdia across the parking lot, head down, unaware of her surroundings, so I walked up, pressed my dick against her ass, and put my hand over the phone.

"You was tryna leave without telling me bye?"

"Ugh, Dash, will you move? Damn."

"You smell so fucking sweet, and it ain't the perfume you wearing."

"Dead ass, fuck out my face with that shit." Dia laughed, letting me know she didn't mean it.

"Real shit, though, lemme get yo' number. I'on want this to be the last time I talk to you."

"Look, I'ma keep it a hunnid with you. I'm a ho. Matter fact, I was *just* setting up a dick appointment before you came. You don't want me."

"Shiiiiid, I'm a ho too. We can be friends with benefits."

Sighing, she handed me her phone. "Put your number in there. When I'm ready for some dick, I'll call you."

Damn, li'l mama was gutta, and I couldn't do shit but respect it. I handed her phone back, wished her well, and was on my way. When I got in my whip, I readjusted my piece, then called up this li'l Mexican bitch named Daisy to get my shit wet.

"Oh, fuck, Dash, don't stop! Fuck me harder, baby," Daisy screamed. The crazy part was, I was barely knocking her walls down, so I knew it was some bullshit. I was bored as fuck with her loose-ass pussy, but oh well, she was convenient.

"Right there. Fuckkk."

Fed up at this point, I pulled my dick out and walked into her bathroom to clean it off.

"Wait. Why did you stop?"

"Shid, what the fuck you mean? Ain't no way that shit felt good because my meat was just floating around that endless pit of pussy that you got."

"Pendejo! That's your little-ass dick. There's nothing wrong with my cat." Shorty was yelling.

"My piece can't be that little from the way you were just in here screaming like I was murdering something. Fuck out my face, Daisy." I bent down to grab my hoodie from the floor, and when I stood up, this bitch threw a damn vase at me.

"Bitch, have you lost your fucking mind? If you woulda hit me, I was gon' beam yo' ass up like a nigga." This crazy-ass girl had me fucked up.

"Just get the fuck out my house."

"Bet. Fuck you and that swamp pussy," I said as I walked out the front door. The whole way home, all I could think about was Ahdia. She had some walls built up that I wouldn't mind knocking down, figuratively and literally.

Chapter Seven

Ahdia

"Yesss! Ooooh, fuck! Just like that, Double! Fuck me!" I'd been fucking this nigga named Alex, aka Double A, for the past few months. Over time, I thought I would get bored with the dick, but the way he maxed me out kept me coming back and cumming back to back.

Grabbing me by my neck, he slammed into me repeatedly, showing my pussy no mercy. When he started applying pressure to my throat, I came all over his manhood. He pulled out and flipped me over, diving head-first into my good stuff. He pushed my legs back by my thighs and licked me from ass to clit. Grabbing my clit, he gently rolled it between his teeth while teasing it with his tongue at the same time. When he began to suck on my nub like a pacifier with some force behind it, I felt my soul leave my body and enter his mouth. He sucked that muthafucka clean outta me. A wave of pleasure washed over me, and right when I was about to cum, he stopped.

I delivered the ugliest mug I could muster up. When he laughed, I almost showed him what these hands was hitting for.

"Get yo' ass up and come ride this dick. Make it nasty like I like it."

He rolled me over until I was sitting reverse cowgirl. I planted both feet on the bed and guided myself onto his piece. I placed my hands on the bed in front of me and slowly started bouncing up and down, gradually picking up speed. I closed my eyes, biting my lip, and imagined that the dick I was riding belonged to Dash. When he slipped his thumb in my ass, I threw my pussy back hard as hell, because that shit pushed me over the edge. Digging his left hand into my waist, Double A matched me thrust for thrust, slapping my ass with his right. When I spun around, he sat up, pulled my nipple into his mouth, and teased my nipple ring.

"Gahdamn, Dia, this pussy so fucking wet," his ass whispered over my breast. I threw my head back as my clit rubbed against the base of his dick, creating just the right amount of friction, because at this point, I just couldn't take anymore.

"Ooooh, Double, I'm about to cum, baby. Fuck! Ooooh, shit!"

Still holding on to my waist, Alex slammed me up and down, building his nut the same way I built mine.

"Cum right now. When I bust this pussy open, you cum."

He pushed into me one last time, and when I felt his dick in my chest, all the cum in my body squirted out of my vagina. I fell on the side of him, spent, knowing that sleep was in my near future.

Alex went into the bathroom to wash himself, brought a wet towel back, and wiped me clean from front to back. As I drifted off to sleep, the last thing I heard was the front door opening and him yelling that he'd be back at the same time next week.

The Next Morning...

Shit! I woke up, and my whole bottom half was sore as hell. It felt like a whole bus ran my shit over. Crawling out of the bed, I slowly made my way to the bathroom to soak my body. I filled the tub with water as hot as I could stand it, poured damn near the whole container of Epsom salt in it, then climbed in.

"Alexa, play Brie's nineties R&B playlist."

The sounds of Xscape began to play, and that shit had me wanting Dash to come visit the softest place on earth. My ho senses were tingling, but it was something about him that made me want to change my ways a little bit. I turned on the jets to help soothe some of the pain while I relaxed.

Two hours later, I was out of the tub, dressed, and ready to begin my day. I kept it simple in some distressed jeans, a black bodysuit, and some red booties. I invited my girls San and Erica out to lunch because it had been a few weeks since I last saw them. Every time we linked up it wasn't nothing but good vibes—super good vibes only. Like always, San and I couldn't decide where we wanted to eat, so we left it up to Erica, and this heffa chose Chili's.

When I arrived at Chili's, late per usual, I saw Erica and San waiting for me at the door.

"Damn, bitch, you gon' be late to your own funeral. You can't be on time for shit." San was screaming with that reckless-ass mouth of hers. This muthafucka didn't give a damn. What came up was what was coming out.

"Girl, shut the hell up. Why y'all ain't inside anyway?"

"We just got here too," Erica said.

"San, you ain't shit. Got me thinking y'all been waiting on me."

San's goofy ass started laughing, and that shit was contagious because I fell out laughing too. We spent two hours chatting about the kids and the things going on in our lives. I filled them in on Dash, and Erica told me the same thing that my mom said: get to know that man because he might be the one to change my life. Then, of course, you got goofy-ass San saying to fuck him and keep it moving. I really needed to get my shit together to see what was up.

We finished up, paid, and parted ways. I decided I might as well do all my running around while I was out, so I went to pop up on Dreux since she thought she was grown enough to leave with some dude she just met.

"Dreux."

When she didn't answer, I knew she was still asleep, sooo my playful ass took the stairs two at a time, and when I entered her bedroom, I slid in behind her and put my arm around her waist.

"Kamron, I thought I told you to go home."

"Oh, bitch, you let him in yo' house."

Screaming, she jumped up, throwing the comforter on the ground. "Ahdia, what the fuck is your problem? Shit, this is the second time in twenty-four hours that you done snuck in my house *and* my bed."

"I mean, you never texted me and said you were okay, so shit, I popped up to check you out." I hit her ass with the Kanye West shrug.

"Girl, you are a freaking idiot. I swear Mommy dropped you on your head when you were little."

"Blahhh, whatever. Get up so you can tell me about Mr. Kamron."

Groaning, she went into the bathroom to brush her teeth, and when she came out, her ass walked right past me and out the door. I followed her to the kitchen, pulling a water bottle from the fridge, and perched up at her island.

"Soooo, come on, spill it."

"Oh God! You are such a bugaboo. Okay, so, about a month ago, I ran into him at Denny's, but you know I wasn't really in the right space to be making new friends. So, last night when he cornered me in the bathroom, I decided to stop running and hear what he had to say. That's it. That's all."

"Well, did you fuck him?"

"Bitch, I am not you. Hell no, I didn't fuck him. I wanted to, though. That man is so damn fine. If he would have asked, I would have threw this ass back on him quick as hell."

"Ayeee! Yesss, ho!"

"Anyway, we made plans to see each other again, so we gon' see how it goes."

I sat with my sister while she ate, getting the scoop on this dude. Once she was dressed, we left to go do what we do best: shop.

Chapter Eight

Jabari Green

I was so sick of these niggas. Every time I turned around, somebody new was on their dicks. Choppa and Dash flooded the streets with the purest of everything you could think of—cocaine, weed, pills. Shit, the only thing they didn't sell was women. I used to push that white girl under this nigga named Mack, but when he got knocked by twelve, my shit dried up, forcing me to go see a man about a dog. Having to hit up Choppa about some work was a blow to my ego, especially since my bum-ass half-brother was his right-hand man. Dash didn't know we shared the same father, just like my father didn't know he had another son up until a year ago. Apparently, his mama was dying, and she was tryna right her wrongs before the Grim Reaper came to suck the life outta her.

Sometimes the hate I had for Dash overshadowed my need to work. I could be on the block getting to the money; then he would come through and throw my mood off. It ain't like he did shit to me. I was just jealous of the shit he didn't go through that I did. Imagine spending fourteen years of your life with an alcoholic father and a weak-ass mama who thought the shit he did was okay. I could remember being as young as four years old, kneeling on rice because I didn't like green beans, or getting beat with a stick at six for not knowing how to ride a bike. How the fuck was I gon' learn if no one took the time to teach me? I bet you I figured that shit out that day. Dash didn't have to deal with any of that bullshit. His mama packed her bags and got the fuck outta dodge, something I wish my mother would have done.

Making sure my hood was secured over my head, I put my gun back in my waist and made my way to the side exit. Yeah, it was me that shot up that bullshit-ass club. I hate that I didn't hit at least one of them niggas, but I fa sho underestimated Choppa. Why the fuck didn't I think that muthafucka would bust back? That's what the fuck I be talking about: blind rage be having me wilding out.

On my way out the door, I spotted a bitch hiding under one of the tables, so I snatched her ass up. "Get the fuck up, bitch. Let's go."

"Please, I just wanna go home. Don't do this."

"Shut yo' ass up and get the fuck out the door. You think I give a fuck about you crying?" Shoving her out the door, I put my gun in her back and told her to walk to the hooptie I had parked near the exit. With my gloves still on, I swung the back passenger door open and made her get in.

"Take them panties off, bitch."

"Please, why are you doing this?" I could hear the fear in her shaky voice, but I didn't give a fuck.

"Don't make me say it again."

She started to pull them down, but she wasn't going fast enough for me, so I ripped the muthafuckas off. With one hand holding the gun, I unbuckled my belt, letting my pants and drawers drop to the ground. I tried to force my dick in her, but it was so fucking dry that I couldn't get in. Spitting on my hand, I swiped it up her pussy, and without warning, I pushed my dick inside, causing her to scream.

"Shut the fuck up, bitch, and take this dick."

As I pumped in and out of her, she continued to yell, so I drew my fist back and knocked her hard-headed ass out. Still fucking her unconscious, I felt her pussy getting wet, and when I looked down, there was blood pooling between her legs, which sent me into overdrive. The sight turned me on even more, and in no time, I was filling her body up with cum and lead. I slid out of her dead body, stuffing my dick back in my pants before I whipped out my phone and made a call.

"Another one."

"Say less."

"How long you gon' keep this shit up, man? You have a disease. It's nothing to be ashamed of," Lonzo came at me.

"I ain't got a fucking disease. Fuck you! She asked me to fuck her."

"Did she ask you to kill her too? No, she fucking didn't, so lose the bass in your voice, muthafucka. You need help before you end up dead, but since you ain't tryna hear shit I gotta say, I'ma stop saying shit."

"Good. You served yo' purpose. Get the fuck outta my house."

Shaking his head, Lonzo looked at me one last time, then was out the door. I ain't give a fuck, either. I was tired of people treating me like there was something wrong with me. All my life, from my parents to my homies, muthafuckas been side-eyeing me, and I was sick of that shit. It started when I was eight and snapped our dog Butch's neck with my bare hands. But shit, I wasn't crazy. I was misunderstood.

The Next Morning...

Waking up outta my sleep to the sound of my burner phone going off, I rolled over and saw that I had a text from Choppa.

Be at the Inferno by 10 or get yo shit pushed back.

This muthafucka thought everybody was scared of his ass, but I was gonna get the fuck up and go. I had a feeling that I already knew what the fuck this was about, and that had me on edge, so I had to shake that shit before I made it to the spot. I took a quick fifteen-minute shower, dressed down in some black Champion joggers with a royal blue Champion shirt and a pair of matching Retro 13s. It was 9:47, giving me thirteen minutes to make it to Prosper, and shit, that was 45 minutes away.

Pulling up to the warehouse, I started to think, if we were at the Inferno, somebody was gon' die today. I noticed that only lieutenants were in attendance, and that damn sure raised red flags. When I opened the door, a bullet whizzed past my head, prompting me to duck, and shit, I even pissed on myself a li'l bit.

"What the fuck is wrong with you, dawg? Why would you do that?" I exclaimed.

"Well, according to the text that I'm a hundred ten percent sure you received, you were supposed to be here thirty minutes ago. You got any excuse for your tardiness?" Choppa asked.

"Nah, because no matter what I say, it ain't gon' be good enough, so I apologize, and it won't happen again."

"Heard you. Now that this nigga done made his grand appearance, I bet you muthafuckas are wondering why we're here. It's because every time something is going right, something *always* goes wrong."

Dash wasn't there yet, which was unusual because them muthafuckas didn't shit without the other wiping his ass.

"Now, if y'all bitches was on yo' shit like you supposed to be, then you would see that one of your own is missing."

Scanning the room, I noticed that the first lieutenant wasn't there, so I sat back, watching to see if any of the other homies peeped game too.

"Aye, boss, Reek ain't here. What, that nigga got a free pass today?" Trell, one of the top dogs, asked.

"You know me better than that. When I call a meeting, *everybody* is in attendance. It's just a matter of which seat you sitting in," Choppa replied, letting out this creepy-ass laugh.

"Yo, Dash, bring Reek in here, fam."

Dash came rolling Reek out of the back of the Inferno in a wheelchair, and I ain't gon' lie. That shit had me shook as fuck.

"Oh, shit! Say, Chop, what the fuck happened to that nigga's legs?" Trell's big-mouth ass asked.

"That's exactly what the fuck happened. I chopped them muthafuckas off. See, when you steal from me then try to run, I get real upset."

When Choppa started walking to that fucked-up-ass knife table that he had, I knew it was about to be some shit, and I was glad I wasn't on the receiving end of this bullshit. That nigga Choppa was on some other shit. I was starting to think that muthafucka was chemically imbalanced, and that alone had me borderline regretting shooting up the fucking club. Nah, it wasn't no way for that nigga to find out it was me because I covered every base.

After the meeting, I swung to the gas station to pick up some Backwoods, and what I saw had me hotter than fish grease. Standing in the doorway of her car, talking to Dash, was Ahdia McCoy, the li'l bitch that I was fucking with about three years ago. My blood started to boil because when she was with me, she never smiled like she was now. I should have killed the stupid bitch when I had the chance. Shit! This nigga was always winning.

I got back in my car and left. That put me in a sour-ass mood, and I felt myself slipping into the darkness. Coming to, I had my hands balled up in some bitch's hair, and she was throwing up from me shoving my dick down her throat. I pulled out when I felt my nut release, and after I fired two bullets in her head, all my problems went with them.

"Another one."

Chapter Nine

Kamron

This shit with the club was really starting to piss me off. As I sat in my office reviewing the security tapes, nothing seemed to stand out. There was a figure in the corner near the DJ booth, but the hood was pulled too low, masking the face.

"Fuck!" I slammed my hand on my oak desk, making the pictures shake. This wasn't the first time a nigga tried me, just the first time they tried me in *my* shit. Security was mad tight that night, so how somebody got inside my establishment with a gun was a mystery to me. Turning off the tapes, I got up to head down to Inferno because I had other shit that needed to be taken care of.

"Oh, shit! Say, Chop, what the fuck happened to that nigga's legs?" Trell's big-mouth ass asked.

"That's exactly what the fuck happened. I chopped them muthafuckas off. See, when you steal from me then try to run, I get real upset," I said, walking to my knife table. "He lost his legs tryna run." I continued my story while grabbing a rusty-ass saw. "So, what do you think is gonna happen for him stealing my shit?" Swinging my saw around, I made my way over to Reek, whose wrists were bound to the wheelchair. "No one wants to answer? Cool. I'll show you," I said.

I took the saw and started cutting into Reek's left wrist. As blood began to pour out, I heard somebody regurgitating behind me, so I stopped cutting and turned around. I looked on as my newest lieutenant, Bandit, continued to vomit.

"Say, nigga, you good or what?" I hollered, irritated.

"Yeah, Choppa, I'm straight."

"Great. Bring yo' nasty ass up here."

As he made his way to the front, I could see sweat dripping from his forehead. This nigga was nervous like I was about to chop his shit off.

"Wassup, boss man?"

"Ight, since this yo' first go around, we gon' strengthen your weak-ass stomach. Get this fucking saw."

I could see how hesitant he was, but he took the nasty-ass saw.

"Good. Now, finish where I le—"

My phone started ringing, interrupting my sentence. I reached in my pocket to check the call. It was my shorty, but she was gon' have to wait.

"Like I was saying, finish this shit. Nobody is to leave this gahdamn warehouse until both of his hands are in that bag. Dash, I'm out this bitch. You know what to do when he's finished. Aye, Trell, drop that muhfuckin' bag on his mama's porch and tell her Merry Christmas."

"Chop, you know damn well Christmas ain't for another five months," Trell's dumb ass replied, laughing.

Shaking my head, I said, "Christmas came early this year, bitch. I'm out."

As I walked out to my car, I pulled my phone out and called my baby back. Shit, I prolly sound like a sensitive thug because it ain't even been twelve hours since we'd officially met, but I didn't give a fuck. That was all me.

"Hello," Dreux answered softly.

"Good morning, beautiful. I'm sorry I took so long. I was handling a li'l business. You okay?"

"I'm fine. You told me last night to call you when I was awake, so I was just reaching out. No big deal."

"Nah, it's gon' always be a big deal when it comes to you. You might not know it yet, but something tells me that you're my end," I said, putting a li'l sum-sum on her mind.

"Aww, Kam."

"Kam, huh? Wifey already handing out nicknames and shit. That's cool. You can get that."

"Whatever. You made plans for your day already?" she asked all low and shit.

"Yeah, my schedule for the day is set. Why? What's up?" Plugging her address in my GPS, I saw I was about an hour away. Baby girl just didn't know my day consisted of doing whatever she wanted.

"Nothing really. I kind of wanted to see you again, but it's okay since you have things to do. I don't wanna come off clingy or nothing. I just like your vibe."

"Well, maybe when I'm done, I can swing by and kick it with you. Cool?"

"Sure, that's fine. Just let me know."

"A'ight, baby. Let me get off this phone. I'll talk to you later."

"Okay, bye." I knew she was probably upset, but it was gon' be worth it to see the smile on her face.

Whipping through traffic in silence, I needed this time to come down and get my mind right. I got a thrill outta that torturing shit, but it took me to a place I never wanted to linger in for too long. After about twenty minutes of peace, I hit play, and "Plug's Daughter" by Kevin Gates started bumping through the speakers of my BMW Coupe. As I vibed to the music, I had to give it to Dash. My mans came through clutch with that text last night.

Chilling in the booth while Dash did his thing, I picked my phone up from the table and scrolled through my contacts until I found The Neurologist. This chick had the best head a nigga done experienced in all my twenty-nine years, and I done been sucked up by plenty broads. Hell, not only did she drop off good-ass neck, but li'l mama could cook her ass off, so no doubt I always left with a home-cooked meal.

While I was typing out a text to see if I could fall through, Dash hit me up, saying my girl was in here. What are the fucking odds of running into her at the same place where I first laid eyes on her? I locked my phone, slid it back in my pocket, and stood up to head over in the direction that Dash went. As I got closer to the table, I locked eyes with Dreux, and she immediately started to grab her shit out of the booth. She flew out that muhfucka, walking toward the bathroom. I wasn't sure if she thought that was gon' stop me, but nah, I wasn't missing out this time. Fuck that bathroom. She clearly didn't know who I was.

Following behind her, I pushed the bathroom door open, and she gasped, startled. "You can't be in here. I know you seen the sign that said women on it."

"And I know you see that I don't give a fuck. When I saw you about a month ago, yo' ass wouldn't give me the time of day, so now I'm taking that shit."

"I wasn't in the right head space to be tryna talk to anybody. I told you that."

"Yeah, I heard what your mouth said, but when I want something, I won't stop until I get it."

"Wow, that sounds a little stalker-ish," she said with the most serious expression on her face.

"Baby girl, that's one thing you'll never have to worry about with me. Let's get out this bathroom and have a real conversation."

"In one mile, turn left on Singapore Road." Siri snapped me out of my thoughts.

Noticing a flower shop on the corner, I pulled over, ran in, and bought a dozen yellow and pink roses. I didn't want to come on too strong, so I left them red shits behind the counter.

When I made it to her neighborhood, I surveyed the area, taking in the beauty of her subdivision that I couldn't see from the darkness last night. Parking in front of her house, I got out, straightened my clothes, and grabbed the roses from the passenger seat. A nigga can't even lie. While I was walking to her door, my nerves started getting the best of me. Why, I'm not sure, because I was *that* nigga. Ringing her doorbell, I peeped the camera right above it, so I slid my finger over the lens.

"Ugh, who the fuck is it? Get your hand off my damn camera," I heard her yell before the locks started turning. When she swung the door open. Seeing it was me, she squealed, wrapping her arms around my neck.

I put my arm around her waist, pulling her into my body. She looked amazing, made up but all-natural. Dreux was stunning. My boo smelled like vanilla or some shit that had me ready to eat her ass up.

"Hiiii! What are you doing here? I thought you had something to do today."

"I do. You. Whatever you have in mind, my day is yours."

"Really? I'm so excited. Oh God, I need to change. I know I probably look a mess."

"I mean, I wasn't gon' say nothing, but since you put it out there . . ."

"You already get on my nerves, and I just started liking you last night." When she rolled her eyes, it turned me on.

"Yeah, okay. Go get dressed so we can head out. Here. These are for you, of course." As she turned to go put the roses in a vase, everything in me wanted to reach out and grab that basketball booty she was hiding under that long-ass shirt.

Walking into her living room, I couldn't help but notice that li'l mama had good taste. Her carpet was chocolate colored, and shit, it looked so soft I damn near didn't wanna walk on it. A cream sectional completely covered the right wall and half of the back. The two windows on the left side were draped with red curtains to throw some color in the room, I'm assuming. Walking over to the fireplace that looked like it had never been burned, I started to scan over the pictures on her mantlepiece. My eyes almost fell outta my fucking head when I came across a picture of her and my connect on what appeared to be her graduation day. Shit. Just my damn luck that I would end up fucking with the plug's daughter.

I got comfortable in the corner of her couch, and before I knew it, I had dozed off. I felt a body lying on me, so I opened my eyes, low-key forgetting where the hell I was until I looked down and saw Dreux's big-ass hair bun thing on my shoulder. I lifted my arm slowly, letting her head fall into my chest, then rested my arm down her body. Damn, it hadn't been a full day and she already had me on this cuddling shit, but if I'm keeping it a hunnid, it felt good.

"Dreux, wake up, boo," I said while stroking her thigh.

"Hmm."

Fuck, the way she moaned had my shit bricking up, so I slick tried to readjust my dick so she wouldn't get the wrong idea.

"I thought we was going out for the day."

She sat up and stretched her arms, making the tiny-ass T-shirt she was wearing rise a little. "I came down when I got dressed and saw you in here asleep. The wrinkles in your forehead kept me from waking you. So instead, I just laid down too."

I checked my watch. It was a little after three. Shit, we'd been sleeping for the past two hours. Standing up, I reached out for her hand and pulled her to her feet.

"Come on. Let's go feed my future wife."

"You better stop saying shit like that before you end up stuck with me in real life."

Looking into her eyes, I cupped her chin. "I think I could live with that, beautiful."

She slid her feet back into her sandals, and I led her to the door, letting her lock up so we could get out of there. I couldn't keep my eyes off that ass as she walked to the car in front of me.

"You must think I'm some kind of sucka-ass nigga, huh? Get this damn card off the table, Dreux."

This girl really had me fucked up. I knew it had to be decades since she'd been on a date, or all the niggas she fucked with before were *poocheese* to make her pull out this baby-ass black card. I let her pick where we went for lunch, and when she chose The Boiling Crab, I damn near took her to my jeweler. Seafood was my shit, so I was extra hyped for this li'l date. On the way, she held my hand most of the time, not all tight and possessive like most hoes, but kind of relaxed, giving off that "I'm with as much of this as you're with" type vibe. We talked a little here and there, mostly about her job as an ultrasound technician, which I thought was dope as fuck, but also had me feeling kind of bad for judging her based on who her dad was.

Dreux picked her card up, sticking it back in her wallet, and put her hands up in surrender. "Well, excuse the hell outta me. You got it, so get it."

"Girl, that smart-ass mouth you got is gon' get you in trouble. Keep playing with me."

"Mm-hmm, I hear you. Excuse me while I run to the restroom. You mind babysitting my purse?" Shorty didn't even wait on me to answer when she said it over her shoulder.

While I waited on her, I felt my phone start to vibrate in my pocket. Seeing that it was Trell, I went ahead and answered. “This better be an emergency. You know damn well to hit Dash before you hit my jack.”

“Aye, boss man, you need to get over to the White House. It’s up in flames, dawg.”

“Fuck, it’s gon’ take me about an hour to get to the Cliff. Call Dash. He might be closer than I am. I’ll get there as soon as I can.”

“Bet.”

Peeling three hundred out of the wad in my pocket, I stood up, grabbing Dreux’s purse just as she came out of the bathroom.

“You okay, babe? You got them worry wrinkles again.” She genuinely looked concerned.

“It’s business. Nothing you need to worry your pretty self about, but I gotta go, so come on. Let me get you back home.”

Pulling up to Dreux’s spot thirty minutes later, I opened her door and walked her to the house. “I hate that I gotta cut our day short, but if it’s okay with you, I would like to come back tonight, just to chill.”

“Don’t apologize. Just make it up to me, and yeah that’s fine. Let me know when you’re on your way.”

“Of course I will. Can I kiss you? Is that okay?”

Biting her lip, she nodded her head. Holding her face between my hands, I pecked her lips, and they were just as soft as I’d imagined them to be, prompting me to deepen the kiss. Teasing, I ran my tongue across her bottom lip, and when she parted her lips, inviting me in, I took full advantage. When I felt her tighten her grip on the sides of my shirt, I knew it was time to leave because my piece was two seconds from poking her in the stomach.

Pulling back, I told her I’d see her later, and once I made sure she was inside safely, I jogged back to the car, frustrated as fuck, knowing I was about to go deal with some fuck shit. Hitting the steering wheel, I pulled off. “Fuck! If it ain’t one thing, it’s another.”

Chapter Ten

Dash

Speeding through traffic towards the White House, my mind shifted into overdrive. When Choppa and I talked the other day, I was only speculating that someone on the inside was a snake, but now, I knew for sure. The White House made us the most money, so only a muthafucka that worked for Block Boyz would know to target that trap. It seemed like every time we turned around, it was some bullshit, so hell, maybe we needed to stop turning the fuck around. Swinging into the driveway of the trap, I damn near jumped the curb from pulling in so hard.

"Trell! Aye, what's up, nigga? What the fuck happened?"

"Maaaan, say. So, the old broad that I fuck with across the street hit my line talm 'bout my house was on fire, and at first, I thought she was tripping until she FaceTimed me, and hell yeah, our shit was up in flames. By the time I got here, it was damn near burned to the ground. Somebody is tryna take us down, man."

"Shit! I know it ain't a single piece of nothing left in that bitch. I'm glad I came and collected yesterday, or we'd be down bad."

As I was shooting the shit with Trell, Choppa came thumping down the block. This nigga barely had the car in park before he jumped out with his chest puffed up. "Y'all muthafuckas really got me fucked up. Who the fuck was supposed to be here watching my shit? I'm real confused on how somebody had enough time to set this shit on fire."

"Aye, Choppa, hold all that shit down. This ain't my location, so you coming at me real reckless on some bullshit that ain't on me. Jabari and Lonzo oversee this spot, and conveniently neither one of them niggas was here when I pulled up," Trell said, defending himself.

Lately, every time some shit popped off, Jabari and Lonzo was never around. Now, me being me, I'd been keeping my ear closer to the streets more, because if some snake-ass shit was going on with them, the streets would know first.

"Say, li'l nigga, remember who you talking to next time you decide to come out yo' mouth foul. You know I'on play that disrespect shit," I heard Choppa say to Trell.

"Heard you."

Reaching in my pocket, I grabbed my keys, got in my whip, and rode off. Choppa was there, so shit, ain't no need for both of us to stick around. Halfway to the crib, my gas light came on, and as much as I didn't wanna stop, I knew I had to. I pulled into the nearest Valero, mad as hell for leaving my wallet when I rushed to the trap. While I was inside, I grabbed a Core water and some Skittles, then made my way to the register to pay for all my shit.

It was just my luck to run into Ms. Ahdia, who'd been ducking and dodging me since I ran into her a month ago. Walking up on her, I set my stuff on the counter and pressed into her, resting my chin on her shoulder. "Ring all that shit up together, my man."

"Oh my fuck! How is it that you manage to keep finding me? And back up!"

"Well, I wouldn't say I've done a great job considering you ain't hit me up yet."

"I remember saying when I want some dick from you, so I guess that explains why I haven't hit you up, right?"

Sliding my card across to the cashier, I was low-key floored by how this fine-ass girl was really on some mo' shit. "You know what? Cool. I ain't ever been fucked up behind no female, and as cute as you are, I ain't gon' start with you. Don't worry about hitting me up at all. I'm sure there's enough dick out here for you."

The cashier handed me the sack with my water and candy in it, and I walked out coolly, heading back to the car to fill up. In all my years, no woman had ever acted the way Ahdia did. It was something to her, and even though I told her not to, I hoped she'd hit me up because I wanted to know what went wrong that made her so detached.

"Wait."

I turned around to see her jogging over to me, titties bouncing with every step she took.

"Wassup?"

"Okay, so, it's been a while since I've done this whole 'talking' bullshit with anybody, so I'm sorry if I'm doing it wrong, but I am attracted to you, and I want you in the worst way."

"Word? Now, was that so hard to say?"

"Yes, it was actually. So what's next?"

"Next, you gon' shoot me a text. G'on do it. Good. Now *you* gon' wait for *me* to hit you up, and that's *if* I'm still interested. You have a good day." I kissed her on the cheek and left her standing there, probably wondering what the fuck just happened. She must have thought shit was sweet. Nah, it don't work like that, not with Dashir.

Pulling out of the gas station, I checked the rearview. I saw a car that looked a lot like Jabari's turning in. *This crash dummy,* I thought to myself.

Hooking my phone up to the Bluetooth, I scrolled my contacts until I found my grandma's name. It had been a few weeks since I'd last seen her, so I knew a visit was well overdue. I listened to the line ring until it finally went to voicemail, so I figured I'd just pop up on her. As I drove out to her house, I bobbed my head to Don Trip's "Like Me," feeling everything this nigga was spitting.

Pulling up to my grandma's house, a sense of peace washed over me. Grammy was my whole world outside of my ma, and it was nothing but good vibes every time I came around. I inserted my key into the door, pushed it open, and stepped in.

"Grammy, it's me." I walked into the house, going from room to room. When I didn't hear her call back to me, I made my way into her kitchen. I saw what looked like blood on the floor, and when I rounded the corner, there she was.

"Grammy, noooo! Who would do this to you? Come on, Grammy. Wake up!" I wailed, heart crushed as I dropped to my knees, cradling her head in my lap. Her body was still warm, so whoever killed my grandma hadn't been gone for too long. I slid my phone from my pocket and dialed 911, hoping and praying they could save my baby.

"Nine one one, what's your emergency?"

"Somebody killed my grandma. Help me, please!"

"Sir, I need you to calm down and tell me your location so I can send you help."

Doing my best to contain myself, I rattled off my grandma's address and hung up. I rocked my queen back and forth, more so to comfort myself than anything because in my heart, I knew she was gone, and there was nothing anybody could do.

Twenty minutes later, the ambulance and the police arrived, and as they bagged up my grandmother and rolled her away, my heart broke into a million pieces. I cried from my soul, and I ain't give a damn about being a grown-ass man. I picked up my keys from the hall table and got in my car to leave because I knew they'd be taping her house up within minutes as a crime scene investigation.

Something in me said to call Ahdia. I don't know why, because other than our brief encounters, we'd never talked, but I called anyway. The phone rang a couple of times; however, as I went to hang up, she answered.

"Hello." Her sweet voice sang in my ear.

"Wassup, ma? You busy?" My voice was shaky.

"No, what's wrong? You've been crying."

"Can you meet me somewhere around seven? Please?"

"Uh, yeah, sure. Just send me the location and I'll be there as soon as I can."

"Cool."

Hanging up, I sent her the address to the old, abandoned warehouse I used to escape to when I needed to clear my mind. This was probably the worst feeling I'd ever felt, and right now I just needed somebody.

As I drove back to the house in silence, blood staining my clothes, my mind raced, filled with thoughts about who could have killed my grandmother and why. As far as I knew, I didn't have any enemies. I did what I did in the streets, handled my shit, and minded my own fucking business. The more I thought about it, my hurt quickly turned into anger. Not only was someone fucking with my bread and butter, but somebody was fucking with my personal life, and that was no good.

Pulling up to my condo, I parked and sluggishly walked inside, feet heavy, heart heavier. I went straight to the bathroom, fully dressed, and climbed in the shower with my head down, watching the water wash the blood and all the hurt I felt down the drain. I snatched my clothes off, grabbed my Dove Men's Body Wash, and cleansed myself, paying more attention to the areas that were still bloodied. After I got out of the shower and dried myself off, I grabbed some solid black track pants, shirt, and shoes to blend in with the darkness. It was six ten, which gave me a few extra minutes to make it to the warehouse. I picked up the keys to my all-black Altima, aka my hitman car, and headed to my destination.

I arrived at the warehouse a little before seven, so I turned on some old-school Prince and grooved to the low sounds of the radio. I must have dozed off for a second because when I opened my eyes, it was seven thirty, and Ahdia was nowhere in sight. I checked my phone, but there were no missed calls or texts, so I said fuck her, fuck this shit, and this is why I don't let bitches in my personal world.

I called the one person that I knew had my back no matter what—my fucking brother.

"Yooo, G, what's good wit'cha?"

"Not shit, family. You get that bullshit straightened out earlier?"

"Ugh, yeah, man. Lonzo and Jabari punk asses showed up, and I fired both of them, then moved Spank and Gusto to head a different department."

"That's what's up. Aye, you busy? Can I fall through?"

"You ain't even gotta ask. My shorty here, but I'm about to put that ass to sleep, you feel me?"

"You a fool, man. Ight, here I come."

Not giving a fuck about too much of shit right now, I did one ten, weaving in and out of traffic all the way to Choppa's spot, cutting a forty-five-minute drive down to twenty. I put my hand up to the palm reader at the gate, and it slid open. For the life of me, I didn't understand why the hell this nigga needed a forty-mile driveway. Like, bitch, you gotta drive to the mailbox. Ain't nobody got time for that fuck shit.

Walking in the door, all I could hear was moaning and skin slapping, and that shit damn near made me go the fuck home.

"Ooooh, shit, Kamron! Yesss, baby!"

"Aye man, shit! Don't nobody wanna hear that bullshit. Close the fucking door," I yelled from the foyer.

"Muthafucka, nobody told you to just walk in either," Choppa shouted back.

Going in the kitchen, I could still hear the fucking, but I bet you I ain't hear another moan. I'd been around Dreux a few times to know that her embarrassed ass wasn't coming down here to speak tonight. I grabbed a Corona out of the fridge and chilled in the den, smoking an L until my boy got himself together. Not too long after I finished my first blunt, Chop came strolling in with a Corona and his box of Cuban cigars. How the fuck he smoked them large ass cancer sticks was beyond me. I stuck to my herbs.

"What's up, bro? What brings you by tonight? Not that you aren't welcomed, before you say some dumb-ass shit."

Dragging my hand down my face, I rested it in my palms, and like I knew they would, the tears came rushing down. This was my mans, so I ain't give a fuck about crying in front of him.

"Aww, dawg, this gotta be some serious shit if it got you like this, fam." He rested his hand on my shoulder, giving me a minute to gather myself.

I wiped my hand down my face again and delivered him the news that I'd been holding on to since it happened.

"Nawww, man, nawww! Not Grammy. Who the fuck would do this to her, man? What the fuck?" Choppa let out the most gut-wrenching cry for my grandma because she was as much his as she was mine, and that shit shook me to my core. My guy sobbed. I could damn near see his heart weeping for Geraldine Edwards, just the way mine had.

"Baby, what's wrong?" Dreux appeared in the doorway, respectfully dressed, to check on Chop. He looked up at her with tears in his eyes, and when sis walked over to him, cradling his head to her chest while he cried, I knew she was it for him.

"Dash, what's going on?"

"My grandma was killed earlier today."

She gasped, bringing her hand to her mouth. "I'm so sorry. I am so sorry. What do you need? Is there anything I can get you?"

I debated on telling her about Ahdia, but I decided against it, since it really wasn't anything between us. Yeah, I was feeling shorty, but I had bigger things that I had to deal with.

"Where she at, man? Where's my Grammy? I gotta see her."

"Man, Chop, I ain't dealt with none of this shit yet, but she's at the morgue, man. I'm gon' try to go handle everything tomorrow, but if not, sis, I know you didn't get the chance to meet her, but if I can't, can you get it together for me? I don't care about the cost. Just make sure it's nice."

"Absolutely. Whatever you need me to do, I got it."

"Thanks. It means a lot to me. Chop, you mind if I crash here, man?"

Nodding his head against Dreux's stomach, he replied, "My house has always been your house. Ain't no need to ever ask me if you can stay here."

"I know it. Formality, fam. I'ma catch the room in the basement. I'll holla at y'all in the morning."

“Night, Dash. Come on, babe. Let’s go to bed.”

I grabbed my beer from the table and made my way to the basement, which was set up like a small-ass apartment. I took the rest of my drink to the head and lay down for the night. I tossed and turned for hours, images of my grandma’s body constantly surfing through my head. Finally, after three hours, I said a prayer for Grammy, for God to rest her soul, and I drifted off to sleep.

Chapter Eleven

Dreux

These past few weeks with Kamron had been some of the best of my life. After I let him know about my past, he'd been so patient and kind. This man was so sexy without even trying, and it had my hormones raging. He had yet to try to have sex with me, which had me wondering what his problem was. Did he have erectile dysfunction, was he uncircumcised, or just didn't know how to put it down? Nahhh, there was no way a man that fine had problems fucking.

Rolling over, I felt around for Kam's warm body, and when I didn't feel him, I jumped up, only to find him sitting in his recliner, staring at me.

"You're so beautiful when you're asleep. The way your hair sprawls out all over the pillows and the little humming noise you make is probably the cutest thing I've heard outside of your laugh." He got up from the chair and started walking toward me. "But my favorite is when you press your ass up against my dick once you think I've fallen asleep. You want me to fuck you, Dreux? All you gotta do is say it."

My heart began to race, watching Kam crawl up the bed, looking like the whole damn dinner plate. He hovered over me, forcing me to lay back, and when he smashed his lips against mine, ignoring my morning breath, I knew this man was my husband.

"Answer me," he said against my lips. "You ready for me to break this li'l pussy in? I smell her. Just tell me you want it."

I nodded my head because my voice was caught in my throat.

Sliding his hand into my panties, baby gripped my whole kitty, and when he dipped that long-ass finger in my lake, she overflowed. Gliding his fingers in and out of my wetness, he began to suck on my neck so hard I could feel the passion mark forming.

"Use your words, Dreux. I don't understand that nodding shit you doing." Taking his middle finger, he started circling my clit slowly, gradually picking up the pace.

I closed my eyes as my head fell back and rode his wave of ecstasy. The throbbing of my nub told me that I was near climaxing, and I guess Kam felt it too because, unexpectedly, he removed his hand. Popping my head up and my eyes open, I delivered the meanest mug that my face could form.

"Baby, what the fuckkkk? Why did you stop?"

"I asked you a question, mama, and I need you to open your mouth like a grown-ass woman before I give you this grown-ass dick," Kam said with his lips still pressed against my neck.

"Yes, bae, I want that grown man dick, I wanna feel you." I swear I know how Beloved felt when she told that man to touch her on the inside part.

He tugged at the bottom of my shirt. I raised my arms, and he pulled it over my head. He hiked my leg up around his waist, and my hands instantly found the back of Kam's head, pulling it to my left breast. While his tongue flickered over my nipple, his hand found its way back to my hidden treasure. Sliding down my body, he kissed down my stomach until he was at eye level with my pearl. With his thumb, Kam massaged my clit, and when my juices pooled at the opening of my vagina, we locked eyes. I wanted to feel him on me. In me. But being the man that he was, Kam was taking his time, so I decided to speed up the process.

"Kamronnn, fuck me, please." I couldn't take any more of this caressing shit he had going on. I needed something. Mouth, dick, both—I didn't give a damn at this point. He gave me that sexy-ass smirk I'd grown to love.

Lifting my ass up, with my legs in the air, Kam sucked my pussy from the entrance to the clit like his name was Bissell. I gasped, clutching the sheets, taken aback by the sensational feeling that radiated all over me. As he circled my button with his tongue, he slipped his finger back inside of me, tapping that G-spot in a "come here" motion.

"Ohhh, shit, bae. Eat this pussy. Make me feel good. That's it right there. Don't stop, right there. Mmmm fuck!"

Gripping the back of his head, I pushed his face further into my vagina, and that only fueled him to go harder. My pressure began to rise, and before I knew it, an orgasm came ripping through me, raining my love all over Kamron. Coming up for air, his face was glistening with my essence, making me curious to know what I tasted like. I crashed my mouth to his, sucking on his lips, savoring the sweet taste of my honey.

"Damn, Pooh, I've wanted to taste that shit since the first night I met you. Turn over. Put that ass in the air."

Doing as he said, I dipped my back down until my breasts were touching the bed, creating the perfect arch. Looking behind me, I saw Kam stripping out of his clothes, and when that dick sprang out of them boxers, my jaw hit the floor. It was long, thick, and chocolate with a slight curve to the right. The muthafucka had to be at least ten inches, and I wanted it down my throat.

Before I could get up, Kam started rubbing that monster of his up and down my slit, coating the tip with my moisture. As he poked at my entrance, I could feel him struggling to gain access.

"Bae, I can't get in. I'ma have to push hard, and it's gonna hurt a little bit, but work with me. I swear I'ma be as gentle as possible."

"Okay," I replied softly, bracing myself. I was nervous because this was hands down the biggest dick I'd seen in a long time.

Kam grabbed my waist, positioning himself at my opening, and when he pushed into me, it had to be the most painful feeling I've ever felt. He pulled in and out of me at a slow, steady speed, and eventually, the pain subsided and was replaced with pleasure.

"Ohhh, fuck, Dreux. This some dangerous-ass shit you got between your legs. It's so fucking tight and warm."

"Babyyyy! Shiiiit!"

He was hitting me so deep I could have sworn his dick was in my chest. He was smacking my right ass cheek, and I caught his rhythm and started matching him thrust for thrust, because this muthafucka wasn't about to outfuck me.

"Hell yeah, just like that, mama. Throw that shit back for a real nigga. Show me what it's made for." Kam hit me with a stroke so long and strong that my juices began to run down my legs, and I knew that I was about to explode. Toying with my clit, he quickened his pace, maxing me out, and when he pushed into me the last time, I came on him as he came in me. I collapsed on the bed with him following behind me.

"You on birth control?"

"Nope."

***

While I waited for my next patient, my phone vibrated on my desk, lighting up with a text message.

TheMister: I miss you already.

I couldn't help the grin that formed on my face. I'd spent the last few days with him, boo'd up, ignoring everything that wasn't business related for him. I'd become just as addicted to him as he was to me. It had only been about a month, but I knew that I could love this man for the rest of my life.

Me: I just left Kam lol

TheMister: And? So you don't miss daddy?

Me: LMFAO! Boy do NOT start calling yourself that lol, but yeah I do.

TheMister: Jokes. Dinner tonight?

Me: Raincheck, date with my parents.

The nurse peeked her head in the door, letting me know that my patient was ready, so I dropped my phone in my purse and went to check on Ms. Johnson.

Closing the office after my last patient, I searched my purse for my keys and phone before heading out. Checking my messages, I had two apiece from my parents, making sure we were still on, and three from Kam.

TheMister: That's cool. I love you.

TheMister: Damn that's cold. You ain't gon' reply?

TheMister: I feel dumb as fuck for saying that shit. Bet.

Once I was in the car with my phone connected to the Bluetooth, I called my man, but like the stubborn-ass dude he was, I got no answer. I'd grown to learn that when things didn't go Kam's way, whether it was business or personal, his attitude shifted drastically. Now, what I needed for him to learn was, quite frankly, I don't give a damn. Typing him a quick li'l message, I made my way home to get ready for dinner with my parents.

Later that night . . .

Dressed in a white off-the-shoulder crop top, burgundy bell bottom type pants, and black Steve Madden pumps, I exited my car, doing a happy dance because we were at my favorite restaurant, Ruth's Chris. Once I spotted my parents at the entrance, I made my way over and kissed both cheeks, greeting them individually.

"Hey, Mama. Hey, Daddy."

"Girl, don't be putting' yo lips on me. I don't know where they been." Leave it to Lo McCoy to pop slick at the mouth.

"Whatever, lady. How are you guys? Shit, feels like weeks since I've seen y'all."

"Aye, watch your mouth, girl. I know I raised you better than that." My daddy scowled at me.

"Sorry, Daddy."

"Anyway, your father is taking me to Punta Cana for two weeks since he's been working so much, and I was wondering if you and your sister wanted to join me," my mom said.

"Wellllll, I do have some vacation time that needs to be used. What day are you planning to leave, and are significant others invited?"

I watched the color drain from my daddy's face. *Sheesh, I'm twenty-five. I'm sure he doesn't think I'm not dating—or fucking, for that matter.*

"Who the fuck has a significant other at this table other than me?"

"Daddyyyy. Don't start acting crazy. I'm almost twenty-six years old. It's time I start taking dating seriously."

"Seriously enough to have you wanting to bring him on a family trip? Shit, how serious are y'all?"

"It's still fairly new, but I want him to meet you and Mom, so what's better than a vacation?" Beaming at Big Drew, I hoped that eased him into it.

"Damn. Okay, but I wanna see this young man before the trip, so bring him to Sunday dinner."

"Yayyyy, okay. Thank you, Daddy. I love you so much."

"Mm-hmm."

For the rest of dinner, my parents caught up on the things that were going on in my life, occasionally asking about Dia, but hell, what could I say about that crazy-ass girl? Big Drew paid for the check, and we parted ways, them to a blues lounge, and me to the house, of course.

It was creeping up on twelve a.m., and I still hadn't heard from Kam, which was unusual. I guess he was still in his feelings about me responding late to his text, but oh well. Restless as hell, I headed to the kitchen for a late-night snack, hoping it would help put me to sleep. I grabbed the Genoa salami, some Colby cheese, and crackers from the refrigerator, then made a small pot of hot tea to soothe me.

As I sat down at the table to begin eating, my doorbell rang. It was after midnight, so I pulled the 9 mm from under the island and walked my ass to the camera system, and of course, it was black. Kamron. Swinging the door open, Kam stumbled in, almost knocking me over in the process, and when I went to help him, he reeked of a mixture of Hennessy and weed. This didn't seem like the thing Kamron would do on a regular, so I made sure to handle this situation with care.

"Baby, come on. You're kind of heavy, so you gotta help me. Come on. One step at a time."

He groaned but shuffled into the house, allowing me to close and lock the door behind us. Slowly but surely, we made our way over to the couch, where I sat him down and started removing his clothes. I pulled his shirt over his head, exposing the tattoos that adorned his chest, and as I scanned his body, one particular tattoo stood out.

Rest In Peace
Santino Luis Vega
10/23/1966 - 08/14/1995

I covered the tattoo with one hand and my mouth with the other. He was hurting today, and I missed all the signs. The extra neediness, the quick attitude when I didn't answer right away. I missed it all.

"You didn't know, Pooh. Stop that."

"Oh, baby, I should have. We've talked about everything but that, and now I feel awful for not being there for you."

"You good. I sat at his gravesite all day getting fucked up. Shit, I even think I fell asleep at some point." Kam shrugged his shoulders as he spoke. His head fell back against the couch, giving me the opportunity to squat down and remove his shoes. Tugging at his belt, he lifted up enough for me to pull them down his legs, and when I got them past his waist, that big-ass dick damn near took my eye out. Licking my lips, all I wanted to do was taste it, wrap my lips around it, and ease his mind.

"Don't touch my shit if you ain't gon' handle it right."

Smirking, I didn't even bother saying anything. Instead, I slid my hands in his boxer and freed the beast. As if it was made for me, my mouth started watering, ready to eat this dick like Thanksgiving dinner. Gently circling the head, I licked the pre-cum that was oozing from the tip of his dick, enjoying the salty taste.

"Ssss."

I opened my mouth, letting my saliva fall, and stroked him up and down as I sucked the head. Dropping my jaw, I took him in inch by inch as he stretched my mouth wider, challenging me to go hard. When I had half of him in my mouth, I pulled back, then swallowed all of him down my throat. I ain't ever been more thankful for my lack of a gag reflex.

"Oh, fuck. Do that shit again, baby. Show me yo' mama made a ho."

Flattening my tongue against his shaft, I took him back slowly, feeling the meaty veins that ran down to the base. I held him in the back of my throat and hummed for a few seconds. I massaged his balls with my hand and started to pick up speed, creating the perfect suction with my jaws.

"Dreux, gahdamn! Suck that shit, Pooh. Eat this dick up." Kamron grabbed two fistfuls of my hair and began to fuck the shit out of my face.

Being me, I had something to prove because ain't no way this nigga was gon' one up me. I didn't give a damn if he was drunk or not. I sucked his balls into my mouth, letting my tongue tickle the gooch while I stroked his dick. I felt his hands tightening in my hair, indicating that my baby was ready to bust.

"Fuck, I'm about to nut. Come catch this shit, baby."

Covering his tip, I sucked the head slow and hard, until I felt him filling my throat with hot cum, and I swallowed every bit. I got off my knees to go upstairs, brush my teeth, and finally take my ass to bed.

"Oh, dinner with my parents. Sunday at eight."

Coming out of the bathroom, I noticed that Kam had made his way upstairs and into my bed. This was his first time being in my bed, because usually, I'd spend the night with him, so this was different for me. Sliding in beside him, I turned on my side, facing away from him, and closed my eyes.

"Pooh, get yo' ass over here. You know damn well we don't sleep like this." His deep baritone voice scared the hell outta me. I rolled over, and as soon as my head hit his chest, I heard light snoring.

"Baby."

"Wassup, boo?"

"I love you too."

A few hours later

I felt the bed shift, and when I turned around, Kam was up, getting dressed.

"Where are you going so early? Come back to bed with me."

"Can't. I got a few runs to make, and I don't wanna be out all day, so I'm getting started now."

"Can I go with you? I don't have anything to do today, and I promise I won't get in the way. You won't even know I'm there."

I could see him battling with himself, deciding if he was gonna let me go or not.

"Ight, that's cool. Come on, get ya ass up."

I jumped up, rushing to the bathroom to take a quick shower because Kam was damn near ready to walk out the door. Throwing on some jeans, a tank top, and my black Retro 13s, I was ready in twenty minutes flat.

Vibing to Ella Mai's new album in my headphones, I sat with my hands tucked between my legs as Kam wove in and out of traffic, heading toward Oak Cliff. He reached over and pulled my earbud out of my ear and grabbed my hand.

"What you come along for if you were just gon' ignore me?" he said with a smirk on his face.

"I ain't tryna bother you. I just didn't want to sit in the house by myself. What you gotta do in the Cliff, if you don't mind me asking?"

"Look at you. What the hell you know about the Cliff?" He laughed.

"Boy, whatever. My best friend was from around the way, so I was out there every now and then."

"Why I ain't ever see you then?"

"I don't know. Maybe you weren't looking hard enough."

He licked his lips and put my AirPod back in my ear. I made a mental note that he never answered my question, then went back to grooving to "Trip."

Fifteen minutes later, we were pulling up to this house on Polk that was halfway burned to the ground. I looked over at Kam, who was texting somebody, and when we made eye contact, he leaned over and kissed my cheek.

"Lock the doors when I get out."

I wasn't locking shit because what he didn't know was that I had my baby Desert Eagle in my purse, and I wouldn't hesitate to let that bitch rip. I liked for Kam to think that everything with me was sugar sweet, but if the time ever came, he'd see first-hand why I was named after my daddy. I saw Dash pull up behind us, so I figured we'd be sitting here for a while. Out of the corner of my eye, I saw a bitch in some little-ass shorts with her ass hanging out, a tank top that hung so low her titties were almost on the floor, and a dirty-ass weave. I cracked the window a bit to see what was going on, and I heard her screaming about some nigga named Reek. Since it wasn't shit that concerned me, I started to let my window up until I saw that bitch put her hands on my nigga. Aww, she had me and him fucked up. Dropping my AirPods in the cup holder, I threw the door open and stepped out of the car.

“Aye, listen, bitch. Don’t put yo’ fucking hands on my man again. Anything you gotta say, say it, and keep them dick beaters to yo’self.”

“Ho, this ain’t got shit to do with you. The fuck yo’ uptight ass doing in the hood anyway?” she popped slick, rolling her neck and shit.

“You worried about the wrong shit. Like I said, keep yo’ hands in check, and I’ll let you get back to what the fuck doesn’t concern me.”

“Bitch, please. No, like I was saying, what the fuck did you do to Reek?” she said to Kam, mushing him in the head.

That shit sent me over the edge, and before I knew it, I had that dirty-ass ponytail wrapped around my hand, and I was giving her the same business that she insisted didn’t concern me.

“Baby, let her go. You done fucked her up enough. Dreux!”

After I punched the ho in her mouth one last time, I coolly walked my ass back to the car and got in.

“Maaan, let me get this crazy-ass girl outta here. Stay up, my nigga.” Kam got back in the car, and before he drove, he asked me where I got hands so cold from. I just shrugged my shoulders. He laughed as he pulled away from the curb.

“Can we go eat now?”

Chapter Twelve

Jabari

One trap down, four more to go. After I dropped the match through the back window, I got the fuck out of the area. Lonzo had ran to get him some food while the other niggas were hitting the block, giving me the perfect chance to set that shit ablaze. I had no doubt that if I tried to do this shit with Lonzo around, that nigga was gon' fold, and I'd hate to have to kill my best friend. I hated that Dash had already cleaned house because that would have been extra money to execute my plan. I'd spent the last two weeks gathering everything I needed to destroy these bitch-made niggas.

I felt my phone vibrate. It was Choppa, just like I expected.

"What's up with it?"

"Muthafucka, what you mean? Where the fuck you at? The White House up in flames and you missing."

"Maaaan, I stepped out for a few minutes to get some food. What the hell you mean it's in flames?"

"Bruh, you know what? Don't even worry about it. You and ya fucking sidekick Lonzo can kick rocks. I'on need no muhfuckin' body on my team that can't make sure shit doesn't go south."

"Kick rocks? Nigga, you firing me?"

Click

"Fuck!" I yelled, beating on the steering wheel. This bitch-ass nigga fired me *and* hung up in my face. That's cool, though. I had something for him and Dash's pussy ass.

Pulling up to the trap in the Cliff, I scoped the scene, ready to light this muthafucka up just like I did the last one. Since the whole hood was out today, I had to play it safe, so instead, I decided to make a trip to see a special lady until the block cleared out.

"Mmmm! Mmmm!" Dash's grandma Pearl struggled to say due to the tape on her mouth.

This nigga had fucked up bringing people to the place where she laid her head, especially since you can never be too sure about someone's intentions.

"So, let me tell you a story. Once upon a time, there was a little boy who was born to an alcoholic and a weak-ass bitch who was too afraid to stand up for her boy. Imagine getting your ass beat every day for twelve years until you're old enough to fight back, and you end up killing your father. The feeling you get, the rush of knowing the person who caused you so much pain your whole life, was now suffering at your hands. See, I believe in karma, and this, sweet Grammy, is divine intervention. You know, I really hate to do this, but I don't think it's fair that Dash not only gets to reign in these streets, but he also didn't have to deal with the same abuse from our father that I did." I watched her eyes grow wide as realization set it.

"Yep, that's right, Grammy. Dash is my brother, and even though he didn't do shit to me, I can't fucking stand him, so this makes you a casualty of war."

She began to squirm, knowing that her time was coming to an end, but there was nothing left for her to do. Lifting her from the chair, I placed her on the sheet of plastic I had on the floor, knees propped up with her hands behind her back. Going into my bag of toys, I pulled out my switchblade and placed it to her neck. Removing the duct tape from her mouth, I allowed her to speak her final words.

"I hope you can live with yourself after this."

"Ehh, I think I'll be fine."

Slicing into her carotid artery, I watched with a smile on my face as blood quickly poured from the wound in her neck. Dropping the knife in a Ziploc bag, I carefully packed my tools, leaving Grammy bound and bleeding, and exited through the back door. I had parked my car two blocks over to keep someone from being able to identify my whip. Once I made it to my car, I stripped out of my hoodie, putting it and the mask I had on in a bag too. I pulled off because I'd already been there longer than I needed to be.

Making it back to the Cliff, I checked my console for some 'gars, and when I didn't find any, I decided to swing by the Valero. As I got closer, I remembered that earlier, I threw them in the glove compartment instead. I reached over to grab them, and as I lifted my head, something at the gas station caught my eye. Dash's dumb ass was leaving out, and when I scanned the parking lot, Ahdia was getting in her car.

Turning around, I pulled up to one of the pumps and sat waiting for her to leave as well. I got out, acting like I was pumping gas, and as soon as she put her car in reverse, I hung up the hose and followed out behind her. I let three cars in between us, keeping me at a far enough distance so that she wouldn't suspect that I was tailing her. After about forty-five minutes, she pulled up to a nice two-story house in Richardson, which I assumed belonged to her. I watched as she entered, still unaware of anybody following her.

"You're still a stupid-ass bitch," I said out loud.

I overheard her telling Dash that she would meet him somewhere around seven p.m., so I guess he found my little gift.

I took two pictures—one of her address, and one of her license plates. I couldn't wait to show her what I had in store because I'd learned some new shit in three years.

It was a little after 5:30. My stomach began to rumble, so I drove out of her subdivision and went to find me something to grub on. I pulled up to the Popeyes down the street, ordered my food, and sat in the parking lot eating until it was time to make my move. These niggas really thought no one could get close to them or they couldn't be touched. Shit, all it took was the right muthafucka, and it was lights out for their asses. One by one, I was gon' take down everyone close to them, until they were too fucked up to even worry about the street business, and then I'd swoop in and knock their asses off, keeping everything they'd built.

I picked up my phone to call Lonzo, just to see where his head was at.

"Yeah."

"Damn, nigga, what the fuck you on that got you sounding all dry and shit, fam?"

"Maaan, I already know you heard about our shit burning down, then Choppa had the fucking nerve to fire me because I wasn't there. Like, my nigga, I got a whole fucking family to feed, and we just found out that Sherene is pregnant again."

"Fuck, bro, another one? That's six gahdamn kids. Look, Choppa called and told me that same shit, but I got another plan. I just need to know if you down or not."

"Bro, I'm not looking for one of your get-rich-quick schemes. I need to know that whatever this is, it ain't gon' have me dead or in jail."

This pussy-ass nigga. I already saw that once I got him to help me with this shit, I was gon' have to kill his ass too, homie or not.

"Man, hell naw. This shit is legit. We gon' be set for life, so you ain't gotta worry about jail or no shit like that."

I had to butter this shit up real good because I knew any sign of bullshit, and I was on my own.

"Ight, bruh, I'm down. Swing by the house later and let me know what the plan is. I got money put back, but with six kids, bills, and a wife, I know that shit is gon' dry up faster than pussy."

"One hunnid. I'm about to tie up some loose ends real quick, and then I'll pull up on you."

"Solid."

Night was starting to fall, and when I checked the time, it was inching up on 6:30, so I threw my box of bones in the backseat and started back toward Ahdia's house with a sinister smile on my face. I couldn't wait to get inside of that sweet pussy again. When I met her, she had told me she was a virgin and she was saving herself for marriage, but I had other plans for her.

We dated for six months, so one night, we were "studying," and when I leaned in to kiss her, she accepted. I tried to take it a step further, but when she denied me, my anger got the best of me, and I beat her ass until she was unconscious, then took what the fuck I felt belonged to me.

The next morning, I knocked on her door, and she opened up, visibly shaken. I pushed my way inside. I was gone off of that piece of ass that quick, and I was ready to break in the rest of her. I made her get on her knees to suck my dick, and when she started puking everywhere, I punched her in the top of her head repeatedly, dazing her a bit. I forced my way inside of her again, and the way her pussy felt around my dick, I knew there was no way I could pull out. This went on for three weeks until one day, I showed up to her apartment, and it was vacant.

For three years, I looked for this bitch, and she was right under my nose the whole time, making me regret not killing her ass when I had the chance. It was time to reclaim what was mine because I refused to let Dash get in between those caramel legs.

When I pulled up to her house, I saw lights in various rooms being switched off, letting me know that she was on her way out the door. I stepped out of my car, coolly walked up to her porch, and waited. I heard the locks begin to turn, and there she was, looking back at me like a deer caught in headlights.

“Going somewhere?”

Chapter Thirteen

Ahdia

"Jabari," I whispered, frozen in place.

"The one and only, baby. What, you thought I wouldn't find you?" he asked with the wickedest grin on his face.

"What is it? What do you want from me? It's been three years."

"You. That's what the fuck I want. Now, you're gonna walk out this door like nothing is wrong, and if you try anything stupid, you already know how I give it up."

Turning around, I locked my house door and slowly made my way to the waiting car. I was terrified out of my mind, but I refused to give him the satisfaction because fear fueled his fire. He reached around me, causing me to flinch a little, but I quickly gathered myself and slid into the passenger seat. When he opened the driver's door, I noticed the gloves that weren't on his hands a few minutes ago.

As he drove away from my neighborhood, I pressed my luck one last time, trying to pick his brain. "Jabari, what is this? Why are you doing this?"

"Shut the fuck up. What? You think I'm about to let you and that muthafucka Dash ride off into the sunset, knowing that pussy belongs to me? Nah, ma, you got me fucked up."

"I've never—"

"I said shut the fuck up. You know what? I was trying not to use this, but it seems like you don't know what shut the fuck up means, so let me help you."

He pulled a white, weird-smelling cloth from his pocket, and the last thing I heard before I passed out was Jabari saying no one would ever find my body.

Coming to, I was naked, handcuffed to a bed in a house that resembled a cabin. I immediately started to panic because other than my mom, no one knew about the things I went through while I was in college, so I knew if he did kill me, people wouldn't suspect that it was him. I listened to see if I could hear anyone else in the house, and when I was sure that I didn't, I yelled out.

"Hellllp! Somebody help me! Please!"

"Tsk, tsk, tsk. Now, why would you try that, Ahdia? What kind of idiot do you think I am? There isn't another house for at least seven miles, sweetheart."

I could no longer hold back the tears that had been threatening to fall from my eyes the moment I saw him on my porch. Fear was an understatement. I was terrified. Flashbacks of the things he did to me three years ago began to flood my mind, and the tears were coming at the same rate.

"What are the tears for, Ahdia? The last time we were together was so special, wasn't it? I'd like to think so." He licked his lips with the creepiest smile on his face, making my skin crawl.

Years ago, when I met Jabari, I thought he was the finest man that this world had to offer. He stood around six feet even, towering over me the way that I liked, with a muscular build. His skin was the color of brown sugar, and he kept his hair cut in a low fade that was tapered on the side. His golden eyes accented his complexion, and his succulent pink lips pulled it all together.

Jabari was the perfect gentleman until I denied him access to my hidden treasure. It didn't take long for the monster to appear, and when it did, he violated me every day for almost a month, tearing down my self-esteem. I dropped out of school, and shortly after, I found out that I was pregnant. I told my mom about the things that had happened to me, and she accompanied me to get an abortion because there was no way I could look into the face of a child that reminded me of him.

"We can do this the easy way, or we can do this the hard way. Your pick," he stated as he walked over to me while unbuckling his pants.

"Jabari, please don't do this. Just let me go, and I won't say a word to anyone about this," I pleaded.

"Okay, I see we're gonna have to do this the hard way." He dropped his pants and climbed on the bed, causing me to squirm. "You can either get still, or I can knock yo' stupid ass out and get you still myself."

I knew that no matter what I did, he was still going to rape me, so I closed my eyes as tight as I could and lay there, preparing to lose myself all over again. I could feel his body hovering over me, and I could instantly feel the bile rising from my stomach. He leaned down to peck my lips, and when I didn't reciprocate, he squeezed my throat until my mouth fell open, and he shoved his tongue inside. I wanted so badly to clamp down on it, but I knew if I did, there was no way I'd make it out of this situation alive. Feeling his nasty-ass dick poking at my opening, I tried my best to close my legs to keep him from entering my body.

"Open up. Don't fucking play with me, Ahdia."

"No, I don't wanna do this."

I saw his eyes turn as black as 2 a.m., and I knew nothing good was coming from this. He delivered three hard smacks across my face, making me open my legs because of the excruciating pain. As he rammed his dick repeatedly inside of me, I hollered out in horror. He was ripping my kitty apart, showing no remorse, even when he noticed that I wasn't getting wet.

"Ohhh, fuck, this pussy is still as tight as when I broke it in three years ago. Too bad that muthafucka will never get to feel it."

As he was pumping in and out of me, I tried everything I could to hold my tears in, but I felt them sliding down the side of my face.

"Aww, shit, you might as well stop that crying bullshit because that ain't gon' do a damn thing but make me go harder. That's the type of shit I like."

His body began to shake, and I just hoped and prayed that he would pull out this time because I didn't want to go through another abortion—if I made it out of this alive. Sure enough, he pulled out and nutted all over my stomach and the top of my vagina. The bile that I'd been holding in came up, so I turned my head and puked on the side of the bed.

"Bitch, I should make you clean that shit up."

He went into a bag that he'd brought into the room and grabbed a liquid-filled syringe. Walking over to me, he took the needle, inserted it into my neck, and within seconds, I was out again.

"Nigga, what the fuck is this? This ain't what I signed up for, bro."

"Yes the fuck it is. You said you were down to get this money with me, and this is the way to do it. That's Dash's bitch in that room, or at least he thinks it is, so when she wakes the hell up, we gon' record a video, send it to him, and request a million-dollar ransom."

"Maaaan, hell naw. You don't think that nigga is gon' take that shit to the police the first chance he gets?"

"Nah, family, you know damn well Dash ain't no fan of the boys in blue, so that'll be the least of my worries. You sure you don't want a piece of that pussy?"

"Bro, you mean to tell me you been in here raping her too? Dawg, you sick as fuck, man. I keep telling you to seek some medical attention for that shit."

I overhead Jabari talking to somebody whose voice I didn't recognize. I'd finally awakened from what seemed like an eternity. Shit, I didn't even know what day of the week it was. I'd yet to be removed from these handcuffs, so there was dried-up semen on me, and I was starting to form an odor.

"JB, come on, man. You really got her laid up in here like this? Damn, I knew you had your ways, but what the fuck? Go run her a shower or something. Unlock these cuffs, dawg."

"Aye, you bet not try no funny shit when I let her loose. You starting to look real suspect to me."

"Man, whatever. Just get her in the shower. How you gon' get ransom money and you already fucked her up? Think, nigga."

"Fuck, you right. Ight, man, get her together."

I wasn't sure who this man was, but I was more than grateful he showed up to talk a little sense into Jabari. My vagina was on fire, which let me know that even while I was unconscious, he still got his rocks off on me.

"All right, look. I don't know your name, and nine times out of ten, I can't save you from him, but I will try to intervene as much as I can. This isn't my type of wave, so I'm really not trying to be a part of this."

"Thank you. I really appreciate whatever at this point."

"Cool. Can you stand on your legs? I need to get you to the bathroom."

"Yeah, I can. I may need to use you as a crutch, though."

"All right, let's go."

I stood up on shaky legs, and when I looked down and saw the excessive amounts of blood that covered the sheets, my joints almost gave out on me. Like, what could have gone so wrong in a person's life to make them wanna treat somebody like this? I hobbled to the bathroom, avoiding eye contact with Jabari, and climbed into the shower.

"You got eight minutes to wash your ass and make yourself presentable. Let's see how much you're really worth to that little boyfriend of yours."

Not bothering to reply, I washed my body as well as I could, being especially gentle to my genital area, and cried my last set of tears. I ain't gon' lie and say I wasn't scared wondering if this nigga was gon' kill me or not, but Drew and Lolita McCoy ain't raise no bitch, and I wasn't going out like one.

"Let's fucking go!" this psycho-ass nigga yelled, snapping me outta my thoughts. I stepped out, and the mystery man handed me a towel, a big T-shirt, and some boxers to put on.

"Even in that big-ass shirt, you're still fine ass fuck, and it's taking everything in me not to knock that pussy down again."

"Aye, man, chill out. Get the damn phone. Let's record this stupid-ass video so we can get this money, and then you're free to do whatever you need to do on your own time."

"Fuck you, bitch. Say, unlock this muhfuckin' phone and FaceTime that nigga Dash right fucking now."

Something in my heart said that Dash wasn't gonna answer considering the fact that I was supposed to meet him the night before and never showed up. Hell, he was liable to tell this psycho-ass bastard to go ahead and kill me anyway.

I hit the FaceTime button. The phone continued to ring until it finally ended the call. Jabari snatched the phone from my hand and started recording a video.

"Hahaaaaa bitch-ass nigga! I heard you was looking for the muthafucka that killed ya granny and burned down ya li'l trap house. Well, here the fuck I am. See, y'all fucked up when y'all underestimated my ass. How the fuck y'all gon' fire the nigga that was running the spot that ran y'all the most money, huh? How the fuck does that work? Y'all thought you couldn't be touched, but guess what? You touched. I'm coming for everything you muthafuckas got, and look, I started with you, Dash." He flipped the camera to me.

"Yeah, that's right. I got ya li'l girlfriend, and I'ma have a real good time with her. Matter of fact, I already started, and I must say that pussy is probably some of the best I've ever had. Maybe you'll get your chance—if I don't kill her first. I'll be seeing you niggas again."

"Nigga, what the fuck? You ain't say shit about the ransom money. Fuck you on?"

"Chill and be still, kinfolk. I got something even better."

Listening to him record that video, I closed my eyes and prayed that Dash gave a damn about me enough to send me help, but above all else, I prayed that he would forgive me.

Chapter Fourteen

Dreux

Sunday

Whoo, shit! As much as I enjoyed sleeping wrapped up in Kamron's arms, it always felt like I was in bed with a damn heater. I lifted my phone off the dresser to check the time, and it was almost ten o'clock. I flipped the comforter back, trying to ease out of the bed, and like I knew he would, Kam pulled me back to him.

"Baby, you gotta let me up."

"Unh-uh, why? Where you going?"

"I gotta get home. There's a few things I gotta take care of before tonight. Come on, Kam."

"Aww, shit, my real name. A'ight, can you do something for me first?"

Rolling my eyes, I knew he was about to be on some good bullshit. "What, Kamron?"

"Can you take care of this before you go?" he asked, rubbing his dick against my ass.

"Really, nigga? You make me so sick," my ass replied as I pulled my left leg outta my panties.

"Mmm, you know you wanna feel this shit inside of you. That's why you took them draws off so damn quick." He slid his hand between my legs and started tickling my clit, creating an instant mess.

"Look at my girl. She's ready for Poppa. You know what to do, so stop playing and get with it."

Throwing my leg on top of his, I pushed my ass back as he pushed his dick into its newfound home. I had to hold my breath for a second because I still hadn't fully adjusted to his length and girth.

"Ssss, why this pussy so fucking wet? Gahdamn," Kam said with his lips against my neck, placing soft kisses here and there.

He wrapped his arm tighter around my waist, locking me so I couldn't move, and began to dig me out from behind. He was giving me long strokes, pulling all the way out, then pushing back in slowly, letting me feel every inch of his manhood.

"Uhhh shaaaat, yesss, baby, fuck!"

I couldn't do shit but moan and take what he was dishing out. He was tap-dancing on my G-spot. All I wanted to do was explode, but I knew he wasn't ready, so I tried to hold it.

"Nahhh, bae, I feel it. Let that fucking nut go. What you holding that shit for?" He began playing with my nub, and just like he said to do, I let my first orgasm go.

"Ooooh fuck. Messy just how Poppa likes it." His pace began to quicken, and he was slamming into me aggressively, knocking my bottom out.

"Oohhhh, shit, Pooh! It feels like this nut is coming from my muhfuckin' stomach. Fuck!" He slammed into me one last time, holding me in place by my belly as he sprayed my womb with his semen.

"Kamron, we've had this birth control talk seven thousand times. You don't wanna wear condoms, the least you can do is pull out. Damn! You know how the hell babies are made, nigga."

"Aye, tone that shit, Dreux Ali. You ain't fucking with no ho-ass nigga. Now, my fucking bad. That shit was too damn good to pull out, and yes, I know how the fuck babies are made, so shit, oh well, if one of my boys hit yo' egg, then we just got a fucking baby on the way. I know we still kind of fresh, but we grown, mama. I already told you that you gon' be my wife, so what if we go a little outta order? We in this shit, ight?"

The way his ass bossed up and put me in my place had me ready to throw this pussy on him again. Hell, I couldn't even open my mouth to respond, so I hit him with a head nod.

"Use your words. You know I ain't wit' that Silent Bob shit you be doing."

I fell out laughing because this muthafucka didn't care what came out of his mouth.

"Yes, baby."

"Good. Now, gimme a kiss with yo' funky-breath ass."

"No. Why would you say that?"

"Man, gimme a fucking kiss." Kam was talking as he turned my head. I lifted up a little to give him a peck, but he had other plans. He kissed me so deep I had to take a minute to catch my wind.

When I got up to finally take a shower, Kam smacked my ass so hard I damn near punched his big ass.

"Mmm. Fine-ass li'l bitch."

I rolled my eyes and went to handle my hygiene. I was excited as hell to have both of my guys in the same room for Sunday dinner tonight, but I couldn't lie and say I wasn't nervous. This would be the first guy that had ever met Big Drew. Wasn't no telling how he was gonna act. I washed my body, brushed my teeth, and walked out of the bathroom to air dry. I grabbed my shea butter/ coconut oil mix and began to oil down my body.

"Lay on your stomach, baby."

"No, Kam, I'm not fucking with you again."

"Ain't nobody tryna fuck. Shit, if I wanted to, I could. Just lay yo' water-head ass down and say gimme the shit."

I didn't even bother responding to his dumb ass. I just handed over the shea butter and laid my ass down. He melted the mixture between his hands and slowly massaged my body from my shoulders down to my ass. He kneaded my cheeks with just the right amount of pressure. As he rubbed me down, I felt him slip a finger in my vagina.

"Kammm, stopppp."

"I'm just playing, baby. Come on so you can go handle your business."

"Ughhh. Okay. Can you get me something to wear out the closet, please?"

"Yeah, wit'cha spoiled ass."

I watched as he walked into the closet, his broad back and shoulders glistening with drops of sweat. I was on cloud nine with this man, and I hoped he believed everything he said about me being his one. He came back with a black Champion sweatsuit and some red Vapormax that he bought me last week, and I instantly frowned.

"What?"

"Bae, I know you fucking lying. What is that?"

"Shit, you ain't doing nothing today that requires you to be all dolled up. Hell, at least I picked the one with the crop top instead of the full damn sweatshirt. I'm wearing the same thing, so shit, you just gon' match my fly." He pointed to the chair.

When I came out of the bathroom, I hadn't even seen it sitting there. I rolled my eyes and went to the drawer I kept my panties in. I picked a red matching bra and thong set and started putting them on.

"Aye, hold the fuck up. Where yo' drawers at?"

"Boy, I know you see me putting them on. What the hell?"

"Nah, baby girl, you got me fucked up. Where the shits at you be wearing on yo' cycle?"

"Kamron, you can't be serious right now."

"Yes the hell I am. You about to put on these loose-ass sweatpants with that damn string? Hell naw. You got more than a little bit of ass, and it ain't about to be jiggling around for these thirsty-ass niggas."

"Ohhh my gawwwd."

"I'on give a fuck about yo' attitude. Here, put these muthafuckas on." He handed me a pair of red "period panties," as I called them. I snatched them from his hand so damn hard I'm surprised I didn't take his wrist off. Shoving my legs into my drawers, I mumbled some bullshit under my breath about him not being my daddy.

"But I'm that baby's daddy."

"Kamron, shut the hell up, for real. Ain't no damn baby, so you can get out my face with that."

"Yeah, okay, we gon' see."

After I tied my shoes, I grabbed my keys and phone off the nightstand and headed downstairs to leave. I stopped in the kitchen, picking up a banana from the island, and when I turned around, I bumped into Kam's hard-ass chest.

"You were about to leave without telling me bye? You that mad?"

"No, I figured you would walk me to the car like you always do when I leave, so relax, Mr. Vega." Reaching up to touch his face, I wiped a droplet of water from the corner of his mouth and gave him a light kiss. I grabbed his hand so we could walk outside, and as I was opening the driver-side door, he pinned me to the car, one arm on each side of my head, and his body pressed against mine.

"I'll see you later, Pooh. Wear something sexy tonight, and I'll be there around seven to pick you up."

"Okay, babe, I love you."

He kissed my forehead, the top of my nose, and then my lips before he opened the door, letting me in. "I love you too."

"You give good love to me. Babyyy, so good. Take this heart of mine into your hands. Yesss, Muva Whitney." I sang all out of key at the top of my lungs. After I left Kam's house, I went home and switched into my convertible Audi A5 since it was such a pretty day out. I started to invite Ahdia out, but for some reason, around this time of the year, she always disappeared and shut herself off from the world, so I didn't even bother. My first stop was to Lucy's Nail Shop because these nails were growing something serious, and baby girl always got me right. She was one of the few Black women killing the nail game in Dallas.

Parking in front of her shop, I was glad to see that I was the only one here.

"Hey, welcome to Lucy's."

"Chile, it ain't nobody but me." All I could do was laugh.

"Oh, hey, girl. You never know, so I gotta make sure I keep it professional. Lock the door, flip the sign to closed, and come sit down. I already know how this is about to go."

An hour and thirty minutes later, I was walking out of her shop with a simple set of long white coffin-shaped nails, and both pinky nails were black with Kam's initials in gold. My next stop was the beauty bar to let Keeva beat my face because I wasn't in the mood to deal with it myself.

I was finally finished with my shit for the day, so I swung by Starbucks for a Mocha Macchiato and then took my ass home to chill before it was time for dinner. As I pulled into my garage, I saw that I had a missed call from Ahdia, so I tried to call her back, only to be met by a voicemail. Oh, well. I was used to these mood swings, so if she called back again, okay. If not, that was fine too.

"I'm pulling up, Pooh. Lock up, and I'll meet you at the door."

"K, I'm coming down the steps, so hurry up."

As I went through the house, turning off the lights, I heard Kamron knocking on the door, so I put a little more pep in my step. I picked up my clutch from the kitchen table, flipped the hall light on, and when I opened the door, Kam was standing there looking as handsome as ever. Dressed simply in a pair of light blue jeans, a white long-sleeve shirt that had his muscles on display, and a pair of all-white Air Max 95s, he had me ready to take him down in my doorway.

"Hey, beautiful, you ready?"

"Yes, sir. Let's go."

We rode to my parents' house in silence, stealing glances here and there, just enjoying each other's company. An hour later, we were pulling up to my childhood home, and I watched as Kam admired it.

"This shit dope as fuck, shorty. You lived here your whole life?"

"About half of it. Lean back so I can let us in."

I scanned my palm and waited for the gate to slide open before we made our way up the driveway. Parking, Kam got out, opened my door, and we walked hand in hand up to the porch. Instead of using my key, I rang the bell so my parents could meet Kamron the proper way.

"Hi, my baby. Ooooh, look at you. You must be Kamron."

"Yes, ma'am, that would be me. How are you?" he asked while planting a kiss on her hand, making Lolita blush.

"Whooo, chile, I'm doing just great. Come on in. Your daddy is in his office tying up some last-minute things for work."

My mama already knew how I was when it came to my daddy. I loved her to death, but my daddy was my entire heart. Kam opted to help my mom finish up in the kitchen while I went and sought out my dad. Gently knocking on his office door, I entered with the biggest smile on my face. My dad's eyes lit up like they always did when Ahdia and I came around.

"Baby girl, I'm glad you made it. You bring your company with you?"

"Yes sir, I did. He's in the kitchen helping Mama. I came to drag you out of here."

"Aww, you ain't gon' have to drag me. I'm ready to meet this little friend of yours, so I'll voluntarily leave this stuffy old office."

"Good! Come on. I'm so excited."

We left the office, making small talk as we walked toward the kitchen to join Lo and Kamron.

"Choppa?"

Kamron turned around, and I noticed the look on his face that he quickly tried to change.

"Who the heck is Choppa? His name is Kamron, Daddy."

"I'm sure that's what he told you."

"Wait. You know him? How?"

"Well, young man, you wanna do the honors, or shall I?"

Kam dragged his hand down his face and looked back at me with an expression that I couldn't read. I folded my arms across my chest and waited to hear what he had to say.

"Dreux, baby. Come here."

My feet wouldn't move. it was like cinderblocks were weighing them down.

"Dreux." The authority in his voice caused me to walk in his direction slowly, side-eyeing him the whole way. He unfolded my arms, rubbing them up and down, and when he blew out his breath, I just knew I was about to get the worst news of my life.

"So, look. There's certain things about myself that I haven't told you, not because I don't trust you, because I do, but I felt it was safer for you to not know. I don't just own the clubs that you know about. I also own these streets." He looked over at my dad and asked him if I knew, and my daddy nodded.

"I'm head of the Dallas Block Boyz, and your dad is my connect."

"Wowwww, are you fucking kidding me? Did you know that when you first met me? Is that why you approached me?"

"No, I didn't."

"So, when? From the look on your face, you weren't surprised when he called your name. Tell me when."

"Baby, calm down, please."

"Don't tell me what the fuck to do. I'm waiting."

"The day I took you on our first date, when we fell asleep on your couch. I saw the picture of you and him on your mantelpiece."

"Weeks. You've been knowing for weeks, and you didn't say a thing. Get out."

"Dreux, come on, ma."

"I said get the fuck out." Looking at Kam, I knew he thought I was crying because I was hurt, but hell naw. I was pissed. This muthafucka was flaw as fuck, and that was some shit that I just couldn't get down with. What he didn't know was that he just unleashed a beast, and I was about to show him how shit really got with me.

"Baby girl." My dad tried to calm me.

"I'm good, Daddy. Don't worry about me."

"You got that look in your eyes, and all I'm gonna say is whatever you do, be careful. I taught you well, but these streets ain't shit nice."

"I said I'm good." I leaned up and kissed his cheek.

Taking the steps two at a time, I went up to my old bedroom, stripped outta this funky-ass dress, and changed into an all-black ensemble. I grabbed my Glock off the top shelf of my closet and tucked it in my waist. Throwing my hair up in a bun, I made my way to the garage and jumped in the all-black Camry, heading to fuck some shit up.

I parked at the end of the street, watching these niggas chill outside one of the traps that Kam had brought me to. I guess he figured I'd never find out this was what he did, so it was no big deal. Thinking back, I don't know how I missed the signs, like the way niggas would damn near freeze up when he came around or the way he would wave off the fiends who had no problem approaching him when I was there. Talk about blinded by the dick. I screwed a silencer onto my piece because it was about to get real messy real quick.

I pulled off down the street, and when I reached the front of the trap, I rolled down the passenger window and let my Glock sing, laying down everything moving. I took the Polaroid I kept of us in my purse, got out, being sure to check my surroundings, and left the picture on the porch steps.

I headed back to my parents' house because something told me that Kam would be waiting on me at home, and I just didn't feel like hearing that bullshit. I called myself sneaking back in, but as expected, my daddy was up waiting for me.

"Baby D."

"Yes, sir?"

"Give it here."

Without hesitation, I handed over my gun and fell into my daddy's arms.

"I loved him, Daddy."

"It's all right, baby girl. You'll figure it out. If he loves you the same way, y'all will get it together. Go get some rest, and I'll see you in the morning."

Taking my clothes off piece by piece, I climbed in bed with thoughts of Kam running through my mind. I knew after tonight, this was the end of us.

Chapter Fifteen

Dash

I finally left Choppa's spot and came back home. I sat in my office going over my financials and the insurance policy my grandma had, so I could start preparing her funeral services. As I was flipping through papers, my phone lit up with a text message.

BeautifulDia: Attachment: 1 Video

As fucked up as she was for leaving me hanging, I decided to open the video and see what she had to say.

"Yeah, that's right. I got ya li'l girlfriend, and I'ma have a reallll good time with her. Matter of fact, I already started, and I must say that pussy is probably some of the best I've ever had. Maybe you'll get your chance—if I don't kill her first. I'll be seeing you niggas again."

Fuck fuck fuck! That's why she didn't show up the other night. This bottom-of-the-barrel-ass nigga kidnapped her, and now I had no idea where she was. Then, to make matters worse, he killed my grandma, but for what? Before Choppa let him go, he was eating good. Shit, the muthafucka was running our biggest trap with no issues, and we were getting ready to promote him. All I could do was sit there and rack my brain, wondering how the fuck we dropped the ball to make this nigga flip the way he did. Or was he always jealous-hearted?

I watched the video seventeen times, each time paying attention to a different aspect of it, trying to get even a small idea of where he could possibly have her, but I came up short every time. Guilt washed over me because all that came to mind was that if I'd never approached her, she'd be fine. Picking up my burner, I sent out a mass text for everybody to be at the warehouse in the next thirty minutes, and anybody who was a minute late was dead on arrival.

The last three muthafuckas had less than a minute to walk in the door before they ended up as maggot food. Two foot soldiers came rushing through the door, outta breath, but shit, they made it. Five minutes later, the last nigga strolled in on the phone, smiling, and with no warning, I hit him with a single head shot.

"Moving on. Eyes forward."

I played the video on the projector at the warehouse where I had every fucking body in attendance. Over and over again, I kept that video playing, until these muthafuckas was tired of it and decided to speak up.

"Feet to the muthafuckin' street. I want everybody in this bitch looking for that nigga high and low until he's found, and if you find him before I do, bring his ass to me. I don't give a fuck if you niggas gotta work in shifts. Twenty-four hours a day this nigga needs to be looked for. Everybody get the fuck out." It had been a fucking week, and this shit had me falling off the ledge a little more every day because if I didn't catch up to Jabari and that nigga soon, I was gon' completely lose my shit.

"Aye, Dash, we gon' get that nigga, real shit. I'm sorry again for the loss of Grammy."

"Feet to the street, Trell. We ain't gon' find that bitch in here." I dapped him up and left to pay a special visit to somebody.

***

As soon as she opened the door, the barrel of my gun was pressed to her dome. I didn't come to play with this bitch.

"Oh my God. What's this about?"

"Where the fuck is Jabari? I ain't got time for the gahdamn theatrics today."

"What did he do? I always knew his ways would catch up to him."

"It don't fucking matter. His time is up, but if you must know, he killed my grandma, then kidnapped, raped, and beat my girl. Now, where the fuck is he?"

"I don't know. I swear I don't know, but please, when you find him, instead of killing him, help him. He's sick."

"Why the fuck would I help him after everything he's done to me?"

"Because he's your brother."

That shocked the fuck outta my trigger finger because a bullet was in her head as soon as the last word left her mouth.

My fucking brother.

The bomb she dropped on me really fucked my head up since I'd never met my father, so I decided to call the one person who did.

"Hey, baby, how are you?"

"I'm fucked up, Ma. This shit with Grammy is still fucking with a G, but I'm tryna make it. Lemme ask you something. What you know about my sperm donor?"

There was a long pause before she spoke again.

"Well, son, there's really no grand story about him. We met one summer when I'd come down to visit your Grammy, and he wore me down. I ended up sleeping with him the night before I came back to Chicago, and six weeks later, I found out you were baking. I tried reaching out to him several times, and when he told me that I was better off getting rid of you, I was done. We were better without him."

"Hmm, no surprise there. Apparently, he had another son, but whatever. We good. I love you, Ma."

"Love you too, baby."

"Damn, my nigga, that's some cold-ass shit. If his mama knew, then I know that nigga had to know."

I was sitting at the bar, stressed out, throwing back shots with Choppa. This nigga had been in his head since the night Dreux put down everybody at the Green House. I knew my brother had it bad when all he did was call up the cleaning crew, drop twenty Gs to each family, and go the hell home. He kicked some real shit to me when he said he didn't give a fuck about the drugs and money. All he wanted was her, and to have a chance to apologize.

"Hell yeah, that nigga knew. She said some shit about him being sick, but if he knew I was his brother, then why the fuck would he do this? You ain't even my muhfuckin' brother by blood, and I know damn well you wouldn't ever do no fuck shit like this, so help me understand that shit, man."

"Aye, fam, everybody ain't cut from the same cloth, so everybody loyalty ain't set up like mine. Just know, as long as I'm breathing, you ain't gotta worry about shit."

"One hunnid. I'm about to get at Sherene and see if she's seen her fuck-ass baby daddy." I pulled Chop into a brotherly hug and bounced.

Until I had answers, everybody connected to these niggas was getting hit up. The only thing keeping me from offing Sherene was those babies she had. I'd never leave a child motherless, but I was gon' make her ass a deal that would have her rolling over on her nigga.

"Hold on. I'm coming. Who is it?"

I didn't say anything, just in case Lonzo tipped her off.

"Hey, Dash, what you doing here? You never make house calls."

"Can I come in? I have some important shit to talk to you about."

"Oh. Well, okay."

I entered her crib, impressed because for having five kids, it was clean as fuck. I walked to the couch and got comfortable.

"Umm, can I get you anything to drink?"

"Nah, I'm straight. Sit down, Rene." I cut the pleasantries and got right to the reason why I was there.

"So, your nigga done got himself wrapped up in some bullshit fucking with Jabari, and I'm here as a courtesy to let you know that he is gonna die."

"Wow. I always knew that JB would be his downfall. So where does that leave me? I have babies that need me."

"I'm not here for that, Rene, but I do know that he's your only source of income, so without that, you'll be ass out."

I could see the wheels starting to turn in her head, trying to figure out where this was leading.

"What do I need to do?" she said with her head down, realizing that she had no choice but to turn on Lonzo.

"Next time he shows up here, you call me. After I get him, I'll pay your rent up and put twenty bands in your account on the first of every month for a year."

She was hesitant to accept my offer, so I told her I'd give her 24 hours to decide what she wanted to do, but either way, he was dying.

Leaving her spot, I ran up on all the places I knew Jabari used to hang out at, starting with the hole-in-the-wall-ass strip club off of Ledbetter. I walked in, looking around for Trixie, the stripper JB took to a private room every time he came through. I spotted her at the bar, so I made my way over.

“Meet me in the back,” I said against her ear.

“It’s gon’ cost you.”

“When the last time you seen JB?”

“Five thousand dollars. I already heard about the bounty on his head, so this shouldn’t be shit for you.”

Pulling out a wad of cash, I handed it over. “Talk.”

“He was in here yesterday around eight o’clock. He slipped in through the back exit and left out the same way. He had that dude with the funny eyes with him.”

“Good looking out.” I thanked her and peeled off an extra five hundred dollars.

214-985-3521: He’s on his way here.

Like I knew she would, Sherene accepted my offer, and now I was on my way to putting my plan into motion. I parked a few houses down, waiting until I seen his bitch ass pull up. Rene shot me a text, letting me know that she unlocked the back door like I asked, and by the time I was finished reading the message, Lonzo was pulling in the driveway.

I sneaked in through the back. Lonzo was sitting on the couch, watching the game with a beer in his hand. As quiet as possible, I walked up and choked him from behind, making him pass out. Dumb ass fucked up by coming here, and I was about to show him why. After I got Lonzo secured in the backseat, I shot Kam and Trell a text to meet me at the Inferno. Shit was about to get real.

Smack!

I backhanded this muthafucka so hard, I could have sworn I heard his neck snap.

“Wake the fuck up, bitch. You can rest when you dead.”

As he came to, I decided to pull a Choppa because an instant death wasn't enough to satisfy me.

"Lonzo, tsk tsk tsk, you know you fucked up, right? How you thought turning against me and Choppa was a good idea is beyond me."

"D-D-Dash, I swear I wasn't trying to, man. JB said he would rape and kill my girl if I didn't help him."

"And nothing in you said let me go holla at Choppa and Dash about this shit? Instead, you chose to fuck with a nigga that's gon' get you killed. Good look." Walking over to Chop's table of gadgets, I picked up a hammer that Choppa had added nails to.

"I'ma ask you three questions. Depending on your answers, you'll either die real fast, or you'll die real slow, but first—" I raised the hammer, slammed it into one hand, then the other. When I pulled it out, blood poured from the holes. "That's for touching something that doesn't belong to you." Lonzo began to scream out from the pain, and a smile formed on my face.

"Now, first question. Jabari raped my girl?"

"Yes."

I smashed the hammer into his left thigh. "Is she still alive?"

"For now."

I smashed the hammer into his right thigh. "Where is she?"

"I don't know."

"Ah, see, we were on a roll. You were giving me the answers I needed, but now you dropped the ball. You're telling me that you know she's still alive but can't tell me where she is? Cool." I grabbed a corkscrew-style knife from the table, and without hesitation, I shoved it into his chest. His eyes got wide, waiting to see what my next move was gonna be

"Try again."

"Man, all I can tell you is that it's somewhere near Fort Worth, and if you want her, then you better start working faster. He's gonna ask for ransom money, but he still plans to kill her."

Hearing that not only was he raping her, but he planned to send her to her maker, I became enraged.

"Just like I was coming back, so is he. He's in the shadows watching, man. I know it's too late because ya girl is already missing, but that nigga ain't right in the head, so you gotta play his game. Stop looking, and eventually, he'll show himself."

With the knife still in his chest, I beat Lonzo's ass until my hands were numb, and if Trell hadn't grabbed me, I don't think I would have stopped. I twisted the knife into his chest, and when I yanked it out, blood came rushing down his body. He gasped, struggling to breathe. Since he answered my questions, I decided to take him out of his misery with two to the heart and a dome shot.

Pew! Pew! Pew!

"Fuck, man. I feel like I'm racing against a clock that I didn't know was there."

"How you wanna play this, bro?" Trell asked, ready to get to it like always. That's why I fucked with him.

"Man, I'on know. It's been a week, and the muthafucka ain't said shit else, dawg. Damn, speak of the devil and he will appear." My phone started ringing, flashing JB's name across the screen.

"You got these niggas going dumb looking for me, and I been right here the whole time. I know pussy-ass Lonzo tried to sell me out. That's why I made sure that nigga didn't know shit."

"Man, look. Kill all the noise. What's up? What the fuck you want?"

"Five hundred thousand in forty-eight hours, or she dies."

"Say less."

Two days later, 10pm

I had to give it to Jabari. This nigga was calculated as fuck, and if the situation was any different, I'd applaud him on a job well done. He gave us forty-eight hours to get the ransom for Ahdia squared away, so here we were on hour forty-six, duffle bags full of money, waiting on a drop-off location. Our whole team, plus the unit that Ghost had assembled, met up at the Inferno, going over our plan one final time because there was no way Jabari was touching that money. None of us were tryna be out of that much, even though Dia was worth it. Ghost put up 250K, and I put up the other half. Choppa offered to split with me, but this was my girl, so I was good.

JB: Attachment: 1 image

"Load up. Choppa, lemme holla at you real quick."

"Wassup, family?"

"Check the picture. You ever heard of this place?"

"Greenhaven? Shit, I think it used to be a camp in Fort Worth for kids with behavioral issues."

"Well, that's where he has her, so you, me, and Ghost in his whip. Everybody else load up in the vans."

"One hunnid."

The hour-long ride from Prosper to Fort Worth was filled with nothing but silence as we all mentally prepared for the possibility of shit going wrong. Nobody knew what we were walking into or if Ahdia was even still amongst the living. Before this shit happened, I ain't have a chance to romance her and make her my girl, which was the part that had been fucking with me. She got caught in the shit of a nigga that wasn't even hers. On my soul, if and when we made it out of this, I was giving her the world.

We arrived at Greenhaven, signaling for the vans to stay parked down the street, and they proceeded on foot, posting up in the shadows. Pulling out my phone, I hit JB to let him know that it was time to get this shit over with, and when I looked up, he was coming out of a cabin carrying a limp-bodied Ahdia. He tossed her on the ground like she was trash, and it was then that I lost it. Throwing the door open, I took off full speed to get to her, but when Jabari drew down on me, I stopped in my tracks.

"Aht-aht, that's not what we're gonna do, brother."

"Why'd you do this, JB? If you knew I was your brother, then what's the point of all this bullshit, dawg?"

"Because I hate you. You were living the good fucking life while I was getting my ass beat and raped by our sick-ass father. You had people who loved you enough to protect you from him, whether it was on purpose or not. Then you come down here and steal my best friend too. That was supposed to be *me* running shit beside Choppa."

This nigga was really sitting here sounding like a female. I stole his best friend? The fuck? Nigga, we grown. But to keep from making matters worse, I humored him.

"Bro, it wasn't shit good about my life growing up. I grew up in a shit-ass neighborhood where your only options were to use drugs or sell 'em. I watched my childhood Day one get his brains blew out two feet away from me, and instead of staying with him, I ran. Nigga, I ain't no better than you."

"Fuck that shit. What you need to do is turn around and get my money. This li'l heart-to-heart is over."

I wasn't dummy enough to turn my back to JB, and Choppa, being the type of nigga he is, was already on his way with the bags, dropping them at my feet.

"So, this is what the fuck is gonna happen. We gon' trade places. You gon' get your money, get the fuck outta Dallas, and I'ma get my girl. Plain and simple."

"Cool."

We changed sides, maintaining a safe distance between the two of us, and after I bent down to pick Ahdia up, I ran toward the car, throwing her inside. When I saw Jabari running toward the woods, I got shit popping.

"Light 'em up."

Guns started banging left and right, but what I wasn't expecting was the handful of our soldiers, who teamed up with Jabari and were bussin' back at us. Bodies were dropping like flies on both sides, but I was glad to see Choppa and Ghost still standing, putting in work. Out of my peripheral, I peeped Jabari coming from the other side, attempting to take Choppa out. I dipped low, as if I was changing my clip, and circled around the back of the car. When he lifted his gun, aiming at my brother, I left off a shot that ripped through his hand, causing the gun to go off.

"Aargh, shit!"

"You really thought you could take my woman and live to tell about it? Nah, bro, you'll never be able to say you got one up on me. Anything you wanna say before I send you to hell with your sick-ass father?"

"Fuck you."

"That's cool," I replied, then without a second thought, I dumped one clip in his body for Ahdia and a second for my grandma.

Running back toward the car, I saw Ghost laid out on the ground, holding his chest. Blood was spilling from between his fingers, and it wasn't looking good. I eyed the scene. The muthafuckas that turned on us was good as gone, with only two men from our side killed.

"Choppa, we gotta go. We gotta get him to a hospital, man."

"Shit! Load up. Head back to Inferno and get rid of your shit. Move now!"

We grabbed Ghost, placing him in the backseat as easy as possible, trying not to fuck shit up even more. I pulled my shirt off and applied pressure to his chest. Choppa jumped in the car, threw it in drive, and peeled out. Going 100 in a 75, we made it to the Fort Worth Medical Center in fifteen minutes.

"Help! I need a doctor, nurse, something. I got a gunshot victim and a rape victim that need help."

Muthafuckas started rushing from all over the place with gurneys and shit, making me nervous, because the last time I was at a hospital, they were confirming the death of my grandma.

"Do you have any information on the victims?

"No, I only know her first name, Ahdia, and nothing about the male."

"Okay, that's fine. We'll worry about that later. How about you have a seat, and a doctor will update you as soon as possible."

An hour later, the doctor came from the back to give us an update on my baby girl. "There's a significant amount of swelling on her brain, so we had to remove a piece of her skull to relieve the pressure. Her ribs are bruised and cracked, which must heal on their own, and her hCG levels are elevated."

"Elevated? She pregnant?"

"Yes, it's still very early, but it appears so."

Damn, man. Ahdia was the epitome of everything I could see myself loving in a woman, but could I really deal with raising a baby that was a constant reminder of this fucked-up situation?

"What about the male that was brought in with her?" Choppa asked, snapping me outta my thoughts.

With a solemn look on his face, he gave us the news. "I'm sorry."

Chapter Sixteen

Ahdia

I couldn't take this shit anymore. I was getting my ass beat and raped, day in and day out. The only time I got some kind of relief was when that Lonzo muthafucka was around, which was only for a few hours at a time. I was handcuffed to this fucking bed twenty-two hours of the day, getting bed sores to add to the bruises. I'd lost track of time because he'd boarded up all the windows, so I never saw the sun. I used to *be* the sun; now I was nothing but a mere shell of darkness. The very man that stole my innocence had unlimited access to do whatever he wanted to me.

I heard the door rattling, making me cringe. *Fuck! Here. We. Go. Again.* Every time he climbed on top of me, I grew physically sick, which I tried to control because that made him go even harder.

"Wake the fuck up. I know you ain't sleep."

"What the fuck else could I possibly be doing then?"

"Oh, you got a mouth on you today, huh? Let's see how well you use the bitch for more than just shit-talking."

Ugh! Why did I have to open my fucking mouth? I'd gone this long without having to suck his dick, but I guess my luck had finally run out. He unbuckled his pants, pulled them off leg by leg, and climbed on the bed. I already felt like a low-class ho, but when he stood over me, looking down as if I were beneath him, my self-esteem completely diminished. He gripped my hair so tight it felt like it was being torn from my scalp. As he shoved his dick into my mouth, my teeth scraped his shaft, and I felt a hard blow to the top of my head.

"Watch your teeth, stupid-ass bitch, or next time I'll knock 'em the fuck out," his ass hissed at me.

He pumped in and out of my mouth, occasionally ramming his member down my throat, causing me to gag. Tears flowed down my face, which frustrated me because I didn't want this nigga to think he was breaking me down. One thing Big Drew didn't do was raise a weak-ass daughter, so even if I had to do it while handcuffed, I was gonna keep fighting.

His piece began to pulsate in my mouth, and I was relieved when he ejaculated in his hand and not on me. I waited for him to recover and force himself inside of me, but it never came. Instead, he uncuffed me, pushing me toward the kitchen. I was more than happy to see real food because since I'd been there, all I was given were scraps and water.

"Sit down."

Doing as he said to avoid being beaten, I slowly sat, kind of leery of the way he was acting.

"Why couldn't we just be happy, Dia? Why did you have to leave?"

I stared at him in disbelief that he even had the nerve to let that bullshit come out of his mouth.

"Answer me," he responded, banging on the small table so hard that I almost jumped out of my skin.

"You raped me. Repeatedly, like I was trash. Taking the only piece of innocence I had left."

"You were mine. How the fuck did I rape you if we were dating, huh? Make that make sense to me."

"I said no." With my head down, I continued. "When

someone says no, and you do it anyway, that's rape. I told you I was saving it for the man I married, and still, you took it."

"I didn't fucking rape you," he said, but at this point, I was over it. He did it then, and he'd done it every day since I'd been there, so fuck it.

I ate the food that was on the table, and since I was out, I asked if I could take a shower, which he agreed to. As I stood under the showerhead, thoughts of Dash consumed my mind. All the chasing he did before I went missing, and he hadn't even tried to come find me. Lo, my sweet mama, told me to stop playing with that man, and I didn't listen. I could pretend like I didn't feel the pull between us when we were in the same room, but I did. I was just too scared to act on it.

When I stepped out of the shower, I overheard Jabari talking to somebody about ransom money, and my heart danced a little, thinking it was almost over. I accidentally hit the door, causing me to jump back and him to jump up, and I knew the inevitable was next. He ran full force to where I was, grabbing me up by the throat and slamming my head into the wall.

"You fucking crazy? Listening in on my phone conversations. What you tryna do, escape? Well, sweetheart, the only way out of this is in a body bag."

"No, I was leaving out of the bathroom, and I was coming to ask for a T-shirt since I don't have any clothes here. That's all."

"You think I'm fucking stupid?" He reached back and punched me so hard in the mouth I felt my teeth loosen. At this point, I knew my time was coming. His eyes were empty of all emotion other than rage, and I was genuinely scared.

As he banged my head over and over again, I began to slip in and out of consciousness, my body growing weak.

I saw his hand coming down to backhand me, and out of reflex, I tried to block it.

"Oh, you wanna fight back, huh? Fight me then, bitch," he said, but I could barely stand any longer. My body fell to the floor, and the next thing I saw was his foot slamming into my side. I heard my rib crack, causing me to scream out in agony and ball up into the fetal position.

"Why couldn't you just let me love you, Ahdia? You ran from me when all I wanted to do was love you."

As he punched and stomped me out, my mind went to my parents and my sister, making my eyes fill with tears. I didn't deserve this, and if I died tonight, my soul would never be at peace, knowing they were on this earth, suffering because of me. My scalp was on fire, which brought me back in enough time to see that he was dragging me to the bathroom by my hair.

Holding on to me with one hand, Jabari began to fill the tub with water, and it was then that I realized he was gonna try to drown me. He threw me over, wrapping his hands around my neck, but something clicked in me. If he was gonna kill me, I wasn't going out without a fight, and that's exactly what I did. With all the strength I could muster up, I fought long and hard, wearing myself out faster, which gave him the upper hand.

Ring! Ring! Ring!

Saved by the fucking bell. He let me go to grab his phone, and when he said hello, I swear I could hear Dash's voice coming through the speaker. I was hanging on faintly, but I knew he would come for me. Using the last of my strength, I pulled myself out of the bathtub, and when my head clashed against the tile, I passed out.

Slightly coming to, I felt my body being carried in the fall winds, and then my body hit the hard ground. When I heard Dash's voice, I vowed to hang on long enough for him to save me.

"Oh, baby girl, I'm so fucking sorry," he said, cradling me to his chest. "I'm sorry it took me so long, but I'm here, and you're gonna be okay."

Feeling his soft lips on my forehead and knowing that I was finally safe, I let go.

Chapter Seventeen

Kamron

Shit! How did this dinner turn out so fucked up? I thought that keeping my street business from Dreux was for her safety, but all along, she knew her daddy was the plug, so it ain't like she wasn't accustomed to it. As bad as I wanted to stay and fight for her, the hurt in her eyes when she told me to get out was enough to make me leave. I still had the key to her apartment, so instead of going home, I chose to go wait for her. Halfway into my hour-long drive, my lieu over the Green House hit my jack, adding more bullshit to my plate.

"B-b-boss-m-man, we hit," he stated, and I could hear the finality in his voice.

"I'm on my way," I replied, but I got no response.

"Kilo, fuck, man." I hit a U-turn, heading to the trap to survey the damage.

Pulling up, I saw my whole team laid out, and as tough as I am, it was enough to make a big nigga shed a tear. I hit Dash to let him know what I was dealing with, but when he didn't answer, I just said fuck it. Going in through the back, I spent close to an hour clearing house and pulling the tapes, and then hit my homegirl up to have her report the incident. When I stepped on the porch to grab the last of the stash, something caught my eye. Shit!

Jogging back to the car, I pulled my phone outta my pocket and saw that Dash had sent me a video. I done told him about that gay-ass video shit before, but his ass just didn't listen. I pressed play, and when that bullshit started, my blood began to boil, and all I saw was black.

"Ghost, I know it's late, but I got some shit I need to holla at you about."

"If this is about what happened with you and Dreux, we can talk another day."

"With all respect, I ain't got shit for her right now. This is strictly business."

"Cool. When you get to the gate, hit 2467. That'll be your personal code, but it expires in two hours, so you should come on."

"On my way."

"You know him?" Ghost asked his wife.

With a strained expression on her face, she told him to take a seat and she would explain.

"So, you remember Dia's second year of college, when she came home that winter and you said something was different about her? Well, she'd been dating this guy for a few months, and she told me that she really liked him, and they were growing closer. When our baby came home, she wouldn't leave out of that room for anything other than food. Drew, you were working so much around that time, so I don't know if you'd remember."

Drew nodded his head, indicating that she was right, he didn't remember.

"Okay, well, a week or so later, I just so happened to go up to check on her, and I heard her throwing up in the bathroom with tears rushing down her face. She was pregnant, Drew."

From where I was standing, I could see his jaw tightening and the vein in his temple pulsing as he tried to contain himself.

"Continue, Lo."

"She cried for so long and so hard, hurting. I told her it was okay and that we would raise the baby as a family, but she begged me to take her to get an abortion. I couldn't understand why because all her life the only thing she's ever wanted to be was a mom. When she told me what that monster was doing to her, I couldn't take it. For damn near a month, he was raping our little girl, tearing her apart, and we weren't there to save her."

By the time she finished, everyone in the room had tears in their eyes or on their cheeks.

"Fuck! That sick bastard has my baby again. How the fuck did we let this happen? Against my better judgment, I let up on her security, and now my baby is missing."

"Aye, Ghost, something is off with him, so whatever you're thinking, don't. We gotta handle this situation carefully because he will kill her just like he did Dash's grandma."

"Choppa, to my office."

As I followed behind Ghost, I saw Dreux walk past the door that I assumed was her bedroom, and it took everything in me not to run up the stairs.

"Keep walking, son. Not tonight."

When we walked into his office, he offered me a Cuban cigar, which I gladly accepted because this bullshit-ass night had me stressed the fuck out.

"So, here's what needs to happen. You need to get in touch with Dash, and y'all need to get the ball rolling on bringing my baby home. There's no telling what's gonna happen the longer he has her."

"I'll hit my man in the morning and see where his head is at. This nigga targeted him personally, so I'll let Dash take the reins."

"All right, well, you get back to me as soon as y'all figure that shit out. ASAP, Choppa."

"Heard you. Listen, your daughter came through my trap and lit my shit up. I love her, so I'm not looking to retaliate. I just ask that you try to convince her to give me a chance to explain myself."

"How do you know it was her?"

"I found this."

I tossed the picture of Dreux and me on the desk and watched as he twirled it through his fingers.

"She kept that in her wallet, and that's the only one, so it couldn't have been anyone else's."

"You keep your word that you won't strike back, and I'll talk to her for you. Deal?

"Deal."

I stood up, shook hands with Ghost, and headed home.

Lying in bed, staring at the picture of Dreux as my screensaver, my heart ached. It had been days since I'd heard her voice or even laid eyes on her, and I was going out of my mind, trying to find a way to make this right. She was that kind of love that I'd been looking for. In this short amount of time, baby girl had my nose wide open, but I didn't give a fuck, because I knew we were meant to be, and after Grammy's funeral, I was getting my girl back.

Dressed in all black with a gold Ferragamo belt, I secured the purple flower to my button-up. Dash hit me up to let me know they were here, so I grabbed my shit and headed down. My brother was standing outside the limousine, dressed identical to me, only he added a pair of gold-rimmed Versace glasses to his unit.

"How you holding up, bro?" I asked, pulling him into a hug

"Man, honestly, shit's mad crazy that I'm even having to do this at all."

"It's gon' be all right. I got you, no doubt."

Twenty minutes later, we were pulling up to the church where the funeral was being held, and it took us both a minute to get out. My steps grew heavier the closer we got to the doors, but when I walked inside, sadness dissipated, and relief came over me. Looking back at me was a big picture of Grammy, smiling that beautiful smile I'd grown to love over the years. Even though she wasn't my biological grandmother, she loved me just as much as she loved Dash.

Taking our seats, I stared at the purple casket, wanting nothing more than to avenge her death properly.

After the pastor delivered the eulogy, Dash's cousin stood to sing as the funeral director prepared to open the casket. "Oooon that morniiiiing, when this life is oooover, I'll fly away."

When Grammy's body came into view, silent tears fell from my eyes, but when I saw my brother hit his knees, that shit rocked my core. I grabbed my boy and let him cleanse his soul because once this was over, I knew he was gon' slip into a dark place until Jabari was found.

After the burial, I went home to decompress before I put my plan into motion.

"Hey, this is Dreux. Sorry I missed you, but if you leave me your name and number, I'll be sure to return your call. Thanks."

This shit was starting to frustrate the fuck outta me, and I knew I couldn't really blame anybody but myself. Maybe I should have told her that I knew her pops, but shit, I didn't think it was this big of a deal. Shit, let's argue about it, then move on. I had started getting used to the idea of sharing my crib with a female, and now her scent no longer lingered in the room the way it used to, and I missed that shit. This wasn't my house anymore. It had become our home, and I hated not having her here. I couldn't dwell on that, though. Jabari was still missing because every lead we thought we had turned out to be bullshit.

A Week Later

It was go time, and even though I'm the nigga that I am, I was nervous as fuck. We had the whole unit suited up because this nigga was unstable, so wasn't no telling what the fuck he had up.

When we pulled in, JB was walking out with Dia, who was either dead or barely hanging on. I looked over to Ghost, and there were tears rolling down his face. Dash took off toward her, and when Jabari pulled his gun, I had one chambered. As they argued, I grabbed the bags from the car and dropped them near Dash, because it ain't no way I was letting my brother turn his back on this snake-ass nigga. Dash came running back to the car with Ahdia, and the next thing out of his mouth was music to my ears.

"Light 'em up."

Out of the woods came half of my team, bussin' on behalf of Jabari. This shit fucked with me that we had all these snakes in our grass. Like, what the fuck did that nigga tell them to get them to fold?

"Oh, shit!" It had been too long since I had a good-ass shootout, so my adrenaline was pumping. I reached in the car, dropped my Glock, and picked up the Draco. I held my finger on the trigger, spraying anything that was moving on that side of the woods. They unleashed the beast in me, and it was up from here.

"Choppa, we gotta go! We gotta get Ghost to a hospital."

Looking to my left, I saw Ghost laid out, with blooding spilling from his chest.

"Fuck! Ghost! Round it up back to the Inferno. Move!" I jumped in the car and flew to the FWMC.

"Ch-chop, if I don't make it, the business is yo-yours. Lo knows what to do. J-just promise me you'll t-take care of my girls," Ghost struggled to say.

"Man, you gon' be straight. Save your breath."

"Promise me. You've been my son for eleven years. Promise me."

"I promise."

We pulled into the hospital, and Dash jumped out before I could park the car to get help. People started rushing around me doing shit, but I was stuck in my thoughts, praying Ghost came out of this alive. Time was moving at turtle's pace, frustrating me because all I could think was how the fuck was I gon' tell Dreux if the news wasn't good?

"Family of Ahdia?" My head popped as he gave us the rundown on Dia's condition. I was glad she held on long enough for us to get her there, but I had to find out about Ghost.

"What about the male who came in with her?"

"I'm sorry. We did everything we could, but he flatlined on the operating table."

"Fuckkkk!"

Sitting in Ghost's living room, knowing he wasn't there was fucking with me. He'd been my mentor and connect for the past eleven years, so to know that he died behind some shit that started with my team was a hit to my heart. It had been almost two weeks since the funeral, and I was finally ready to deal with the aftermath.

Lolita came down the hall with a briefcase and a solemn look on her face. Standing up, I kissed her cheek and allowed her to sit before I took my place back on the couch.

"Hey, beautiful lady, how you holding up?"

"I've been better. I'm taking it one day at a time."

"I ain't gon' lie and say it'll be okay, but it will get easier. I'm here to step up for whatever y'all need."

"Thank you, baby. I know you've had it rough, too, but give her some time," she said, patting my knee. She opened the briefcase and started pulling out different kinds of papers that she said I needed to sign. "Everything you need to run this business successfully is in that briefcase, but if you don't mind, I'd like for you to keep it here. It makes me feel close to him."

"Yes, ma'am. Anything you ask is done."

This was the first step to healing for Lo, and I wanted to make the transition as easy as possible, even though she wasn't directly involved. From this day forward, I'd do my best to honor Ghost's legacy.

Chapter Eighteen

Unknown

I'd been Choppa's left hand for years, making sure when shit was going wrong, I got it back right. When he caught chain, Dash wasn't the only muthafucka that kept this ship from sinking. I put in just as much work, but for some reason, I didn't get the same recognition that Dash did, and I was tired of it. Everybody looked at me as the clown of the operation, always cracking jokes, but shit, it was easier to do that than keep up an attitude like crybaby-ass Jabari.

For the past week, Choppa had taken a backseat to the business, since him and that li'l bitch fell out. He'd been sulking around here like a female, so guess who was picking up his slack? Me. Dash been off his rocker since his grandma died and Jabari went missing, and guess who was picking up his slack? Me. Here I was doing twice the work of two niggas, and all the fuck I got was a pat on the back. Not that I needed a muthafucka to reward me, but it would be nice if he did.

For three days, I'd been following her. I knew where she worked, where she lived, even where she got her hair and shit done. Today, I followed her to the mall. She was walking in my direction with her head down, looking at her phone. Since she wasn't paying attention to where she was going, I stepped in her path right as she passed me, bumping into her and knocking her bags from her hand.

"Shit. My bad, beautiful. Let me get that for you."

"Oh, it's okay. I got it. Thanks."

"You mind if I ask your name, pretty lady?"

"It's Dreux.

"Nice to meet you, Dreux. I'm LT."

"Likewise. I gotta go, but thanks for helping me pick up my bags. See you around," she said and disappeared into the crowd.

"Yeah, you will, sooner than you think."

The way she knocked Choppa off of his square made her the perfect pawn for this dangerous game I was about to play. When it was all said and done, I'll finally be the one saying checkmate.

Leaving the mall, I texted Choppa and Dash to see if they wanted to fade the strip club tonight, and surprisingly, them niggas said yeah. Even though I didn't like the way they got down on me, I had to keep the family close and continue to play my role.

"Do it, baby. Stick it, baby. Move it, baby. Lick it, baby."

We were sitting in The Playhouse, watching two fat-booty-ass bitches fuck it up to that new twerk shit all the hoes was banging. There were bottles on the tables, but it seemed like I was the only one drinking.

"Y'all niggas good? Usually we getting it poppin', but y'all over there looking real funny in the face."

"Shut the fuck up, nigga. Cousin Skeeter-looking-ass bitch," Dash rebutted.

They finally got with the program, and by 3 a.m., we were all crossfaded, heading home.

The next day . . .

"I'm starting to think you're following me, beautiful."

When she looked up, a small grin appeared on her face. "I most certainly am not. I was here first, so I'd assume that you were following me."

"Nah, you cute and all, but I ain't on that type of time. Chipotle is my shit." I was lying like a ho because I ain't ever had this bullshit a day in my life.

"Mm-hmm, that's what you say," she replied, flashing those pretty-ass teeth. Hell, I could see why that nigga was losing his mind behind her, and after this shit was over, I just might keep her for myself.

"What can I get for you, sir?" the chick behind the counter asked.

"Lemme get the same thing she got. I'ma try something different."

I grabbed my food, putting on like I was really looking for somewhere to sit, and when she invited me to sit at her table, I knew I had her. We kicked it, getting to know each other. Well, she was talking, and I was fucking up this bowl shit.

"Damn, that was good as fuck, ma."

"For this to be your favorite, you sure ate that like you'd never had it before."

I watched her laugh as I licked my lips. "Maaaan, say, you just had some shit I never tried before. Don't do that."

"I hear ya. Well, let me get outta here. I gotta get back to work."

"That's cool. I'll walk you to your car."

Dumping our trash, I held the door open, and she led us to her whip, which was different from the others I'd seen her in.

"I like your vibe, ma. I was wondering if we could exchange numbers so I could take you out some time." I saw the hesitation written in the wrinkles of her forehead before she answered.

"Umm, I guess that's okay, but I just got out of a situationship, so I'm not really looking for anything other than a friend right now."

"I can dig it. That's all I'm tryna be."

"Cool. Lemme see your phone." She locked in her number and was gone.

Step one was complete, so now all I had to do was get next to her without catching any feelings. I got in my car and made my way to Tonya's Beauty Shop to get my dreads re-twisted because lately, I'd been letting it do whatever, so the new growth was crazy. While I sat under the dryer, I shot Dreux a text, asking if I could see her later this week, and surprisingly, she agreed.

I'd been taking Dreux out on dates for the last week, and this muthafucka was expensive. It ain't like I was a broke-ass nigga, but shit, this wasn't my bitch. Like now, we were at some seafood-ass shit where the muthafuckin' crab leg platter was damn near fifty dollars. Something seemed to be bothering her, but when I asked her what was up, I wasn't expecting the answer I got.

"My situation keeps blowing up my phone, and it's taking everything in me not to answer. My sister has been missing, and he's the only person I wanna talk to about it, but I don't know. I'm sorry. I shouldn't even be talking about him."

Damn right, she shouldn't be talking about him when she got me spending a hunnid plus on some damn food.

"It's cool. I understand. Shit like that is hard to get over for some people."

"Yeah, I guess you're right. Thanks for listening."

For the rest of dinner, we made small talk here and there, and after I paid the ticket, I invited her back to my spot to chill, which she accepted. While we were chilling, my burner phone went off with a text from Dash.

Dash: It's hour 45, Inferno now. If ya late, it's DOA.

Fuck!

"Say, li'l mama, I gotta end our night. Work's calling."

"Oh. Well, okay. I guess I'll talk to you later."

After she was gone, I suited up in my bulletproof vest and an all-black unit. It was time to put in work.

Two days later . . .

I hadn't heard from Dreux since the night I had to cut our date short, which wasn't normal since we talked damn near every day. I picked up the phone to dial her number, only to find her calling me.

"Wassup?"

"Hey, sorry to bother you. You got a minute? Can you meet me somewhere?"

"Yeah, pull up to the house."

It was gon' take her at least an hour to get to where my house was, so I went ahead and finished my business.

"Lemme get the Draco, the AR-15, and the two Glocks."

"Damn, my nigga, what you tryna do? Take down a small army?"

"Shiiiid, something like that." I paid for my shit, loaded it in the trunk, and left to meet Dreux.

I pulled up at the house, and since she wasn't there yet, I went ahead and brought my shit inside. While I was putting my tools away, the buzzer sounded off, letting me know that she had finally arrived. I swung the door open, and baby girl looked like she hadn't slept in days. There were dried-up tears on her face, and her eyes were puffy as hell. Shit, ma looked a mess.

"Fuck, what's wrong?" I asked, pulling her into a hug like I really gave a fuck.

"My father was murdered two nights ago. He died trying to save my sister." Now she was crying.

Two nights ago? The muhfuckin' connect was her daddy? Yeah, I definitely had to keep this bitch now. This was gon' be my come-up.

"Damn, I'm sorry to hear that. What you need from me?"

"Can you just hold onto me? Everything else is going wrong. Can you be the one thing that's right?"

Shiiiiid, if only she knew. I was the worst part of it all.

"Yeah, I can do that." She was vulnerable, which made her easy, so shit, I figured, why not get some pussy? I walked over to the couch, pulled her into my lap, and stretched us out so her head was lying on my chest. I started massaging her scalp, and when she let out a low moan, my dick responded. She must have felt it because she looked up at me with lust in her eyes. Moving her big-ass hair out of her face, I leaned down and kissed her, giving it everything I had. Might as well.

She sat up, made me put my feet on the floor, and straddled my lap. Not knowing how this would go, I let her take the lead when all I really wanted to do was rip her clothes off and fuck. Her shirt came up over her head, and when those titties bounced out, I couldn't resist pulling her chocolate nipple in my mouth. I alternated swirling and sucking, fast then slow around her areola, while rolling the other between my fingers. Her head fell back, giving me access to her neck, and I attacked with hunger. Rolling over, I stood up to come out of my pants, with her doing the same. Her pussy was so fucking wet just from the tongue lashing I gave her nipples, and I was happy as fuck because even though she looked sweet, pussy eating was not for a real nigga like me.

Grabbing a condom from my wallet, I slid it on and dove dick first into her sopping wet pussy. The way that thang clamped down on my dick had me ready to bust already. Shit, I saw why the fuck Choppa was trying so hard to get back in. I wasn't into that slow lovemaking shit, so when I got in it, I drove her ass until she was out of breath and sweaty.

"Oh god, what did I just do? Shit!" She jumped up, pacing back and forth while grabbing her clothes.

"Aye aye aye, calm down. We both grown. Chill."

"I can't. This was a mistake. I have to go." She threw her clothes on, and before I could say anything else, she was out the door. Oh, well. Kept me from having to kick her ass out.

I was sitting at the shop, cutting heads and shooting the breeze with my niggas, when a text from Dreux came in. She'd fallen back almost completely since the day we fucked almost two weeks ago, but that didn't stop me from keeping my eyes on her.

D: You busy?

Me: Li'l bit, wassup?

D: When you get free, can I see you? I need to talk.

Me: Yea that's cool, come by the shop at 5.

D: Okay.

"Ight, niggas, it's going down this afternoon. I need everybody on point so we don't get caught by the boys in blue."

I hit Choppa on some “I need to holla at him” bullshit and started to put my own into motion.

Checking the time, I saw Choppa had hit me to let me know he was on his way. He was a punctual-ass nigga, so as soon as that clock said 4:59 p.m., he would be getting out his car. It was slowly inching up on 5:00, and everybody was trained to go. I had my niggas Spank and Whoodi waiting in the alley, since I knew Dreux would park in the end of the block like always. I locked the shop door, leaving the open sign on, and dipped out the back. Like clockwork, Dreux and Choppa pulled up at the same time, her parking exactly where I thought she would, and he parked directly in front of the shop. When Dreux opened her door, I signaled for Spank to snatch her ass up.

“Ahhhh, get off of me. Help! LT!”

Choppa turned around as Spank threw her in the van, her eyes wide with fear, and when I saw him going to his gun, I mashed the gas, and Whoodi let that thang rip.

“Hello, beautiful.”

Chapter Nineteen

Choppa

I'd been trying to talk to Dreux for the past few weeks, but since the night we got her sister back and her dad passed, she'd been avoiding me. Li'l muthafucka really had me doing pop-ups at her house and job and sending dinner invites. However, nothing was working in my favor. Somebody told me they saw her with some dude about a week ago, and it took everything in me not to show up at her house and wring her neck.

My phone started vibrating on the desk in Ghost's office, and when I saw that it was my mans, I answered.

"What up, boy?"

"Say, boss, you got a minute to link up today and shoot the shit? I got something I wanna run by you."

"Yeah, that's cool. I got some shit I gotta handle with my girl, but after that, I'm good for it."

"Bet that. Just meet me at the shop at five."

"One hunnid."

Since Ghost died, I'd picked up where he left off in all aspects of his life. I checked on Lo every day since she was struggling to shake back. Ahdia was still in a coma three weeks later, and even though Dash was there, I still made sure I talked with her at least once a day. The only one who wouldn't budge was Dreux, but today was the end of all that.

I heard the alarm go off, and when I looked at the cameras, I saw Dreux walking in, disarming the system. She went up to her old bedroom, so I stood up to go follow. I crept up the stairs, posting up in her doorway, admiring the way her body moved as she stripped out of her workout clothes. No longer able to contain myself, I walked up behind her, pinned her between my body and the wall, placed my lips to the side of her neck, and inhaled her natural scent.

"Baby, stop running from me. From us."

"Kamron, move. Whatever us was died when you lied."

"But I didn't lie, Pooh."

"Don't fucking call me that. Failing to mention is the same damn thing."

She fought against me, but I wasn't letting up. I was done with this cat-and-mouse shit. Pushing further into her, my dick began to swell against her ass, and a soft moan escaped her lips.

"You feel that? That's what you still do to me, Dreux. He only responds to you," I said, grinding my pelvis into her.

She turned around, looking up at me with those big, beautiful eyes that had me from day one. Tilting her chin up, I met her lips to mine, and she resisted at first, which I expected.

"Love me, baby." I repeatedly smacked my lips against hers until she opened her mouth, granting me access to what I really wanted. "Tell me you still want me."

When I kissed her, she buckled at the knees, so I lifted her up, and her legs were like magnets around my waist. I walked over to the bed, laying her down, and hovered, just taking in her beauty. She thrusted her hips upward, wanting me to put out the fire that was now burning between her legs. Slowly unbuckling my pants, I let them fall to my ankles, and with no warning, I plunged deep into her ocean, making her back arch off the bed.

"Ssss, Kam. Oh, fuck. I missed this." Shorty was gripping the sides of my shirt, pulling me in.

"What about me? You missed your man, Pooh?" I started long-stroking her pussy, balls slapping against her ass.

"Mm-hmmm, gahdamn, nigga, shit!"

Pulling out, I threw her legs over my shoulders and put my face between her plush-ass thighs. I stuck my tongue in her opening, drawing out the cum that was settled there. The more I slurped on her pussy, the wetter she became, so I licked and sucked on her clit, with my fingers tickling her G-spot. I pushed her legs to her ears. I ain't even been the type to eat no ass, but shit, today I was going all out. When I dipped my tongue in her ass, she creamed all over.

"Let me take you out, Dreux. Say yes."

"Fuuuuck, yesss!"

I stood up and flipped her over, driving my dick into her stomach. I grabbed a handful of those big-ass curls, making her meet me thrust for thrust. I fucked up when I looked down at the way she was cumming all over my dick because that shit turned me on so much I was coating her walls with my nut in no time.

"Whooo, shit." Smacking her ass, I watched it jiggle. "Be ready around six."

"Mm-hmm."

I looked over, and she was falling asleep. I went to her bathroom and cleaned up before letting myself out to go get ready for this date tonight.

When I made it home, I took a quick shower, washing the remnants of Dreux down the drain. Letting my body air dry, I called The Boiling Crab, since it was her favorite, and made reservations to have the restaurant shut down just for her. After I was dressed, I grabbed my phone and shot Trell a quick text.

Me: I'm heading your way playboy.

Trell: Bet that.

As I rode down 635, heading to Trell's shop, "You Might Be" by Ryan Destiny and Quincy was playing in the background, and my mind drifted to Dreux. I forgot she put this shit on my phone one night when we were cruising the city streets. I took a second to listen to the lyrics, realizing this song was written for us.

Got me coming out of my comfort zone, got me feeling like love ain't wrong.

Tonight was my chance to fix my fuck up and get this shit right for her because, in my heart, I knew she needed me as much as I needed her.

I pulled up in front of Trell's barbershop, and I instantly got an eerie feeling, causing me to check my surroundings twice. As I walked toward the door, I heard tires screeching and what sounded like my baby. When I turned around, my heart sank as I watched my everything get snatched from right in front of me. The van came speeding in my direction, and by the time I could bust my gun, it was too late.

Brrrraaatttt-tat-tat!

As my body hit the ground, all I could think was, *This nigga Trell set me up.*

Chapter Twenty

Kamron "Choppa" Vega

Fuck, man! I pulled my shirt off as best as I could, considering my shoulder was on fucking fire. Putting pressure on it to slow the bleeding, my big ass struggled to get off the ground.

"Sir, are you okay? Can I help you?" Some Mona Lisa-looking bitch stood over me. I mugged the fuck out of her and got in my whip. On set, I couldn't wait to catch up with Trell and Dreux's snake asses. Something special was in the works for them. Dreux was going to find out firsthand why they call me Choppa. All that bullshit screaming she was doing was an act to catch me slipping.

Reaching into my pocket, I grabbed my phone and rang Lou, the doctor on my payroll. This muthafucka better beat me to the fucking crib, or he was gon' feel my wrath. Thirty minutes later, I pulled up to the house to find Lou waiting at the gate. *That's what the fuck I thought, nigga.*

"Thanks for patching a nigga up, my G."

"It's all love, family."

I slid him some bread, and he dipped.

I took the steps two at a time. My clothes came off as soon as I hit my bedroom carpet. I stepped into the steaming shower, and the events of the day flashed through my mind on replay.

"Arghhhhh!" Screaming out in frustration, I slammed my hand against the wall. How the fuck could she do this to me? We were supposed to be better than this. After Dreux lit up my trap, I let that shit go because I loved her. Hell, I still loved her, but for the bitch to stoop this low was beyond me. The cold part was that she got down on me with a nigga she barely even knew. Word around town was they had been fucking around long before he shot me. Shaking my head, I let a tear or two loose. After this, there was no room left for tears. My ass was now on straight go mode.

Once the suds were rinsed off, I wrapped a towel around my waist and found something to throw on. Dressing down in an all-black Adidas tracksuit, I grabbed my keys and flew the hell out of the house.

"Aye, Siri, call Dash." Waiting for the call to connect, I weaved in and out of traffic, doing a hundred and ten to get to the Inferno.

"What's good, Choppa?" This shit with Ahdia was really taking Dash through it. I could hear it in his voice.

"A whole lotta nothing, man. You got a few minutes to run down on me? I'm headed to the Inferno, and there's something I need to kick to you. It ain't gon' take up too much of your time, knowing you hate to leave Dia."

"Say less."

I hit shuffle to fill the silence of the ride, and the moment Big Moe started playing, thoughts of Dreux flooded my mind—all our late-night rides, her rapping along to "Just a Dog." This broad really had me wide open. I laughed out loud because the only bitch that my ass let get close to me turned out to be flaw as hell. That shit was pure comedy.

Finally pulling up to the warehouse, I felt tranquility take me over. I put in my code and headed straight to my tool room. Busting a gun wasn't shit. It don't take rocket science to shoot, but that knife play is a skill. I pulled my katana sword from the casing and ran it over my palm. The speckles of blood that appeared made me smirk. It had been a minute since I put it to use, which made me even more anxious to catch up with Trell's bitch ass. One by one, I took the time to sharpen every knife on the leather strap hanging on the wall. My ass low-key felt like Celie when she was getting ready to shave Mister.

Fifteen minutes later, the room lit up blue and flashed three times, letting me know that Dash finally showed up.

"Fuck you got going, bro? What happened to your muhfuckin' shoulder?" Dash walked in and dapped me up.

I dragged my hand down my face before I ran down what happened. "Maaaan, so check it. I slid on Dreux this morning and dropped this donkey dick off in her 'cause I planned on getting my bitch back today, right? I leave the house and get a text from Trell, telling me to pull up at the shop to shoot the shit."

"Aww, hell."

"Naw, for real. I get there, and before I can even make it inside, I hear screaming, turn around, and it's Dreux getting drug into a van. The muhfucka come speeding towards me, lo and fucking behold, Trell hanging out the window letting that thang rip. Bitch ass only caught me in the shoulder, but that nigga was tryna take me out."

"Yooo, square bidness? What type of time is that nigga on? Fuck you do to him?" Dash pulled a Glock from the wall and screwed a silencer on it.

"Bro, I ain't did shit, but what I'm gon' do is show his ass why my name is Choppa in these streets. You hear me?"

"Shiiid, I'm on whatever you on. I ain't wit' that knife shit, but you know these hands are certified. What you gon' do about yo' girl, though?"

"On set, that bitch dead as fuck. How I leave her, then show up to the shop, and she there too? Make that make sense."

"Can't call it. That shit flaw, but lemme ask you something. You really tryna start a war with her people?" Letting loose, Dash emptied the clip into the target at the back of the room.

"Maaaan, I don't give a fuck about that shit. Dreux started this shit when she decided to spread her pussy around town."

"I understand where you coming from, bro, but you at her mama's house every day, running her father's business. Not to mention the fucked-up position you would put me in since I'm fucking with her sister, dawg." Dash reloaded the gun and then looked up at me.

"She gotta pay for that bullshit, bro. I just need to know if you riding."

"Chop, you already know. You my bro and shit, so I'll choose you every time, but my nigga, don't make me if I don't have to. All I'm saying is think of the consequences of your actions before you act." He unloaded the clip again, and I could see the frustration all over his face.

"You good, dawg?"

"Yeah, man. I'ma skate and get back to the hospital. I'll get up witchu later."

"One hunnid." We shook up, and he left.

After all my knives were done, I locked up and took my black ass home. I needed all my rest before I went and delivered the news to Lolita in the morning.

Pulling up to the McCoy mansion, I scanned my palm and watched as the gate slid open. The last thing I wanted to do was face Lolita knowing that her fuck-ass daughter did me wrong in the worst way, but business never stopped. I rang the doorbell instead of using my key to respect Lo's privacy. She opened the door, looking like an older version of Ahdia, and my heart ached a bit for her. The dark circles accompanied by the bags under Lolita's eyes showed the toll life had taken on her.

"Boy, you have a key for a reason. Use it." In pure Lolita fashion, a simple hey wouldn't suffice.

"I ain't wanna barge in on you. I wouldn't disrespect Ghost like that, Lo." I stepped inside and kissed her cheek. As much as I wanted to, there was no reason for me to trip on her for what Dreux did.

Closing the door to Ghost's office, I grabbed a bottle of Crown Royal from the bar and poured up a double shot. The heat from the liquor eased the rage that was blazing inside of me. I sat down behind the desk, going over the numbers for all business, legal and illegal.

Two hours had passed when I heard a knock so soft I damn near missed it. Lolita peeked through the door, so I waved her in.

"I'm not trying to disturb you. I just figured you'd wanna put something on your stomach. Here." She passed me a plate of eggs, bacon, grits, and toast. I was glad she remembered I wasn't a huge breakfast eater because it wasn't a lot on the plate.

"Thank you, beautiful. How you holdin' up?"

"I'm doing the best that I can considering I have a dead husband and a daughter in ICU." She hung her head to keep me from seeing the pain that was permanently etched in her eyes.

I chopped it up with her for a few minutes before she excused herself. My ass felt like shit knowing that the moment we caught up with Dreux, I was bringing a new wave of hurt to Lolita.

Oh, well. Shit happens.

Chapter Twenty-one

Dashir "Dash" Edwards

As Ahdia lay in that hospital bed, hopeless and bound, I wanted nothing more than to scoop her up and take her home with me. There were wires coming from damn near every hole in her body. Four weeks. I'd been by her side, waiting for the smallest sign of life for four weeks. If it weren't for the heart monitor, there would be no indication that she was living.

"Fuck this shit, man." I ran my hand down my face and left out. Jogging out of the hospital, I jumped in my ride, flying down 635 toward my house. I reached into the console for a rolled blunt and faced it the whole way. I needed a break from this stress.

Chilling in my man cave, I replayed the chain of events that led me to this moment. These past two months had been hell on me and Choppa. First, the bullshit with JB, and now this Trell situation. Like fuck, man. The weight of the world was resting on our backs with no way to lift it. Normally, I'd be hitting the streets with Chop, hunting down the nigga that had us fucked up, but this shit with Ahdia was throwing a nigga off his game. I devoted so much time to sitting at the hospital that I'd dropped the ball on my personal shit. Business was still flowing as it should be, but for how long? Half of our unit jumped ship with Jabari, leaving the remaining ones with extra work.

My phone started ringing on the table, so I jumped up, hoping that it was the hospital. It was Choppa.

"Yerrrr," I answered, knowing damn well I wasn't from New York.

"Bro, what's good witchu?" His voice came booming through the phone.

"Gahdamnm, nigga, come up off the mouthpiece hollerin', my G."

"Shit, my fault. Impromptu meeting in an hour. You good for it?"

"Straight. I'll meet you."

"Cool." Choppa hung up.

I got up from the couch and jogged up to my room to change for this meeting. My ass slipped on my black Jordan sweatsuit because knowing Choppa, there was no telling what was about to go down.

Walking into the Inferno, I already knew some shit was up because Choppa was leaned back in a chair with one leg crossed over his knee, rubbing that baby-ass beard. I couldn't help but laugh at his prepaid mob boss–looking ass.

"What the fuck you on, Li'l Scarface?" I slapped his foot to the ground.

"Fuck you, bitch. Money been looking funny, and I know where it's coming from, so I'ma switch some shit around before I cut this nigga up."

"Here yo' muhfuckin' ass go. Ight, I'm on whatever you on."

"Fa sho."

One by one, niggas started coming through the door. Everybody got in their respective places around the warehouse, then Choppa stood up. I stayed seated with my Desert Eagle in my lap in case a nigga got reckless.

"Ight, so first order of business. As y'all can see, Trell, Spank, and Whoodi ain't here. JB wasn't the only snake in the grass. I'ma go ahead and say this. If you're thinking about crossing me, get the fuck up now and let this bullet push you out the door."

Choppa pulled his gun from his waist and cocked it. Nobody moved, but I peeped one nigga shifting from one foot to the other. Either he was going to be a problem, or he was the problem Chop was talking about.

"Cool. I'm assuming everybody know what's gon' happen if you fuck up. Next order of business. I'm changing some shit up. We run a tight ship, but we can never be too careful. Tonight, we gon' rotate the traps. Spooty, you and your team taking over the Green House. Cheese, y'all got the Red House. Ralph is Blue House, and Damu, you got the White House."

I looked over at Choppa, knowing this nigga was on some bullshit. Everybody knew that the White House made the most money, so if Damu was skimming off the top, that shit was going to show.

"Dash, you good on that, bro?" Choppa had a smirk on his face, confirming everything I had already figured.

"Like I said, I'm on whatever you on."

"One hunnid. Ight, so midnight, everybody needs to be shifting their shit around. No exceptions. Meeting dismissed."

Once everybody was gone, I dapped Choppa up and left. Instead of going back to the hospital like usual, I got to business.

I pulled up to the beauty bar that my godsister, Téa, owned out in South Dallas. Most niggas didn't think to invest in some shit like this, but one that was about money knew what was up. She had three locations spread out around Dallas, and I had money in all of them. Normally my ass wouldn't pop up on her, but I was doing anything that would keep me from sitting in the hospital for the day.

"Ladies, ladies, how y'all doing?" I strolled in, greeting everybody before reaching my baby sis.

"Hey, brother, what's got you stopping by on a Wednesday?" Téa came from behind her chair and wrapped me in a hug. From the outside looking in, you'd think she was blood.

"Shit, I didn't know I had to have a reason to come see my favorite girl." I pushed her ass off me.

"Boy, shut up. You only slide by on Mondays, so excuse me for wondering what the fuck your unexpected visit is about."

I ran my hand down my face and sat on the stool beside her station. "Man, sis, I feel like a broken record, but this shit with Ahdia is fucking with my mental. It's not even the point of her being in the coma. She's pregnant by the nigga that violated her. How the fuck am I supposed to love and raise a kid that came from a place that caused my girl so much pain, man?" Baby sis was the first and only person I'd expressed my real issues to.

Knowing that Ahdia was carrying JB's kid has been fucking with me since the doctor told us she was pregnant. He also let us know that her body was too fragile for an abortion, so she'd have no choice but to have the kid. I wasn't the type of nigga that believed in that abortion shit, but I couldn't front like I didn't want her to get one.

"Well, son, if what you've told me about her is true, then you need to step up and love her through the hurt. That baby didn't ask to be here, so don't act like that. She's gonna need you to be there for her. You gotta put your ill feelings to the side, 'cause this ain't about you, bro. Remember that." Tea hung her arm over my shoulder while I sat in my thoughts for a few minutes, digesting everything she'd said.

"I hear you, baby sis. I'll try. I came over here to run them books, but I'on even have it in me no more. I'm finna fade back to the hospital, so I'll get up witchu later."

"Okay, brother. Just remember what I said and take it one day at a time. You got this."

I hugged her and dipped out.

Driving back to the hospital, everything she said weighed on me. I knew this was something I'd have to sort through before fully pursuing things with Ahdia. I sparked up another blunt and bobbed to "Drip 4 Sale" by Plies. Thirty minutes later, I was pulling into the parking lot. Sighing, my ass got out and headed back to Dia's room.

Here we go.

Chapter Twenty-two

Ahdia McCoy

Beep! Beep! Beep! The annoying sound of these damn machines was enough to drive a sane man mad.

Voices. A voice. His voice. Dashir.

"Baby, you gotta wake up. I know we ain't official. Hell, I don't know if you even like me the way I love you, but you gotta wake up. Come back to me, beautiful Dia."

I'm right here!

"If I could, I'd trade your life for mine, but I can't, so you have to fight your way outta this bullshit, ma. You got a real nigga damn near in tears. If not for me, come back for our baby. We're having a baby, Ahdia."

Baby?

"Ahdia! Nurse! Something is wrong! Somebody!"

The monitors started going haywire. My body began to shake violently, sending me into a world of darkness, and then I no longer heard that voice. His voice. Dashir.

Three days later . . .

Bright blinding lights were the first thing I saw when my eyes finally opened. I looked around confused, gathering my surroundings, and to my left was a very handsome man. He had to be the most beautiful man I'd seen in all my years. I tapped weakly on the bed, and his eyes met mine, causing him to jump up.

"Beautiful! Hi, baby." This strange man spoke in the smoothest tone I'd ever heard. It was like ribbons of velvet wrapped around my body.

My hand went to my throat, irritated by the tube that was there. I guess he caught my drift because he went to the door and called for a nurse. When she entered the room, a doctor followed close behind. The doctor, whose name was Susan, removed the tube, and it felt like my throat was on fire.

"Here. Drink this slowly." The nurse handed me a cup of water with a straw, but my arms refused to lift.

"I got it. Don't worry." Mr. Handsome stepped up to help me, and I appreciated it because the dryness of my throat ached something serious.

"It's so great to have you back, Ms. McCoy. You gave us a real scare a few days ago." The doctor was too chipper for me, like the bitch ate sunshine for breakfast every day. My head was banging, and her vocal volume was on ten.

"Why am I here? What happened to me?" I looked between the doctor and my perfect stranger, hoping somebody would shed some light on my confusion.

The doctor looked from me to the man in the chair, and when he nodded, Susan proceeded to speak. "Ms. McCoy, you were brought here five weeks ago, unconscious, with broken ribs and swelling on your brain. We had to remove a piece of your skull to relieve the pressure."

My hand went to my head, and I felt the gauze that covered a missing patch of hair. Tears began to fall from my eyes as I sobbed uncontrollably.

"Why can't I remember anything? What's wrong with me?"

I saw dude's jaw flex from clenching his teeth together, and frustration written over his face.

"Like I said before, there was swelling on your brain, which was brought on by repeated blunt force trauma. What you're experiencing is a bout of amnesia. Unfortunately, I can't tell you how long it'll last, but visiting familiar places and doing familiar things should help." She directed the last part to the perfect stranger, and he nodded his head.

"Also, there was severe vaginal as well as anal tearing."

When she said that, I immediately zoned out. Vaginal and anal tearing could only mean one thing. Someone raped me. I'd been violated. Looking over at the handsome man, I could see the tears on his cheeks and his head hung so low.

"Who are you? Tell me your name." The words came out low and hoarse. His eyes met mine, and the sadness in them shook me a little.

"Dashir, but Dash is cool. Whatever you wanna call me, I'm good with."

"Why are you here? Do we know each other?"

Before he could answer, the doctor and her nurse excused themselves to give us privacy.

"Listen, you just came to after five long and stressful weeks. I really don't wanna overwhelm you, beautiful."

"No, don't do that. This is already gonna be too much for me, so please, just tell me," I pleaded with him in hopes that he'd tell me what the doctor refused to share.

The distressed look on his face told me that whatever happened to me wasn't going to be a pretty story. Dash ran his hand over his face and let out a deep breath.

"Ight, so a few months ago, we ran into each other at the mall. You legit ran into me 'cause ya head was so deep in the phone. We started this game of cat and mouse, and I was chasing the hell outcha ass, but you wouldn't give me the time of day." He laughed, which made me giggle a little bit, and then he continued.

"Some shit happened, and I'd finally got yo' mean ass to meet up with me, but you never showed. I waited for you, ma. For hours, I waited, and you never came."

He choked up, and I could see the tears he refused to let fall. I sat silently.

"I was mad as hell at you for days, until I got the call that someone took you from your crib. I spent all that time in my bag when you were somewhere hurting, and I couldn't do shit about it. When I found you—"

I watched the tears fall.

"When I found you bruised and battered, that broke something in me. We ain't known each other long, but you got a hold on me. I've been here every day, thirty-two days, waiting on you to come back to me. Now look, you don't even know who the fuck I am."

Hurt and frustration was etched on his face, and all I wanted to do was hug him. Dash wiped the tears from his cheeks and stood from the bed.

"Can I hug you?" My voice came out as a whisper.

He walked over to me, and as heavy as my arms felt, I managed to wrap them around his waist. Dash buried his face in my neck as I held him, and I could feel the tears falling down my collarbone.

"Ma, on set, I swear I ain't no soft-ass nigga. This shit just really fucked me up."

I let out a low chuckle. "Thank you for everything. You stayed when you didn't have to, and I'm forever grateful."

Dash and I kicked it for a few hours, talking about nothing but everything all at the same time. He filled me in on the things he knew about me and my family. I could sense there were things that he wasn't quite ready to share, and for now, I'd let him make it. My body started to ache, so I hit the button to the morphine drip. Before drifting off, I asked Dash to climb in and lay with me. He happily obliged, and once my head hit his shoulder, sleep found me.

“Knock knock.” The overnight nurse slowly opened the door. “I’m just here to check your vitals and I’ll be out of your hair.”

I looked down at Dash, who’d somehow ended up with his head in my neck and his arm draped across my stomach. I smiled at how peaceful he made me feel, like this was where I belonged.

“That’s fine. Just please don’t wake him.”

“Of course not.” She put the blood pressure cuff on my arm and proceeded to do her job. Once that was done, she checked my head, which had healed perfectly.

“I’m gonna take the gauze off. Is that okay?”

I was kind of hesitant but went ahead and told her it was okay.

After she removed the gauze, I stroked the patch of hair that had slowly grown back and wept. My shaking body caused Dash to stir, so I tried my best to stop. I glanced down, only to find him staring up at me. He reached up and replaced my hand with his, softly caressing my head.

“Aye, mama, you’re still the most beautiful girl in the world. You hear me? Don’t let this get you down, and don’t let it define you, okay? This is small shit to a giant baby girl.”

He spoke life into me. I nodded as he placed a light kiss on my temple.

“Now lay that big-ass head on me and go back to sleep. I got you for life.” He moved up, and I rested my head on his, once again letting sleep take me over.

“All right, Ms. Ahdia, everything looks good. Your ribs have healed up nicely, but I still want you to take it easy. You'll feel some discomfort, which is normal, so there's nothing to worry about." Dr. Susan came in with discharge papers and instructions.

It had been three days since I came out of the coma, and I'd been up walking the halls to get my legs back in shape. Other than the times he had to handle business, Dash was here every step of the way. He'd gone down to pull the car in front of the hospital.

"I'm gonna have the nurse bring a wheelchair, and we'll get you out of here."

"As happy as I am to be leaving here, I'm so nervous. I feel like my ass is walking into the world blind," I finally admitted more so to myself than the doctor.

"Honey, you'll be fine. You have a great man who's dedicated to making this as easy on you as possible. You're not alone." She hugged me just as Dash came through with the wheelchair.

"You ready, beautiful?" He bent down and kissed my forehead.

"More than you know."

Chapter Twenty-three

Dreux McCoy

How did I end up here? We just got Ahdia back, and now my ass was missing in action. I was starting to assume that snatching bitches was the new wave for these niggas. It had been a solid three days, and LT—or Trell, apparently—still had me hostage in some random-ass house.

Lying across the bed, my mind drifted to my dad, bringing tears to my eyes. He was everything a daughter needed in a father, and now he was gone. Listening to the lock click, I sat up and gave Trell the ugliest glare my face could form.

"I don't know why the fuck you got yo' face bunched up like that. It ain't gon' change shit but my attitude." This muthafucka always had some smart shit to say.

"Who gives a damn about your attitude, nigga? All I wanna know is why you have me here and when are you gonna let me go. Shit."

"It's cute that you think you're leaving here anytime soon. When your boy gives me what the fuck I want, then *maybe* I'll let you go. Until then, eat this shit and chill. You lucky I'm even doing that."

I rolled my eyes from here to the moon and back because he was on some real bullshit if he thought my ass was staying here too much longer.

Tossing the bag of Rudy's on the bed, Trell stalked out of the room, and I was mad as hell at my body for even reacting to his trifling ass. He was a good six feet, easily towering over my small frame, with butterscotch skin. He wasn't as built as Kamron, but the definition in his back made between his shoulder blades the best place for his sandy brown dreads to lay. The best part of him was the hazel eyes that made my pussy betray me every time he was near, but shit, fuck that nigga. He wasn't fucking with *my* nigga in the least bit.

As I tore into a chicken wing, I wandered to Kam and our last encounter. All the time my ass wasted hating him meant nothing the moment he slid into this wet kitty. Trust me when I say he made this twenty-two go *pew pew pew*, honey. Even after almost a week, I could still feel him between my legs and all over my body. After he put that thick-ass piece of meat on me, I was ready to hear what he had to say. Who knows if we'd ever get the chance again, but I missed the shit out of my man.

Finishing up the food, I knocked three times on the door, so this nigga would let me wash my ass. I swear this shit was for the birds. Every fucking door in this house had a lock on it, so even though I had free range, this shit was locked down like Fort Knox.

"What, bitch?"

Bitch? This weak-ass nigga had me fucked up.

"Bitch? Nigga, if you don't open this fucking door so I can wash my pussy. Stop playing with me, muhfucka." If I was a cartoon, there would be steam coming from my ears because this dude had me hotter than fish grease.

The door swung open with his fine/ugly ass standing there holding a towel set. Walking over to Trell, I snatched the towels from his hand and headed to the bathroom.

"Rude-ass bitch," I heard him mumble under his breath. It was crazy how I wasn't a bitch a week ago when my pussy was in his face. Whack ass.

Standing under the shower with my head tilted back, I let it wash the troubles of the past few days down the drain. Tears and soft sobs were drowned out by water drops hitting the tile floor, but my tears stopped when I felt a cool breeze from the door opening. I'd be damned if I let him know I was breaking down.

"I brought you some shit to put on. Be grateful."

"Yep." The more Trell talked, the higher my irritation levels were starting to rise. All I wanted was to click my heels three times and poof my ass back home. Mumbling under my breath, I knew there was a way to break free from this prison. It was time to boss up and show this nigga who Dreux Ali McCoy really was.

"Trell, the least you can do is take me to get some fucking clothes. I'm not about to keep wearing your shit like you my nigga." I swear I'd never been this frustrated in my life.

"Say, li'l mama, you gon' have to wind that mouth down before I put something in it, and that's law. Put some shit on and get yo' dumb ass in the fucking car."

I stomped off with a fake attitude, knowing that part one of my escape plan was underway.

Before I hopped into the car, Trell stopped me and covered my eyes with a blindfold. I guess he had a little more sense than I thought, but that wasn't fucking up my shit. The ride to the mall was silent, other than the sounds of Moneybagg Yo blasting through the speakers. After what felt like a two-hour drive, we came to a stop. The door opened, and I was pulled from the car.

When the blindfold came off, I was standing face-to-face with Spank, who had a dumb-ass smirk on his face. Trell fucked up by sending me to this crowded ass mall and leaving Spank as my bodyguard. This man had been eye-fucking me since I'd been locked down, so my plan to play on his infatuation was in full effect.

Spank grabbed me up by my arm and stared dead into my eyes. "When we get in this fucking mall, you better not try no slick shit, or I'll blow your shit back. You can try me if you want to. I'd hate to show you what it's made for in a room full of people." He squeezed my arm so hard, a bruise instantly started to form. For the first time, Spank had me shook, but that wasn't enough to divert me from my plan. He grabbed my hand, and we walked into NorthPark.

"Smile, bitch."

I'll be damned if I didn't put a fucking smile on my face. As we strolled through the mall, Victoria's Secret was the first store I saw.

"Spankkk, can we go in Victoria's Secret, please?" Running my hands through my hair, I laid it on thick.

"Man, li'l mama, I ain't even fucking witchu like that. You can go in. I'll stay outside."

His dumb ass made that easier than I expected. Power-walking to the other end of the mall, I did my best to shake Spank, but surprisingly, the fat-ass nigga kept up. We reached the store, and I dipped inside while he posted up at the door. Shelf after shelf, I skimmed through the clothes, casually picking up things here and there. Glancing over my shoulder, I saw Spank was still in the same spot, so I made my way to the register.

"Good afternoon, ma'am. Did you find everything you were looking for?" She was chipper as hell. It almost even lightened my mood.

"Yes. I was wondering if I could possibly use your phone. Mine was stolen this morning."

"Umm, we don't have a personal store phone, and I'm not sure about lending out my cell," the cashier replied.

"Look, I know you don't know me, but there's a man standing outside of this store waiting to snatch me up. Please, help me." At this point, my ass was desperate as hell.

Her eyes widened as she discreetly slid the phone across the counter.

"Thank you so much." I grabbed the phone from the counter and rushed to the dressing room. Hurriedly, I dialed Kam's number, hoping and praying that he'd answer.

"Yoooo, who dis?"

Closing my eyes, I relished in the sound of his raspy voice. I missed him.

"Hellooo, who the fuck is playing on my phone?"

My words were caught in my throat, but in the smallest voice, I finally answered. "Kam."

"Dreux? Yo' ho ass got some fucking nerve to be calling my phone. All the shit I've done for you, been to you, and you do some shit like that, snake-ass bitch. Aye, ma, you got two seco—"

"Kam, please. I don't know what you think I did, but I didn't do it. Please come to me. I need you." My feelings were beyond hurt by the way he was speaking to me. This wasn't the man I fell in love with.

"You know what? You're right. Where you at?"

Something in the way Kam spoke made me nervous, but it was too late to back out now.

"I'm at Victoria's Secret inside of NorthPark. Please hurry."

"Bet."

I hugged the phone to my chest, relieved that Kam was coming for me. Grabbing my purse from the bench, I opened the dressing room door, and there stood Spank.

"You know you done fucked up, right?"

Chapter Twenty-four

Choppa

Racing through the mall, my big ass felt like a mad man. My heart was beating out of my chest and my fucking palms were sweating. If she was here, that meant Trell was too. It was murder season, and the whole city was about to feel me.

I dipped inside Victoria's Secret, where she said she was, and hollered her name.

"Dreux! Dreux!" Everybody in there was staring, and I didn't give one piece of a fuck. I jiggled the dressing room doors, but the muthafuckas wouldn't open. I ran up on the cashier, startling her, but I didn't give a fuck about that either.

"Say, li'l mama, I need you to open them fitting closets. I'ono why y'all call that shit a room."

"Sir, I can't do that. It's an invasion of privacy."

"Do it look like I care about privacy? My girl in there and she could be in danger," I barked on ole girl since she wanted to play.

"Oh my God, it's her. She asked to use my phone to call you, I'm assuming. I'm sorry, but some big dude dragged her out of here fifteen minutes ago."

"Fuck!" I slammed my hand on the counter, making the cashier jump. As I left the store, the wheels in my head began to turn. There was no way I was sitting on my ass to wait for this nigga to call and say what he wanted.

Walking through the mall, I spotted a fine bitch going in that fruity-ass bath and whatever store. I'd never been the type of nigga to chase no pussy, but li'l mama was stacked just how a nigga liked them. My mind was telling me to go see what shorty was about, but my heart wasn't on the same type of time. I was off Dreux, though, so my heart was going to have to fall in line. Shit, it wasn't like I was trying to fall in love anyway. My ass just needed something wet and warm to slide into every now and then.

As soon as I hit the door, all those girly smells hit my nose and had me ready to turn the fuck around. I scanned the shelves, picking up shit here and there, until I made it to the section li'l baby was in and turned my mack daddy on.

"If you had to pick, which one would you choose?" I held up some shit called Champagne Toast and Magic in the Air. Shorty looked up at me, and I smirked.

"Hmm, that's a tough one for me. I'd probably go with Champagne Toast. It makes me feel sexy. You buying for a girlfriend?"

"Nah, my mama. I'on need her ass feeling sexy, so I'm getting this other shit. Thanks, li'l mama." I took both to the counter and checked out. While walking out of the store, I heard her voice behind me.

"Hey, you just gon' get my opinion and leave?" *Got her.* "You don't wanna know my name or no shit like that?"

"It's just body wash, shorty. I ain't know I needed your name for all that, but bless me wit' it."

"Lashia, but everybody calls me Lay. Yours?"

"My shit ain't important. I'ma keep it ninety-nine plus one witchu. You bad as fuck, and all I really got time for is to dig in them guts. You down or nah?"

She started chewing on her bottom lip, and I could see the wheels in her head spinning. "Yeah, I'm cool with that, but I'm not a ho."

That's usually what hoes say before they take off like they're training for the 2019 Holympics.

"I ain't saying shit, shorty. We both grown, so let's go do what grown folks do." I left out of Bath and Body Works and made my way to the family bathroom I spotted on the way in.

When I looked over my shoulder, Lay was still talking on the phone, so I pushed the door open and pulled her inside.

"You foreal right now? We finna fuck in here?" She looked at me with wide eyes, and I couldn't help but let out a low laugh.

"My dick don't discriminate. Where I feel like fucking at is where I'ma fuck at. So, you can either grab them ankles or you can step. What you on?"

Like I knew she would, Lay turned around and bent over, pushing the dress she wore over her waist. All I saw was pussy and asshole staring back at me. That little pussy didn't need no help from the way it was glistening. Grabbing two gold wrappers out my wallet, I strapped my dick up and slid in balls to ass.

"Shiiiiiit! Gahdamn, girl, you be doing yo pussy exercises, huh. Shit tight as fuck." Shorty had to have a vice grip in that cat the way it was squeezing my piece.

"Wa-waiiiit, take some outtt."

Blocking out the bullshit she was talking, I continued to hit Lay with strokes so deep my dick was playing patty cake with her kidneys. That ass was crashing like waves against my pelvis, and my balls started tingling.

"Oooh, fuck, I'm finna cum." I hit her ass with a long stroke that had her wetting my shit up.

"Turn around and suck this nut out my dick."

Throwing the rubbers in the trash, Lay swallowed every inch of me. I grabbed the back of her head, fucking her mouth until all my children were sliding down her throat.

"Whoooo, shit! Girl, you got sum'n bout'cha self. Put yo' number in my phone, 'cause I'ma need that shit again." I handed her my jack, and Lay's face scrunched up.

"Damn, nigga, you got a girl?"

Not bothering to address her, I proceeded to wash my dick off. I still had the picture of Dreux kissing my cheek as we sat at a red light as my screensaver, and as fucked up as she did me, my ass couldn't change the shit.

"Helloooo?"

"Shorty, if I ain't answer you the first time, that means I ain't got shit to explain to you. Yo' ass either gon' put yo' number in that bitch or walk the fuck up outta here. Simple." I was damn near regretting the fuck out of dicking her down.

"I did. Hit me up when you ready to cheat on your bitch again." She rolled her eyes before walking out of the bathroom. Funky bitch didn't even attempt to wash that nut off her ass.

After washing my hands, I jogged out to my car and headed to Trell's crib. This was my left hand, so I knew he wasn't shit to be played with, but it wasn't a single muthafucka on this earth that put fear in my heart. When the time came, his bitch ass was gon' feel that betrayal in the worst way.

When I made it to Trell's spot in Plano, I pulled my strap from under the seat and chambered one. His car wasn't outside, but I'd be a dummy to think that he was gone just because his car was. Using my key, I opened the door, and the nastiest smell hit my nostrils. There was old food and trash scattered all over the place, a clear sign that either nobody had been there in days, or niggas was really living nasty as fuck. I went to his office in the back and started going through all his shit. There had to be something in this muthafucka.

Thirty minutes later, I was leaving with the same thing I came with—shit. My ass was getting frustrated as hell. I dialed Trell's number and was met with a disconnection message. Fuck! Now I couldn't do shit but wait on this nigga to hit me up.

While I sat in Ghost's office going over the books to the businesses, my phone lit up with an anonymous call. On high alert, I knew it was Trell.

"Who?" I answered on the third ring.

"You already know who. Cut yo' shit, dawg."

"Say what you want and let's get this shit over wit', fam. You on the same takeover shit whack-ass JB was on?" I humored his punk ass.

"Nah, see, the difference between me and that nigga is I *been* down. We jumped off the porch together. I guess you forgot that part."

"Maaaan, I ain't tryna hear that shit. I never made you feel like you was less than my equal, so if that's what you on, then you did that to yo'self, fam."

"That's bullshit and you know it. That nigga Dash got on *after* we put that time in, but somehow, he eating at the same table."

"Bro, you on some real female-ass shit. You jealous of the next man? He put in work on the same corners as we did and worked his way to the top. You know what's funny? I was already planning to step down and hand this shit to you, but you crossed me instead. Greed is a helluva drug." This muthafucka had me ready to crack his shit with this crybaby bullshit he was on.

"Greed and lust. How does it feel knowing I took yo' bitch from you?"

"You think I give a fuck about that snake-ass bitch? Nah, you keep them sloppy seconds, 'cause bitches come a dime a dozen to a nigga like me. You really want this shit? Meet me at the warehouse tomorrow at seven o'clock. We been boys too long for this shit." I threw the bait out, knowing he was going to bite.

"'Bout fucking time. I ain't wit' that funny shit, so don't try and play me or it's lights out for ya girl."

I laughed at his response because what he didn't know was the minute I got my hands on Dreux, I planned on clapping the bitch like ass cheeks.

"Bet."

This shit was about to get interesting.

Chapter Twenty-five

Ahdia

As I stood in the bathroom mirror, my thoughts began to roam. Who would do this to me, and why? I was frustrated, angry, and hurt. The tears slid down my face, racing one another to see who could reach the sink first. Watching my eyes turn bloodshot red, I hated not recognizing the woman staring back at me. Why couldn't I remember shit? The one thing I did remember was that Dash had clippers underneath the sink. Once I plugged them in, I started releasing all my hurt. As the hair fell into the sink, a gut-wrenching cry pulled from my soul and spilled from my mouth. Dash came busting into the bathroom and stopped at the sight of me.

"Dia, what's going on? Talk to me." Dash spoke so softly as he retrieved the clippers from my grasp.

"Take it off. Cut it all off of me. I'm suffocating."

"Dia, you su—"

"Just do it. Please! Please free me."

With no words, Dash cut while I cried, and after the last piece of hair was gone, I breathed. I leaned my head back on his shoulder, locking eyes with him in the mirror.

"Hi, I'm Ahdia."

"Hi, beautiful, I'm Dashir. Nice to meet you."

I turned into the arms of the perfect stranger and felt more connected to him than anything else in my life. He didn't look at me with pitiful eyes. There was something else there. We stood in the bathroom, wrapped in each other's arms in complete silence.

Once I gathered myself, Dash turned on the shower and undressed me. It wasn't in a sexual way, just a man caring for a woman. I stepped in directly under the showerhead, and he came in behind me, fully clothed. Running his hands over my bald head, Dash gently massaged my scalp. It seemed like with every stroke of his fingertips, the weight shifted from me to him, and I relaxed a little more. I turned around when I no longer felt his hands only to find him reaching for my washcloth and Champagne Toast body wash. Dash lathered up the towel and bathed me from head to toe. When he reached my kitty, his eyes met mine, as if asking for permission to touch me there. I nodded. Dash cleansed my sensitive parts, and when his fingers slid across my clit, a low moan escaped my lips. As he stood, it was hard not to notice the bulge that had formed in his pants. I reached out to touch him, but he lightly nudged my hand away.

"We got time, baby."

I slick felt rejected until it set in that the only thing this man wanted from me was me. Dash got out first, and I followed. He wrapped a towel around my body, then led me to the bed.

"Lay down on your stomach for me. Let me take care of you," Dash whispered in my ear before he disappeared back into the bathroom.

I dried off and then lay down like he requested. When Dash returned, his arms were occupied with oils and a few candles. I waited with anticipation for the feel of his strong hands on my body. My perfect stranger lit the candles, and the smell of vanilla instantly filled the room. My feet were lifted from the bed as the soft sounds of Sade's "The Sweetest Taboo" played through the soundbar. The moment Dash's thumbs pressed against the ball of my foot, shocks of electricity radiated through my body. His hands traveled up my legs, soothing the ache of my thigh muscles that hadn't been moved in weeks. The feel of his fingertips traced under my ass, and when he massaged my cheek in circular motions, a deep groan vibrated in his throat. It was no secret that this turned me on, but the glistening of my vagina must have caught him by surprise. By the time Dash finished caressing my body, I was drifting off to sleep. I felt the bed rise, signaling his departure, which was something my ass wasn't ready for.

"Stay."

Dash paused at the door before turning around and kicking off his shoes. He slowly stalked toward the bed, looking like a chocolate god, as he pulled his shirt over his head. Without another word, Dash climbed behind me, wrapped his arms around my waist, and we fell asleep.

Rolling over, I was greeted by sunshine and empty space. My heart started beating fast as anxiety crept up on me. It had been almost two weeks since I was released, and Dash had been my safety net, so not to see him put me in a bad space. I wasn't ready to be alone. Sweat beads saturated my forehead, but before I could reach full panic mode, he came through the door. Jumping from the bed, I ran into him on the verge of tears.

"Shhh. Hey, you okay, ma? What's wrong, beautiful?"

The anxious feeling slowly left my body as Dash stroked my back and whispered in my ear.

"You weren't there when I turned around. I know I've clung to you while being here, but I'm not ready to be alone. I'm sorry."

"Don't apologize. I'm here, and I swear my ass ain't going nowhere. Come on, cry baby, I cooked for you."

I laughed as Dash placed a small kiss on my forehead. We walked in the kitchen. The breakfast spread he'd set up was fit for a queen. There were waffles, bacon, sausage, and eggs on the island, with oatmeal, fruit, and juice by the stove. My mouth watered at the sight before me.

"Sit down, mama, I got it. What you want? I didn't know how big you wanted to eat, so I gave you options. Light or heavy?"

"Ummm, can I have all of it?"

"Oh, you hungry hungry. Yeah, you can have whatever you want, fat mama." He flashed me a smile that had the seat of my thong wetter than Niagara Falls. My cheeks were turning red, so I dropped my head and fiddled with my fingers.

As Dash fixed my plate, I couldn't help but wonder about my family. He'd asked me before we left the hospital if I wanted to see them, but I wasn't ready. How could I face a bunch of people knowing I had no idea who they were? Would they reject me? Probably not, but I couldn't take that chance then.

The only sounds were forks clinking as we knocked out the meal that Dash had cooked. I didn't realize how fast I was taking that shit back until my ass choked.

"Whooo, shit. Slow down, big girl. It ain't going nowhere." Dash laughed as he held my arms in the air and patted my back. I was slick embarrassed, but hell, I was making up for lost time.

"It might. Don't be laughing at me." I couldn't help but to laugh at my damn self. Whatever this was with Dash felt so natural, so right. This was something I could get used to.

"So, what's the plan for today? You up to getting out of the house?"

"Yeah, I think I wanna see my family. I'm sure they've missed me." My ass was nervous as shit, but I knew this was something I had to do. Not just for me, but for my family as well.

"Ight, that's cool. I'll clean up down here while you shower and shit. Listen, I see the nerves, but it's gon' be all right. I got you."

"What's this?" We were on our way to see my family, and some song about putting ice on his baby was bumping through the speakers.

In the studio, I let you sit in on my session,
I got picked for movie roles. You know I can't be too careful.

"That verse is Kevin Gates, but it's 'Ice on My Baby' by Yung Bleu. You fuckin' wit' it?" He looked over at me and licked that juicy-ass bottom lip.

"Yeah, it's dope as hell."

"Stick wit' me, mama. That's gon' be you." Dash sat his hand on my thigh, and I started dancing in my head.

An hour later, we were pulling in front of a mini-mansion. My stomach was turning as the nerves set in. Dash had spoken with my mother earlier in the week, so she knew I was released. He explained everything to her, and I was thankful that she didn't push. I couldn't imagine how hard it must have been to keep her distance.

Dash pushed the buzzer to the gate, and a sweet voice came through the speaker. My heart fluttered. *My mama.* I tried picturing her face, but I was coming up blank. The gate opened, and Dash drove up the mile of driveway and parked at the front door.

"You ready?" He pulled my hand to his lips and kissed it.

"Ughhh, not really, but let's do it."

Dash got out and walked around to open my door. As I stepped out, the door opened, and standing there was an older version of me. Her hand went to her mouth as the tears came down her cheeks.

"Mama." My voice was low and shaky.

"Oh, my baby. My beautiful girl. Can I hug you?"

I nodded. "Please."

She ran down the steps and grabbed me into the tightest hug. It felt so good to be in her arms. They say there's nothing like a mother's love, and I was feeling all that right now. I melted in her embrace, and despite being with Dash all week, I felt the safest here.

Mama pulled me into the house, telling me to make myself at home. I walked inside the living room, which was decked out in all white, and looked around. There were pictures everywhere, so I took a minute trying to jog even the slightest memory. I saw the childhood pictures of myself, but it was the picture next to it that I picked up.

"Your sister, Dreux. I'm sure you figured that out. You know, I'm giving you a pass considering the things you've been through, but li'l girl, I don't play about shoes in my white room." She chuckled as I looked down at my feet.

"Sorry. I'm so sorry."

"Oh, hush. I'm just messing with you. Are you hungry? I can make you something."

"No, ma'am, I ate before I came, but I would like to sit and talk. This is gonna be a journey for me, and I need you. I need my mom." I fiddled with my fingers.

"Well, come on. Let's go up to your old room. It'll help you get a better sense of who you were before."

Dash came into the room, and after I assured him that I was okay, he left to give us time to ourselves. I looked around my room, searching for things that would help me remember something, anything. The room was painted red with gold trimming and black accents. There was a California king bed with a diamond-encrusted headboard and matching dressers. As I ran my hand over the pictures on the wall, nothing jogged my memory. Further frustrated, I sat on the bed with my head in my hands. My mama sat beside me and rubbed my back.

"It's okay, baby girl. Take your time, and it'll come back to you. There's no rush, sweet pea."

Mama and I spent hours talking, and it crushed me to know my father was killed while I was in a coma. Try pairing that shit with not having a memory. It'll fuck you up in the worst way.

I shot Dash a text, letting him know that I wanted to stay there that night. Sleeping with him every night had become my norm, but I needed to learn how to be without him as well. After a few texts back and forth, he told me that he'd come see me the next day. I spent the rest of the day and into the night loving on my mama. This was going to be my toughest test, but I was determined to succeed.

Let the journey begin.

Chapter Twenty-six

Trell

"Yo' dumb ass had the nerve to call that nigga, and he couldn't care less about you. Pick yo' face up off the floor." I wanted to slap the shit out of Dreux so bad. Bitch damn near fucked up my plan, only to find out Choppa wasn't even worried about her ass.

"Trell, I don't know who the fuck you think I am, but this ain't that. Watch how you talk to me, my nigga."

I didn't know how the fuck Choppa put up with her smart-ass mouth, but I was two seconds off from peeling her muffin cap back blue. Walking into the living room, I slapped the controller out of Whoodi's hand. These niggas didn't do shit but sit on this bullshit all day.

"Fuck is wrong wit' yo' ass, nigga? You been on some other shit since we been here."

"Shut the fuck up. I got a meeting tomorrow wit' Choppa. I want you to stay here with Spank and babysit, 'cause we obviously can't trust him to keep an eye on the bitch in the back."

"Maaan. I ain't Kristy, and this ain't the fucking Babysitter's Club."

I mugged Whoodi hard as hell. "The fact that you know what that is, is a problem. You gon' do what the fuck I said or get yo' ass beat. Ain't no other option."

Whoodi sucked his teeth like a bitch, but he didn't say shit else after that. When I put this shit in motion, Whoodi and Spank were the ones I thought could handle this, but my ass was starting to regret it.

I knew I fucked up when I shot Choppa and kidnapped his bitch, but I wasn't in my right mind. For the past year, I'd been fucking with that white girl, and it was starting to get outta hand. I remembered the day I tried that shit like it was yesterday.

"Aye, bro, we finna bounce. You rollin'?" My homeboy Dank yelled over the music in the strip club.

"Nah, I'm chillin'. I'll catch up with y'all niggas tomorrow."

I was fucking off with this bad-ass stripper named Paradise, throwing hundreds left and right. By the time the end of the night came, she had come up on two thousand dollars from my pocket alone. As I was walking to the car, I noticed her and another stripper coming from the club.

"Aye, y'all tryna come kick it with a nigga tonight?"

Paradise looked to her homegirl, who nodded her head. "Yeah, we're down. We gon' follow you back to your crib."

"Nah, I'm too fucked up to drive to my spot. Meet me at the Omni, and we'll get a room for the night." These were some strippers. Ain't no way in hell I was bringing them bitches to where I laid my head.

Jumping in my car, I sped down Highway 35 with the two slut buckets following behind me. We made it to the hotel, and once we got to the room, I hopped in the shower. When I stepped back into the room, Paradise and her homegirl was licking and sucking all over each other.

"Gahdamn, y'all got the shit started without me?" I slapped Paradise on her fat ass.

"No, daddy, we saved enough for you."

"Enough what? Pussy? Shiiid, I know that."

Her homegirl started laughing. "Nooo, we saved you some candy."

Looking over at the table, I saw three lines of white girl..

"Oh, nah, baby girl, I don't fuck around with that shit. Y'all got it."

"Just try it. The sex will be amazing."

Against my better judgment, I left Paradise lead me to the table. She sniffed her line, then looked up at me to follow suit. Leaning down, I snorted the line of coke, and my body instantly started to tingle. Paradise began to kiss on me, and that shit felt so fucking good. The three of us fucked all night and into the morning. What can I say? I'm a sucker for a big butt and a smile.

Nobody knew because I was a functioning addict, but once I got my hands on Choppa's shipments, it was over. My ass was good for getting high off my own supply. The dude that Chop killed a few months back, yeah, I shorted his ass on purpose. Somebody had to take the fall.

Grabbing my keys from the table, I made my way to the crib in Plano. I dipped back to the city when I needed my fix and some ass. Walking into the house, I saw there was trash and shit all over the place. I was so out of it that the party from last week slipped my mind. Oh, well. I'd call somebody to clean this shit before the meeting the next day.

I plopped down on the couch and pulled the vial of cocaine from between the cushions. Grabbing my phone, I hit up a few of my niggas to fade Onyx tonight, while

I made a line on the table. Choppa handing over his shit called for a fucking celebration. Leaning over, I hit the line and let the euphoric feeling take over my body. Stepping into Choppa's place was going to be straight. Unlimited cocaine? Yeah, I struck gold.

Look, my bitches all bad, my niggas all real
I ride his in some big tall heels

"Gahdamn, the hoes got the club going up on a Tuesday. It's ass everywhere and not just from the strippers." My nigga Jody was acting like his ass had never been in a strip club before.

"Nigga, it's ass. Quit actin' like you ain't ever seen none befo'. Pee, where ya money at? I ain't spotting yo' broke ass like I did last time."

Pee mugged me like I was lying. "Man, fuck you. Ain't shit broke about me."

"Yeah, okay, we gon' see."

We grabbed a table in the center of the floor and flagged down a bottle girl to get this shit popping. I ordered a bottle of Crown before going to the bathroom. Cutting up two more lines, I took them to the head and headed back to the floor.

"This is from the gentleman across the way." I looked up to see Choppa staring back at me. He raised his glass, and I did the same. This shit was going to be all right.

Chapter Twenty-seven

Dash

The next day...

Shit with Ahdia had been cool these past two weeks. She was spending more time with Lolita, but she made sure to come home every night. Home. I couldn't help the goofy-ass grin that was plastered on my face when I thought about sharing space with her beautiful ass. My nut sack was full, and if she kept rubbing that round ass on me, I was going to show her what it was made for.

My head was in my phone, going through some emails, when I heard the bathroom door open. On instinct, I glanced up, and there Dia stood, looking like the whole fucking entrée. Those long caramel legs that I loved were bare, with just a pair of red bottoms on her feet. Gracing her body was a black lace negligee, and for a second, I was jealous of the fabric on her skin. She'd decided to keep her head bald, and the sexy design she got last week pulled her whole look together.

My mans began to rise, but I couldn't bring myself to get the fuck off the bed. That's how stuck she had me.

"You gon' sit there and stare, or you gon' make a move?" She put her hands on her thick-ass hips, and it was over.

Walking over to my beauty, I lifted her chin and kissed those soft lips. Ahdia palmed the back of my head and attacked my tongue with hers. I was sucking on her bottom lip, and she let out the sexiest moan. I came undone. I picked her up by her thighs and walked back to the bed. Laying Ahdia down, I broke the lip lock we were in and stared into her eyes.

"Once we do this, that's it. You're mine, and I'm yours. You ready for that?"

She nodded, but that wasn't enough for me.

"Nah, ma, I need to hear you say it."

"Yes. I been ready."

I didn't need to hear shit else after that. I trailed kisses from her lips down to her neck. Smelling Dia's sweet scent, I licked and sucked, marking my territory. Her nipples hardened against my chest as she moaned in my ear. I stood up and removed the sweats and wife beater to feel her skin on mine.

I took my rightful place between her thighs, and she guided my head to her soft breasts. My ass had been a titty man all my life, so I attacked her nipples with no problem. As I nibbled and sucked, my fingers found their way to her treasure box. The way her pussy was leaking had my mouth watering. I was deep in her shit, digging for that golden G-spot.

"Babyyyy, shiiit!" Ahdia's hands went crazy over my waves as I tapped on her pussy cushion and thumbed her clit.

Removing my fingers, I sucked her juices and was gone that fast. She looked at me with a smirk that had me ready to show her who ran this shit.

"That's what you on? Keep that same energy." I sat up and pulled her legs until they rested on my shoulders with her head on the bed.

"Dash, wait."

"Shut the fuck up and get yo' mind right."

Holding Ahdia up by her ass cheeks, I gave her pussy a long, slow lick. It should be a fucking crime to have that shit sitting between her thighs. I pierced her swollen nub with the tip of my tongue repeatedly until she came. Without giving Dia time to ride the wave, my mouth covered her opening, and I sucked the cum from her body. I tilted her up, giving me a clear view of her ass, and I dove in.

"Mmmm! Stopppp, I ca—. I can't take it. Baeee!" Her legs were shaking as another orgasm took over. Case closed.

Lowering her body, I got up and grabbed a condom from the nightstand. Looking over my shoulder, I saw Ahdia peering back at me with lust-filled eyes. Damn, this girl was so fucking beautiful. When my boxers fell to the floor, I thought she was gon' run. I was blessed with ten long, thick inches of dick, and her eyes showed everything her mouth wanted to say.

"Relax. It's just dick, baby."

"Just diiiiiick!"

I laughed because she'd been doing this shit since she watched that Soulja Boy interview.

"Don't start that shit. I got you, boo. Now, open up and let daddy come home."

Her legs made room for me to climb in between, and I strapped up. Rubbing my piece up and down her slippery slit, I pushed the tip in.

"Dash."

"I know, mama. You gotta relax for me. You want me to stop?"

She shook her head, and I pushed further inside. Dia grabbed my arms, digging her nails into my skin. My mouth met hers, and she bit down on my bottom lip. I was a nigga that loved pain, so I was ready to take off.

Resisting, I rocked back and forth, slowly breaking her in. The grip on my arms loosened, letting me know the pain was now pleasure. I hooked one leg around my waist and put this dick in her stomach. The sex faces she was making almost took me out.

"Ssss, yessss! Fuckkkk me!"

I was giving Dia the deepest strokes, and when she put her hand on her stomach, I remembered that she was pregnant.

"Fuck!" That shit was enough to make my dick go soft.

"Wait. Why did you stop?"

"Shit, I was finna nut up," I lied. "I ain't going out like that. Put that ass in the air." I knew I had to break her off real proper like, so I pushed those thoughts to the back of my head.

Dia was on all fours, and I'd be lying if I said that wasn't the sexiest shit to me. Dropping my dick back in her, I slapped her ass cheeks, and she got in a rhythm. Baby girl was meeting me stroke for stroke. Dipping my thumb in her juices, I circled it around her asshole. When I pushed my thumb in her butt, Dia blessed my dick and stomach with her nut.

"Shiiiiit, I'm right behind you. Gimme one more." As I fucked her pussy and ass at the same damn time, my balls pushed a heavy load straight to my dick head.

"Cum. Now." Her body shook, and it was over for me. I pulled out, and she collapsed on the bed.

"Boo, come on. Come shower with me."

"Dashir, no. Leave me alone. I can't even feel my legs."

Shaking my head, I soaped up a towel and wiped her down.

As much as I wanted to lay up with my baby, I had a meeting to get to. I showered and thought about how I was going to tell Ahdia about the baby growing in her stomach since she still didn't know. From what the nurse said, she should be close to two months. Before long, her ass would be showing.

Pulling my shirt over my head, I admired Dia's beauty. This woman had me on some real creep shit.

"Where are you going, baby?" she turned over and asked.

"I gotta meet up with Choppa in a few. I shouldn't be gone but a couple of hours."

"K. Tell him I said hey. Gimme kisses."

I bent down, placing a few pecks on her lips, and she slipped her tongue in my mouth. Even though she hadn't met Choppa, I was always on the phone with that nigga.

"Aye, you ain't finna have me walking in that bitch with a hard dick, and I don't have time for round two, so stop."

Her spoiled ass had the nerve to pout. Putting one last kiss on her forehead, I was out the door.

"So, you really 'bout to do this shit? Everything we've built on, and you handing it to this bullshit-ass nigga?" I was looking at Choppa with a cold-ass mug on.

"Come on, bro. You know me better than this. Everything costs, and Trell gon' pay with his life. I just want his ass comfortable enough to let his guard down."

"Man, we could ambush the fuck out that muthafucka."

"We could, but we ain't those type of niggas. You're the only one who knows that I'm the plug now, so when it's time for his re-up, I'm on straight bullshit. But you good? Once I step down, you gon' be straight until I take his ass out?"

Choppa knew better than to ask that shit. "Bruh, who you talking to? Yeah, I'm straight. But why you giving this nigga a pass? Just bust his shit wide open as soon as he comes through the door."

"Yeah, under different circumstances, but I want to kill Dreux myself, and he still has her. If I blow his shit back now, I might not get the chance."

"Cool. Say less."

He nodded, and we chilled until punk-ass Trell showed up. In true Trell fashion, he pulled in thirty minutes late. I could feel his fuck nigga vibes before he hit the door.

"Yooo, what's good wit' y'all niggas?"

Choppa's jaw flexed, so I knew he was mad as hell. This shit was going to be good or really fucked up, nothing in between.

"Let's skip the pleasantries. Sit down. Fuck is you on, bro?" My nigga didn't waste no time.

"Shit, like I told you, I'm tryna get what's mine." Trell shrugged his shoulders like the bitch that he was.

"Aye, that nonchalant bullshit gon' get yo' head rocked. Don't play wit' me like I'm some soft-ass nigga. You know what I'm about."

"My nigga, you ain't the only nigga wit' a gun in this muhfucka."

"Shiiiid, he's the only nigga wit' two," I piped up, pulling my piece out and locking one in the chamber.

Trell laughed, and it pissed me off. Aiming my gun at his head, I made sure to let him know what was good. "I already owe you one for shooting my brother. Keep playing."

Choppa took a seat directly in front of Trell, and I didn't say shit else. My silence spoke for me.

"Like I told yo' gluttonous ass yesterday, I already had shit in place to step down and leave this street shit to you. You got greedy, dawg, and that's fucked up, 'cause we supposed to be boys."

"We stopped being boys the moment *that* nigga moved up in rank. I was hitting the streets day and night, while you and ya playmate did what the fuck y'all wanted to do."

I let out a low chuckle. This nigga Trell was really on some high school shit.

"That's on you. I had niggas in place for a reason. You *wanted* to be in the field. You ain't *have* to be. Man, fuck this. Look, this is the name of the connect and the burner he gon' reach you on. Dates, times, and locations, everything you need is right there. Run this shit in the ground for all I give a fuck. I'm straight on it. We'll hold another meeting to let the other niggas know what's up." Choppa stood up, and Trell followed suit.

"Pleasure doing business witchu." Trell held his hand out, being funny, before walking toward the door.

"Fuck out my face. Make sure you find your own warehouse and shit, 'cause this belongs to me."

Trell turned around, and you could see the steam coming off his body. Bitch tried to slam the heavy-ass door on his way out.

"He gon' cry in the car." I laughed hard as hell at myself.

"Get yo' dumb ass on, man. I'm finna go slide in this shorty from the other day, so I'll get up witchu."

"One hunnid."

We shook up and went our separate ways. I jumped in my Hellcat and flew back to the crib to get under my baby.

Chapter Twenty-eight

Dreux

On the other side of town...

Here I was, back at square fucking one. These bullshit-ass walls were starting to close in around me, and on set, I was sick of it. I'd been trying to stay as level-headed as possible, but my ass was about to be on that Uncle Elroy shit. *Day Day, that crazy bitch out here again.* Trell hadn't let me out of this house since the stunt I pulled at the mall. Anything I needed, he'd go and get it himself. I'd been plotting and planning on how to get up out this shit, so the next time Trell left, I was gon' show these niggas why I was my father's namesake.

I went to the kitchen to find something to eat, and Spank was sitting at the table, eating a sandwich.

"Damn, you ain't make me one?"

He looked at me with hardest scowl I'd ever seen. "Who fucking witchu like that? 'Cause I ain't. After yo' bullshit stunt in the mall, ain't nothing left for you over here, li'l mama. Strictly business."

Oh, this nigga was big mad.

"I'm sorryyyy. You gotta know that I'm tired of being here. My sister is in a coma, and my fucking daddy is dead. I just wanna go home." I laid it on thick, even though I really was hurting,

"Strictly business."

Fuck. I guess I had to start working on the friend because this dude was off me. After whipping up a quick breakfast, I took my food back to the living room and sat beside Whoodi. I ate in silence, and I could see him stealing glances out of the corner of his eye.

"Can I help you?" My eyes rolled so hard.

"Shiiiid, I'm tryna figure out why you ain't bring me a plate too. Taking up my personal space ain't free."

"Nigga, please. Do you see me? You should be paying to breathe the same air that I breathe. Cut yo' shit."

"Yo, I see why the fuck Choppa kept you around. That smart-ass mouth is a sexy as fuck."

I swear niggas said the dumbest shit known to mankind. One thing I couldn't stand was a smart-mouth bitch, so how niggas could was beyond me.

"Anywayyy, let me play. What's this?"

"Girl, hell naw. It's Fortnite, some shit that ain't for you."

"So. Gimme the other controller."

He picked the stick up from the table and handed it to me. Checkmate.

I played around with Whoodi for a few hours, getting him comfortable enough to let his guard down. Seven o'clock was quickly approaching, so I knew Trell would be leaving soon. As I hopped off the couch, he was making his way to the front door. When he walked past me, I slapped him on the back of his head.

"That's for calling me a bitch."

"You better keep yo' hands to your fucking self before I break them hoes off yo' wrist."

If he hadn't done shit yet, then he wasn't going to do shit at all.

"Blahhhh, whatever. Tell Choppa I said heyyy."

Trell flipped me the middle finger, and he was out.

I knew there was no time to bullshit around, so I got my ass in motion. I'd scoped the layout of the house within the first few days of being there. There were two entrances to the kitchen, and a door leading into the garage. Two cars sat outside, but the keys were hidden. As I made my way to the back, Trell's bedroom door was open, which was usually locked when he left. This night was getting better by the minute.

Spank and Whoodi went back to playing the game, so I slipped inside Trell's room. I scanned the room to see if any of the obvious things looked out of place. Niggas loved hiding shit in plain sight. Everything looked intact, so the mattress was next. Bingo! There was a slit on the side, and when I reached inside, there was a gun and a set of keys. Now it was time to fuck some shit up.

I heard footsteps coming up the hall, so I slipped into the bathroom, locking the door.

"Yo, you good? We finna order in if you want something."

Shit, they wouldn't be alive to eat, but whatever.

"I'm cool. That breakfast is still on my stomach."

"Ight."

I stuck the keys in my panties and the gun behind my back. Easing out of the bathroom, I was thankful for the ballet classes Lolita put me in. Light feet made it easy to creep up on your enemy. I had to play this smart because both had a gun, and my ass lacked a silencer. Creeping to the kitchen, I crouched down on the opposite side of the island. It was a damn shame how easy a gaming system had these niggas off their square.

With a perfect shot, I pulled the trigger and watched Spank's brain redecorate the living room. Whoodi jumped from the couch, firing into the kitchen. One. As he walked toward the bedrooms, I tiptoed through the living room and sent a shot to the back of his head.

Tucking the gun, I walked to the table and grabbed both cell phones before running to the garage. I hit the key fob, and the lights of a white BMW flashed. It was time to go home.

Two hours. Two whole fucking hours away from home is where that bitch nigga had me. When I finally pulled up to my parents' gate, the tears wouldn't stop falling. Being with Trell was nowhere near as bad as what Ahdia had experienced, but the time spent away without properly grieving weighed on me.

I left the car parked and walked up the driveway and around to the cellar. I stripped from my clothes and tossed them plus the cell phones and gun into the incinerator. My body fell to the ground, and I breathed.

Taking the stairs up to my room two at a time, I stopped dead in my tracks when I saw the light in Ahdia's room. I quietly walked to her door, and there she was. Ahdia had no hair, but there was no mistaking my baby sister.

"Motormouth." Her childhood nickname rolled off my tongue in a whisper.

She looked at me and smiled. "Dreux, hi. I've been waiting on you to show up." Something about her was different.

"How l—how long have you been awake?"

"Two weeks today. I'm still getting adjusted, but between Mom and Dash, I'm doing okay." Something was definitely wrong because she hadn't called Lolita "Mom" since she had been talking.

"What's wrong? You don't seem like your usual self."

"I'm sorry. What am I usually like? When I woke from the coma, I had no memory. There's still nothing, just current things."

Wow. I surely wasn't expecting that. Before the tears could fall again, I turned and ran back to my room. Tears for my father, Ahdia, and my mother soaked the pillow I lay on.

"Did I say something wrong?"

I sat up when I heard Ahdia's voice at the door. "Oh. No, baby, it's me. So much has happened, and I just haven't had time to process it at all."

"Can I stay in here with you? Maybe you can help me figure myself out."

"Of course. Come on." I pulled the covers back, and she climbed in with me.

We talked for a few hours. Well, I talked mostly about our childhood. She laid her head in my lap, and I softly rubbed the scar. Ahdia was dozing off, and before she went to sleep, I asked the question that was burning in me.

"So, how's the baby doing?"

Her headed popped up from my lap. "What baby?"

Oops.

Chapter Twenty-nine

Ahdia

"Dashir! Dashhhh!" I ran into the house, angry and hurt. After Dreux dropped that bomb on me, I couldn't rest, so she brought me home. I left my purse and keys at the front door, taking the steps two at a time. When I walked in, Dash was laid out on his back, with one hand behind his head and the other holding his big-ass penis. My mouth started watering until I remembered why I was even there.

"Dashir, get up. I need to talk to you."

His raggedy ass still hadn't moved, so I picked up a pillow and smacked him across the face.

"What the fuck? Dia, what you on, man?" He popped up, mad as hell.

"I'm gonna ask you one question, and you bet' not lie, Dashir."

"Beautiful, it's damn near three a.m. and you wanna talk? Come lay down, and we can do this in the morning." He lay back down, getting comfortable, and I smacked his ass again.

"Get up. We're doing this right now."

Dash blew a breath out and climbed out of the bed. After he relieved his bladder, Dash sat on the bed with his hands clasped in front of him. "Ight, beautiful, what's so important that we can't wait till decent hours to talk?"

"You said we've never had sex, right? Yesterday morning was our first time, right?" My arms were folded across my chest, with my legs bouncing.

"Yes, and yes. What else?"

This muthafucka was too nonchalant for my liking.

"Then how the fuck am I pregnant, Dashir?"

The color drained from his face, and I prayed like my life depended on it, that he wouldn't lie to me. He stood up, but every step he took forward, I took one backward. My back hit the wall, and there was nowhere left for me to run. Dash put his hands on either side of my head, placing his forehead on mine. As mad as I wanted to be, his vulnerability did something to me.

"I was just trying to protect your peace, mama. You've been through so much already, and this, this was gon' tip you over the edge."

"What, being pregnant? Why would it? Babies are a blessing, and that wasn't for you to decide. Where's the father? Does he know?"

Dash reared his head back so hard I'm surprised it didn't detach from his neck.

"The fuck you mean, where is the father? Shit, I'm right here. The only muhfucka raising that baby with you is me. Yo, you really got me fucked up. Get out my face before I lay yo' ass down, man." He grabbed his shirt and keys from the chair before walking out on me.

This was our first argument, and I knew I needed to set the tone for how this would go. From what Dreux told me, I was a bitch that didn't back down from anybody, so that's what I was going to do.

"You don't get to do that. You don't get to walk away when shit doesn't go how you want it to. I'm talking to you. Come back."

Dash continued to walk down the stairs toward the front door, hurting my feelings, because he was doing the one thing he said he never would.

"You said you'd never leave me." It came out as a whisper, so I wasn't sure if he even heard me.

Dash turned and trudged back up the steps. When he pinned my body against the wall, I didn't know if I should suck his dick or run.

"No, *you* don't get to do *that*. You don't get to pull my card when it's convenient for you. I said what I said, and I meant it. My ass would *never* leave you, not in the sense that you're tryna make it. You went through something, I get it, but I did too."

Standing before me was a broken man. Everything had been about me since I was released, and not once did I attempt to ask how he was coping. Dash was pouring his all into me, and in return, I was leaving him empty.

"I fucking love you, Ahdia. I'll move earth for you, mama, but I can't do this right now. I just need a minute to get my mind right, and when you wake up in the morning, I'll be there."

Dash kissed my temple and was out the door before I could process what just happened. The tears that I refused to let fall in his presence came pouring down. Wiping my face, I made my way back to our bedroom. For the first time, I was going to bed alone.

Waking up to empty space, I sighed, and my lip started trembling. I hated that all my ass seemed to do nowadays was cry.

"You bet' not start that crying shit, Ahdia. I ain't playing witcho ass, either." Dash's voice boomed through the room.

I turned over to find him sitting in the chair by the window. He got me together quick because tears were on the way. Jumping from the bed, I climbed into my baby's lap and laid my head in the crook of his neck. Dash slid his arms around my waist, holding me tightly against his body. There were no words exchanged as we sat wrapped in one another.

"Good morning, beautiful." He kissed my forehead softly, and I blushed.

"Hi. You just getting home?"

"I've been here. I sat in this chair, watching you toss and turn all night. Look, I've had time to calm down, and I would like to have a conversation with you if that's okay." Dash was always so sure of himself, but this wasn't that. He was nervous. "Umm, it's about that day, so just be patient with me."

"Okay."

He blew out a heavy breath, and I braced myself.

"At the hospital, I told you that something happened to me but never said what it was. When I was eighteen, I moved here to live with my grandma. The day that you were taken, someone killed her. I was fucked up. Square bidness, it felt like the wind was knocked out of me." He hung his head. "I hit you a few hours later to come see me 'cause I needed to feel something other than hurt. For days, my ass was shut off from everybody. I figured since you weren't fucking with me, then I needed to fall back." Dash pulled me closer as if I weren't already up his neck.

"On day three, I got a video from this nigga named JB that was working for us at the time. This muthafucka was in my face every day, man, chillin' at my crib, eating up my food. Shit, my grams were his grams, and you know I'on play about my weed." We laughed because his ass wasn't lying. He wouldn't let me hit the blunt even if I begged for it.

"Anyway, I got that video, and everything around me stopped moving. He killed my grammy, and he had you. Do you know how fucked up I was? The shit he said in the video had me ready to take the world down. Yo' mean ass ain't want shit to do with me, but I knew we belonged together. Another two days went by before JB's punk ass said anything else, but when he did, he sent his location. Mama, as soon as that shit hit my phone, I suited the fuck up. My niggas ain't let me go by myself, but for you, I would've." Dash grabbed my chin, looked me dead in the eyes, and I saw love. This man was really for me.

"When JB walked out with your body in his arms, I thought my ass had lost you before I ever had you. Baby, I don't know what happened inside that cabin, but I swear on my life, I'll never let shit happen to you again. You gon' be my wife, and I be damn if a muthafucka touch what's mine."

A big-ass smile spread across my face. "You want me to be your wife?"

"Maaaan, out of everything I just said, that's what you focus on?" He let out a low chuckle. "Yes, woman, I want your beautiful ass to be my wife. Even if you never get your memory back, I wanna spend the rest of my life making new ones wit'cha."

"I wanna go back there, to the place where he had me."

Dash looked at me like I'd grown a nipple on my forehead. "For what? Hell naw, man. Why would I take you back there?"

"Susan said places of significance could help with my memory. I wasn't ready to say anything, but over the past few days, bits and pieces have been coming back to me. The shit is kinda frustrating."

"Word? That's what's up, mama. I got you for life, so if this is what you really wanna do, then I'll do it." He tapped my leg for me to stand up. "I'm going to take a shower. Join me?"

Shit, he didn't have to ask me twice.

***

Dash lifted my hand to his mouth and kissed my knuckles. The car ride to the cabin had been quiet for the most part. Dash was in his head just as much as I was in mine. He wanted to move on as if nothing had ever happened, but I needed to do this. Who wants to go through life with something this heavy on their heart? It was not guaranteed that this would help my memory, but I could at least get closure from it.

We pulled into a run-down place called Greenhaven, and Dash's grip on my hand grew tighter. I looked over, and tension was written all over his face. Grabbing his chin, I turned his head until we locked eyes.

"Hey, none of that, okay? I'll be all right. You got me too, remember?" I leaned over the armrest with my lips puckered. He met me with a slow kiss that made the hairs on the back of my neck stand up.

"For life. You ready?"

"I guess so. You?"

"Hell naw, but come on." He stepped out of the car and came around to let me out.

Dash guided me to the cabin, and the closer we got, the thicker the air started to feel. When we made it to the door, he hung back and gave me time to get myself together. After about five minutes, I slowly turned the knob and opened the door. The smell of death and old food greeted me as I stepped inside. I walked over to the couch, running my hands over it in hopes that something would come to me. Dash followed behind me, close enough to be there but far enough to give me space.

As I made my way up the small hallway, there were specks of blood that led to what I assumed was the room. Pushing the door open, the sight before me was so disturbing I could feel bile rising in my throat. Blood covered the sheets, and old vomit was all over the floor.

I walked in, picked up the sheets, and that's when it happened. Everything about this place came rushing to me, knocking the air out of my body. I fell to my knees, and my body shook as memory after memory flooded my mind.

"Nooo, nooo! Dashhhh!"

I felt his strong arms wrap around my body as he rocked me back around forth. "I got you, baby. I swear I do. Let it out. I got you."

"Whyyy! It was him. Ja–Jabari. He raped me when I was in college, and I was too scared to say anything. I just came home and told my dad I just didn't want to do school anymore." That's when it hit me. My hands went to my stomach, and I cried harder. "Oh God, that means this baby is his. Dash, I don't want this baby. I can't have this baby."

"Shhhh. We'll deal with that later. Come on, let's get you out of here." He lifted me bridal-style and carried me back to the car. Before he closed the door, Dash kissed my forehead and held my face between his hands. "Whatever you want to do, I'll be here every step of the way. You know that, right?"

I nodded my head. "Let's go home."

Chapter Thirty

Dash

Since the day we went to the cabin, Ahdia had sunk into a deep depression. I'd done everything I could to keep her sane, but nothing was working. Dia refused to eat or leave the house, and if I didn't force her, she wouldn't bathe. My ass was trying to be understanding, but that funky shit I couldn't get down with. I wanted to be her Superman, but she decided to shut me out. There's no way I could front like it didn't fuck with me because it did.

Stepping onto the patio, I sparked up a blunt to get my mind right. The energy in the air shifted, and I felt Ahdia before turning to see her. She stood in the doorway, looking between me and the chair, trying to decide where she wanted to sit. I got excited as hell when she chose my lap as her resting place. It had been days since I felt her body on mine because I'd been sleeping in the guest room while she took ours.

Ahdia wrapped her arms around my neck and laid her head on my shoulder. "I'm sorry for zoning out on you."

God, I missed that sound. A home without the sound of Ahdia's voice wasn't a home at all. She pulled the blunt out of my hand, and I let her. This was the only pass her ass was getting.

"Don't apologize, mama. You know what it is with me. I got you."

"For life." Ahdia passed the blunt back, and I put it out.

She smelled like lavender and shea butter, a scent I'd grown to love these past few months. Her beauty was unmatched, and her pure heart had me ready to get down on one knee.

"As long as you know. Lemme get them lips."

She lifted her head, placing a small peck on me. My ass wasn't going out like that, though.

Gripping her chin, I placed my lips back on hers and separated them with my tongue. As my mouth got reacquainted with hers, Ahdia let out a moan that sent chills up my spine.

"Okay, girl, you gon' be getting this dick. Keep playing. You know I ain't been in that good shit in a few days."

She slapped my chest and lay back on my shoulder.

"But real shit, though. You think you're ready to get out the house? Go do something wit'cha man?"

"Yeah, I think so. I'm tired of looking at these walls, and the sunshine is greatly needed. Come on so you can shower. Yo' ass smells like you smoked the whole Ziploc bag."

"You full of jokes today. Let's go, so I can fill you up with something else." I pushed my dick against her thigh.

"Stoppp, Dash."

She had me fucked up if she didn't think I was sliding in between them long-ass legs. Ahdia stood up from my lap and grabbed my hand, leading me into the house. I went into the closet, getting my towel and clothes, and headed to the guest bathroom.

"Wait, where you going?" I turned around to see Ahdia standing there in her birthday suit.

"Shit, uhh, I was going to the guest bathroom to give you some privacy."

"Nah, I said *we* were taking a shower. I need to feel all of that." She nodded her head toward my hard dick.

I should have gotten a trophy for fastest nigga to come out his clothes the way I pulled them shits off my body. When I walked into the bathroom, Ahdia was adjusting the water to the devil's dick. My ass never understood why women had to have the water that fucking hot. I noticed the weight gain in her stomach and hips, but I didn't want to ruin her mood, so I didn't say shit. She stepped in, and the way the water fell down her body was the sexiest shit I'd ever seen. As she stood under the shower head with her eyes closed, I stroked my dick slowly. I bit my lip a little harder every time that ass shook. Ahdia looked back at me with those bedroom eyes, and I damn near nutted up.

"Here, let me." She dropped to her knees and replaced my hand with hers.

Her soft hand caressing my shit had it growing harder with every stroke. My baby put my dick in her mouth inch by inch. When she got to inch number nine, Ahdia gagged.

"Relax ya throat, baby. You got a lot more dick to swallow." She popped it out her mouth and hit me with a hard mug.

"I got me. Make sure you got you." Without another word, Ahdia gripped my thighs and swallowed my dick whole with no hands. Like, she just said fuck a gag reflex. This was the first time baby girl put her mouth on my piece, and she was showing out. Ahdia looked so beautiful with saliva dripping from the corners of her lips.

"Fuckkk, baby! Suck that shit then, girl." My eyes rolled to the back of my head.

Ahdia took my balls in her mouth as she double-handed my dick. I fucked up when I looked down and saw her playing with that pussy as her jaws sank in from sucking. Before I could catch myself, nut shot out my dick and landed on her bald-ass head.

"Damn, nigga. You couldn't wait for me?"

I let out a low chuckle because she was more worried about her nut than the nut that was sitting on her head.

"Come on. It's yo' turn." Sitting on the shower bench, I pulled Ahdia up and placed her legs on my shoulders.

"Put yo' hands on the wall, and they bet' not come the fuck off."

"Okayyy."

She was moaning before I touched her, so my ass knew she was about to go crazy. Gripping her ass cheeks, I licked my lips at the sight of glistening folds. I ran my nose up the pussy and inhaled. Ahdia's natural scent could drive a sane man mad, and I was on my way to being committed. Her clit was peeking out at me, and in one swift motion, it was in my mouth. Holding her pearl between my teeth, my tongue flicked back and forth as it hardened.

"Ssss! Yesss! Don't stop!" I could feel her legs starting to tremble, but my ass wasn't done yet.

Sliding my tongue in her opening, I lifted her body up and down so she was fucking my mouth. Ahdia started banging on the shower wall, signaling that she was near her peak. Replacing my tongue with my fingers, my attention was back on her clit, sending her over the edge. When she put her hands on my head, a smile spread across my face.

"Mmm, your hands came off that wall, beautiful. Daddy's gon' have to do something about that. Assume the position."

Placing her feet on the ground, Ahdia turned around and grabbed her ankles. I bit down on my lip at the sight before me. With my hands on her waist, I pushed into her wet-ass ocean and went to work. As I pounded into her,

Ahdia was matching me stroke for stroke. Her ass cheeks were giving my dick a round of applause.

"Baeee, harder. I wa–wanna feel it in my chessst."

Who was I to deny my baby? Sticking my thumb in her ass, I started beating that little pussy up. I pulled all the way out and slammed back into her. If I wasn't holding her waist, Ahdia would have gone head-first into the wall from the way I was hitting that ass. Her pussy started to contract around my dick, so I slowed my strokes, letting her feel every inch. I pushed my thumb deeper in her ass. Ahdia's legs shook as she wet up my dick and stomach. I couldn't hold back anymore, so I pulled out and nutted on her ass. She turned around and gave my ass the deadliest glare I'd ever seen.

"Since when do you pull out to nut, Dash?"

Aww, fuck. Here we go.

"Maaan, bae, come onnn. We foreal finna do this? I just maxed yo' ass, and this what you on? It ain't that big of a deal."

"It is."

"Beautiful, can we not do this right now? I got some shit planned for you, and we gon' be late."

"No, not until you tell me why you pulled out."

I ran my hand down my face because my irritation levels were rising.

Instead of answering the question, I stepped out of the shower and went into the room to get dressed. Ahdia came fuming from the bathroom, and I knew this shit was far from over.

"So now you don't fucking hear me? Dashir Rhamad Edwards, answer me."

"Because you got a baby in yo' stomach that don't belong to me. There! You fucking happy?" The look on her face told me everything I needed to know. I'd hurt her feelings, and that had my ass feeling like shit. The tears in my girl's eyes shook my heart up, but it was too late to take back what I'd said. I tried to avoid it, and she just wouldn't let up.

"That never stopped you before. You knew it was a baby in there any other time you did, so what's different now?"

"You didn't know, so shit, I acted like I didn't either." This argument was frustrating me, and shit was falling out of my mouth before I could stop it.

"Wow, just fucking wow. That's pretty fucked up, my guy."

Blowing out a heavy breath, I grabbed my shit and went to the guest room. I needed a minute to get myself together because all a nigga was doing was making shit worse. She didn't deserve the weak shell of a man I could become when my anger took over.

"You don't get to walk away. You stay and fix what you fucked up. How do you think I feel, knowing I'm housing the kid of a nigga that raped me?"

I flinched when she referenced JB's punk ass. Instead of blowing up, I took a different approach. "I'm sorry for the bullshit I was spewing. The shit is sensitive as fuck in this house, and I should have been more mindful of what I said. I don't give a fuck about that baby. Well, not that I don't give a fuck, but like, it doesn't change how I feel about you one way or another. You're still the most beautiful girl in the world to me, and I love you."

"That doesn't excuse what you said, Dash. I would never say some shit like that to you, but whatever. It's cool. I think I'ma go stay with Lolita for a few days. You know, give you some space."

Oh, she had me fucked up. If she was going to Lolita's, I was too.

"Baby, we just had all the space we needed. I don't need no more space."

"Yeah, you do. This is obviously taking a worse toll on you than you're letting on."

"Can we at least enjoy the day I have planned before you leave me?" Maybe if I let Ahdia run up a check, she'd change her mind about leaving.

She rolled her eyes before answering. "Come on, dude."

I ran my hand down my face because this girl was about to have an attitude the whole time we were out.

"Bend your back around, drop that booty to the ground. Just as long as you twerk for me. Darling, darling, twerrrk for me. Ohh, twerrrk for me."

I looked over at Ahdia. She was singing the fuck out of this song, but I was focused on that ass bouncing in my passenger seat. "Beautiful, do we really have to listen to this shit?"

"Nigga, you barely out the doghouse, so you gon' listen to whatever I put on this Bluetooth."

"Aye, who you talking to?"

"You."

Oh, she was really feeling herself. I let her make it since my ass was the reason for the attitude.

Pulling up to the Galleria, Ahdia held her hand out, and with no hesitation, I handed over my whole fucking wallet. Her mean ass hardly let the truck stop before she hopped out. Shaking my head, I followed behind her, ready to play bellhop.

We'd been in the mall for damn near three hours, and my ass was starving. The smile on Dia's face every time she swiped my card was worth the damage she was doing. Like, shorty legit ran up four mortgages in Louis Vuitton. Little did she know this was my first and last time shopping with her ass.

"Aye, mama, you just gon' let yo' nigga starve?"

Her pretty ass made my dick jump with the way she looked over her shoulder at me.

"All this food in here? I'm not stopping you from eating, bae."

"Shit, you the one balling. I'm broke as fuck right now."

"You right. I got one, two, three, four, five, six, seven, eight Ms in my bank account."

Her silly ass was dropping hundreds in the middle of the mall, and I couldn't help the smile that she put on my face. If it took eight hundred wasted-ass dollars to change her mood, then so be it. Grabbing my baby around the waist, I lightly kissed her jaw.

"Nah, mama, you got about eighty in ya bank account. Get that shit right. Come on so we can go eat."

"Okay, but I gotta go pick something up from the jewelry store real quick."

I groaned loud as hell because my fucking stomach was in my back. We made it to the jewelry store, and while bae picked up whatever it was that she needed, I replied to a few emails and texts. I looked up to see her bopping toward me with a goofy-ass grin on her face. Ahdia handed me a bag as she bounced from one foot to the other. I opened the velvet box, and there was an iced-out necklace of her initials. This shit was dope as fuck, and I knew after today, it was never coming off.

"Do you love it? Even when I'm not around, I'm always with you. I got one for myself too."

I didn't notice the necklace around her neck until she pointed it out. Her shit said *MrsDash,* and I couldn't hold my laugh in.

"Baby, you got no-salt seasoning dripped in diamonds around your neck. Shorty, that's how you going out?" I was busting up in the middle of the mall.

"Dash! Oh my God! Why would you say that? Now I gotta get another one."

Ahdia's face was beet red, and I almost felt bad for laughing. My boo was excited as hell about her chain. She stormed back over to the jewelry store, and that neck started rolling.

I let Dia handle her business until I saw the jeweler lean over the counter and get in her face. Pulling my strap from behind my back, I bulldozed my way through the crowd of people.

"Say, my nigga, if you don't want three pumps of hot lead in yo' body, you'll back the fuck off this one."

His eyes got wide as hell when he noticed the gun in my hand.

Ahdia leaned in and kissed my lips with those plush-ass pillows on her face. "Thanks, baby. Now, like I was saying. I want you to take this one and add I-R to the end of it. So, it should say D-A-S-H-I-R, cool? Great."

Every day I was starting to see traits Ahdia had prior to her memory loss. She was confident, strong, and loud as hell. Every day I fell more in love with her.

My baby needed a getaway, and I'd been planning one since the night of the cabin incident. She thought I was letting her run up a check for fun, but my ass really needed her to get some shit without actually packing.

When we pulled up to the airstrip, Ahdia's eyes widened in surprise.

"This isn't Lolita's house. Where are we going, Dashir?"

I grabbed her hand and planted a kiss on her wrist. "Turks and Caicos. Let's ride, mama."

Chapter Thirty-one

Dreux

"We're not making loveeeee no moreee. We're not even tryingggg to chaaange. Sometimes, I get little lonely."

"Girl, if you don't shut that shit up. You been singing that sad-ass shit since you been home. Hell."

I rolled my eyes, knowing Lolita would have smacked them out of my head if she saw me. "Mamaaaa, why you can't let me be in my bag? My nigga done left me, and I don't know why."

"Dru Hill ain't gon' help you figure it out either. Get ya ass up and call that man. And go the hell home."

The morning I dropped Ahdia back off with Dash, I went back home and told my mama everything that had taken place. It's not like I was scared to go home. My ass just didn't want to be there without Kam. The last time I was there, we had redecorated damn near every room with our lovemaking.

I walked downstairs. Lo was going dumb in the kitchen, and I couldn't wait to eat.

"How am I supposed to call him with no phone? Trell threw all my shit out when he snatched me up."

"Cuss in my house again, and I'll beat yo' ass like your daddy should have."

I laughed because she was right. Big Drew never laid a hand on me, and I was bad as hell growing up.

"My bad, Ma, but what if I call and he doesn't want to talk to me? You didn't hear how he talked to me in the mall that day. He called me a snake-ass bitch, and he's the one who lied to me. He's the reason we lost all those weeks together." This nigga really had me fucked up.

"Girl, who is yo' mama? Dress it up and make it real for him. If he doesn't wanna talk, then hit that nigga where it hurts. Show him what he's missing."

"You right. I'm about to get dressed and go to AT&T. If he doesn't want to talk to me, then I'll show up at Luxe on my real single shit. Thanks, Lo."

Jogging back to my room, I went to my closet to find something to wear for the day. I decided on a light gray T-shirt dress that hugged my frame just right and a pair of black booties. Simple but cute. After handling my hygiene, I got dressed and was out the door.

"Hi. Welcome to AT&T. What can we do for you?"

Here we go, an overly friendly sales representative.

"I just need a new phone. I already have service with y'all."

"Okay, what's the name on the account?"

"Dreux McCoy." I was not trying to be in this store all damn day.

While she tapped on her computer, I looked out the window, and my heart stopped. Across the street, Kam and some female were going into Chipotle. Anger filled me knowing he was sharing *our* spot with someone else.

"Ma'am, can you put a rush on that? I kinda have somewhere to be." I didn't mean to snap on the poor lady, but Kamron had me fucked up.

"Oh, I'm sorry. Okay, do you want a replacement of your phone, or would you like to upgrade?"

"Give me the Max and charge it to the card on my account."

While she went and got the phone, my leg was bouncing uncontrollably. This nigga was going to give me some answers today—either voluntarily, or I could shoot up his shit again. His choice.

"Here you go, ma'am. I'm sure you know how to set it up, so I won't waste anymore of your time. Have a great day."

I pulled five hundred dollars from my purse and handed it to her. "Commission. Thanks."

Leaving AT&T, I sat in my car and set the phone up. Once it backed up to iCloud, my phone went crazy with text messages and emails from work. The first thread I opened was from my boss.

Denika: Just checking on you. You didn't show up to work, so we rescheduled your patients.

Denika: Okay, this is day two, which isn't like you. Call me when you get this text.

Denika: DREUX! Look, now I'm not playing! What the hell is going on with you!? As your friend AND boss, I need to hear from you ASAP!

Shit! I immediately called her to explain.

"What the hell is going on with you? It's been damn near a month since I've heard from you." *Well, damn! Tell me how you really feel.*

"I'm sorry. Are you in the office?"

"No, I left early today." She huffed, and it irritated the hell out of me. Bitch got a whole attitude and didn't know why.

"Okay, meet me at Chipotle, and I'll explain everything to you."

"On my way."

After she hung up, I scrolled through the rest of my messages until I came across Kam's.

DaddyBae: THAT'S THE KIND OF BULLSHIT YOU ON? You setting me up for muthafuckas now?! You got it. Just know when I catch up to you and that pussy ass nigga . . . yep.

DaddyBae: Damn that's cold. I ain't take you for that type of bitch, but I guess you can beat somebody's pussy out the frame and still not know shit about em. I fucked wit' you heavy as hell. It's good though, he can have yo hoe ass.

DaddyBae: FUCK YOU BITCH!

As I read his messages, my feelings were hurt by how he handled me. I didn't know what he meant by setting him up, but I planned to get to the bottom of it.

Fifteen minutes later, Denika texted me, saying she had arrived. I hit the locks on my A5 and walked across to Chipotle. The closer I got to the restaurant, the heavier my steps became. I couldn't believe this nigga was really sitting there smiling with another bitch.

"Girl, you okay? You stomped over here like you told Harpo to beat me." Denika cracked up, but I didn't see shit funny.

"Shut up. Shit, come on. I'm hungry as hell."

When we walked into the restaurant, I had to keep myself from walking over to Kam's table and delivering him these hands on a Chipotle tray. While ordering my food, it felt like somebody was burning a hole in my back. I turned to sit down, and Kamron's eyes met mine. Shit, how was it possible for him to get any finer? As I moved past him, his jaw flexed, and I knew he wanted to take off on my ass.

"So, that's why you mad. Trouble in paradise?"

I was starting to regret inviting Denika's overly observant ass to lunch.

"Mind the business that pays you. We here to talk about why I've been missing so much, so let's focus on that."

We sat and ate while I gave her the modified version of what had taken place these past few weeks. Denika's mouth hung open in shock like I'd just dropped some heavy news on her, but to me, it wasn't that big of a deal. My ass was just ready to go home.

"Whooo, chile, that's too much. I'm glad you're safe, though. When do you plan on coming back to work? I borrowed a tech from another facility, but I know how you are about your patients."

"Since it's already Thursday, I'll be there Monday morning. I've missed them, especially Ms. Johnson and her rays of sunshine." The Johnson family had easily become my favorite. You could see the love dripping from them.

"Excuse me, Nika. I gotta run to the restroom." I excused myself and walked/ran to the bathroom. My bladder was on some good bullshit lately, and at this rate, I'd be wearing Depends soon.

Before I could close and lock the bathroom door, it was pushed open with so much force. Kam rushed in and hemmed me up on the wall. His eyes no longer held love for me, and it broke my heart. We were really done.

"I swear to God, the only reason you're still breathing is because we're in public and you're carrying my baby."

What was wrong with this nigga? There was no baby.

"Get offfff me! I'm not fucking pregnant by you, nigga. Why are you in here? Your little girlfriend is probably waiting on you."

"This ain't got shit to do with her, so worry about yo'self. That ass looking a li'l heavy back there, and you got some extra meat on yo' stomach. You pregnant."

I swear this man was delusional. I rolled my eyes so hard Jesus could see the pupils.

"Ughhh! Move! You try being held hostage for almost a month where all you can do is eat, and let's see how heavy your ass gets. Get away from me, Choppa."

He stared at me for a second before his lips crashed into mine. His tongue danced on my lips until I finally opened and let him in. Kamron lifted me by my ass cheeks as he explored the depths of my mouth. By natural reaction, my legs wrapped around his waist, and I palmed the back of his head. Kam pinned me to the wall, and his fingers found their way to my slippery folds.

"Fuckkkk! This pussy still gets so fucking wet for me." Kam sucked on my neck as he dipped into my vagina.

"Uhhh, Kammm. Shiiiit, right there."

He removed his fingers, putting them in my mouth, and I wasted no time sucking the juices off. I heard his belt buckle hit the floor before he was filling me up with ten inches of hard dick.

"Mmmm. Daddy's home. This pussy was made for a real nigga." Kam was hitting me so deep I couldn't do shit but hang on for the ride. Every time he slammed me down on his dick, I felt myself getting closer to my peak. I buried my face into his neck and bit down on his shoulder.

"Kammmm, I'm about to cummmm."

"Fuck, me too. Cum with me." He slammed me down one last time, and my love rained down on his penis as he shot his load in me.

Kam let me down on shaky legs and stuffed his dick back in his pants. He looked back at me on his way out.

"Stay the fuck away from me, Dreux, 'cause next time I'ma splatter yo' shit no matter where we at."

Right there, in the middle of Chipotle's restroom, I cried.

Chapter Thirty-two

Kamron

What the fuck was I doing? I was here on a date with Lay and ended up fucking Dreux's ass in a public bathroom.

When she walked into the restaurant, my ass thought I was tripping. She still looked just as beautiful as the day I'd met her, just a little thicker. After I fucked her dumb, reality set it. I owed her fraud ass a bullet or two.

I dipped into the men's restroom and washed Dreux's scent off my dick. Lay was just something to do, but I'd never been a disrespectful-ass nigga and wasn't starting today. Making my way back to the table, I could hear Dreux crying in the restroom, but her feelings weren't mine to cater to anymore.

"You ready?" I held my hand out to help Lay from her seat, but she dodged my shit. Here we fucking go. "What you on, ma? Yo' attitude went from zero to one hundred real quick."

She had the ugliest mug on her pretty-ass face. "The whole restaurant heard you fucking that girl in the bathroom. You know how embarrassing that is? I'm sitting at this table by myself while you're draining your dick fifty feet away from me."

Fuck.

"Man, listen, I'm sorry that you were embarrassed, but we ain't even together like that. You serve the same purpose she does. To keep my balls empty. Until we make some shit official, what I do with my dick is what I do with *my* dick." I wasn't trying to be rude, but damn.

"Wow, okay. That's the type of time we're on? Got it."

I ran my hand down my face. These women were going to send me to an early grave.

She walked to the passenger side of my car and waited for me to let her in. This little attitude she had was cute as fuck, and if I hadn't smashed Dreux, my ass would have fucked it out of her.

"We kicking it, ma. That's all I'm saying. I just got out of something, so I ain't tryna fuck with you knowing I ain't closed that chapter yet."

"That was her?"

Why the fuck did she have to ask that?

"Yeah, that was her. First time we seen each other in almost two months."

"Hmm, and the first thing that came to mind was to max her out. Cool."

The only sound in the car on our way back to her house was *Luca Brasi 3*. Lay was holding on to her attitude, which was cool, but once we pulled up, it was over. She grabbed the handle at the same as I hit the locks. I apologized to Lay again, and once she accepted my apology, my ass unlocked the doors.

"You gon' get out without giving me a kiss?"

"Did you kiss her?"

I shook my head, knowing damn well I was lying.

She leaned over and put those juicy-ass lips on me. I waited for her to get in the house before pulling off.

I pulled a pre-rolled blunt from the console and fired it up. It had been a few days since I checked on Lo, so that's where I headed.

"Damn, for a minute, I thought you forgot how to operate a business. Ain't seen yo' ass around here in days, then used the key like you my man."

I could always count on Lolita to get on my ass when I was fucking up. "Aww, Mama, don't do me like that. You always saying to use my key, but when I do, you chop my black ass down."

"Boy, shut the hell up. You hungry?"

"No, ma'am, I just left Chipotle. Speaking of, I ran into your daughter, and it took everything in me not to send her to God above." Lo already knew what I was on when it came to her daughter.

"Kamron, you know I don't play about my baby. Keep it up. Why won't you just tell her what yo' beef is? I know my child, and that's just not her. How you know she wasn't just a pawn? You ain't even give her a chance to explain."

I heard everything Lo was saying, but I wasn't on that shit. I went into Ghost's office. Lolita had stacked the papers on the desk neatly. It was kind of shocking because she hadn't been in here since he passed.

My phone vibrated with a text from Dash.

D: Handled that situation with Dia. I'm outta pocket for a few days.

Me: Cool. Take care of sis.

D: Always.

When Dash hit me about what happened with Ahdia, I felt for my nigga. She was his match, so to see her broken really fucked with him. We didn't have shit going on in the streets, so I was good with him taking off.

It was almost time for Trell to re-up, and my plan to flush his ass out was in full effect. My whole unit knew about the bullshit stunt Trell pulled, so when I announced that he was taking over, everybody looked at me like I was crazy. I had a private meeting with the lieutenants and gave them the rundown on what was going to happen so that they wouldn't be caught by surprise.

After I sorted through the numbers for Ghost's businesses, I locked up and went to find Lo. She was a street bitch at heart, and I knew she wanted to help take out Trell for fucking with her daughter.

"Mama Lo, where you at?" I walked straight to the kitchen because that's where she spent most of her time. Sure enough, she was leaning on the counter, drinking tea.

"You good, lady?

"Always, baby. What's up? I thought you'd be gone by now."

"Nah, not yet. I wanted to run something by you right quick."

She set her cup down and got comfortable on a bar stool. "Let's hear it."

"Okay. I heard you loud and clear when you said you wanted in on whatever I had planned for Trell. My plan is to flush his ass out before I put a hot one in his head. I got two teams in place, one to run through his traps and another to make sure the right product is still flooding the streets. When it's time for his re-up, it's gon' be a botched shipment. Nobody knows I took Ghost's place except the family, so it makes it easier for me to take his snake ass out."

Lo took a sip of her tea before she said anything. "What you want me to do? I done been around the block a few times, so I'm good with whatever."

"I figured. Ghost told me about your little come-up from back in the day."

Her eyes got big when I said that. "His black ass was supposed to take that to the grave with him."

We laughed and chopped it up for a few more minutes before I had to cut out. When I opened the front door, Dreux was standing there, fumbling with her keys. She looked up with red eyes and a deep scowl on her face. My mans began to rise at the sight of her fine ass, but this wasn't that anymore.

"Why are you here?" She reminded me of that chick on diary of some shit that my mama used to watch all the time.

"Why the fuck you worried about it? My business don't concern you no more, shorty. Move around."

"Get the fuck out of my way, Choppa." Dreux said my name, and it dripped with sarcasm.

"Make me."

"Ughhh! My nigga, I ain't got time for this shit. I'm just tryna get in my house, and you on bullshit. I get it. You don't want me. Cool. Excuse me." She pushed past me, and I couldn't resist smacking that wagon she was dragging. What I wasn't expecting was for her to turn around and rock my shit.

"Don't fucking touch me. You ain't my nigga."

Before I could stop myself, my ass caught her by the throat.

"Say that shit again. I'm yo' nigga. You just ain't my bitch. Play wit' it if you want to. Until the time comes for me to blow yo' shit back, you property of Kamron Vega."

"I hate you."

"You think I give a fuck? I hate yo' ass too." I lied, just like she did. I still loved the fuck out of her. I just couldn't trust her snake ass.

We stared at each other before I pushed her ass back, and she fell on the stairs. Dreux hopped up like she wanted to pop shit, but I raised my eyebrow. She took her ass upstairs.

"Get y'all's dysfunctional asses out my house with that shit. Y'all worse than me and Ghost in our prime. Either get it together or leave it alone." Mama Lo checked our bullshit, and I low-key felt bad for acting up in her house.

"Fuck that nigga. I'm good." Dreux slammed the room door, and I laughed at her childish ass.

"Ight, Ma, I'm gone."

I jogged to my car and left. The whole way home, Dreux was on my mind. Could I really kill her? My heart said no, but my mind wasn't on the same page. I guess I'd see when the time came.

Chapter Thirty-three

Lolita

I was sick of muthafuckas coming for my kids. My ass was convinced they wanted Lolita from around the way to resurface. When Dreux told me how that fuck nigga snatched her up on some get-back shit, my blood started boiling. As soon as Kam left, I grabbed my phone from the counter and called up my old goon, Tiba, knowing she was down for whatever.

"When, where, and what time?"

This was why I fucked with her. No matter what time of day I called, she was always on go.

"Calm down, killa. I'm waiting to get the details from my future ex-son-in-law. I just need to make sure you still down to ride like we used to." I knew the answer as soon as the question left my mouth.

"Hell yeah! It's been a minute since I've busted my bitches."

"So, look. I'ma call up Sommer too. Y'all meet me at the house, and I'll give y'all a rundown."

"Cool. Be there in about an hour."

After Tiba hung up, I shot Sommer a text to let her know to meet us.

Before I met Big Drew, the Three C Girls were in full effect. Our motto was "bag a baller, get the dollar," and we lived by that. Our young asses were fucking with any nigga that had money. We would get in good, rob their asses blind, and put two in the chest with no remorse. Our get-rich-quick scheme was going off until Sommer fell for one of the marks. When my girl met Chris, something in her changed. There was no faking the smile that graced her face, so when she said she couldn't do it, we understood. Tiba and I kept up with the good bullshit, and then her ass had the nerve to fall in love. Issac came in like a smooth criminal and swept her off them red bottoms she loved so much. I wasn't going in the field without my girls, so I sat my ass down too.

By the time Big Drew came along, I was sitting on a cool-ass penny. It wasn't until after we were married that I told him my secret. This nigga looked at me sideways for a year before he figured that I really loved his ass.

When I heard yelling coming from the foyer, I knew it was going to be some shit. Kam was supposed to be gone before Dreux came home, but I saw that didn't work out. Hell, if she was at her own house, they wouldn't have run into each other. I got their asses together quick and went on my way.

Shaking my head, I made my way into the white room. These kids were gon' drive me up a fucking wall. Kamron could front all he wanted to. He was still in love with my girl, and she was in love with his ass too. I told him to sit down and hear what she had to say, but his stubborn ass wasn't trying to hear me. Dreux was the pettiest person I knew, so Kam was either going to get it together, or she was about to be on some real bullshit. Right now, I had other stuff to worry about, so they were on their own.

"I caaan't maaaake you love me if you don't. You caaan't make your heart feel something it wooon't. Here in the daaa—"

"Dreux, shut the fuck up. Gahdamn!" This love-sick-ass girl was about to get kicked out of my damn house. I don't know whose child this was because my ass damn sure didn't raise my girls to get weak behind no dick.

"Mama, I love him."

"Girl, bring yo' ass down here."

I walked around the white room, looking at all the old pictures of me and Big Drew, picking up my favorite, a picture of us on the block. He was sitting on the hood of a 1989 BMW 5 series. It was the first car he purchased when he started making money. His arms were wrapped around my waist, with his chin resting on my shoulder. I had on some hoochie mama shorts and a shirt that tied in the front, showing my belly button. The bamboo earrings in my ears were a gift from Drew on our first date. He said I couldn't be his around-the-way girl without a pair of door knockers. God, I loved that man. I ran my thumb over his face and placed the photo back on the mantle.

"Yes, ma'am?"

I was so wrapped up in my thoughts that my ass didn't hear Dreux come in. "Sit down, ladybug. Let's talk."

"Ladybug. The last time anyone called me that, I'm sure I was in diapers still."

I laughed because she was right.

"Oh, hush. So, get to it. What's going on with you and Kamron?"

She laid her head in my lap, and I ran my fingers through her hair. "Nothing, apparently. He thinks I had something to do with him being shot. Earlier that day, I didn't know he was here. You know I wasn't talking to him at the time. I had just made it from the gym, and he came into my room when I was getting ready to shower. We, ummm, you know."

"Girl, I know you wasn't fucking in my house."

"Mamaaa, can you just listen? Anyway, after that I agreed to go on a date with him so we could talk. I went down to Trell's shop, who I knew as LT at the time, to tell him we couldn't do this anymore. That's when he had those dudes grab me, like I told you. Ma, I didn't know Kam was gonna be there. I swear I didn't. When they started firing on him, my heart broke. I just knew they'd killed him. It wasn't until a few days later that I heard them saying he was okay. Apparently, they weren't trying to kill him, just sending a message to get his attention."

I felt a tear hit my leg. This was hurting my girl more than I thought it was.

"I made Trell take me to the mall so I could get away from him. The cashier let me use her phone to call Kam, but when I told him it was me, he started saying a bunch of hurtful stuff to me. He finally said he was coming for me, but now I know he was only coming because he wants to hurt me."

"That man ain't gon' do shit to you, girl. You know what kind of man Choppa is, so if he wanted you dead, you would be."

"Wow, thanks, Ma."

"I'm just being honest. You're going to have to make him talk to you. From his point of view, it does look kinda suspect for you to be in the same place at the same time. Shit, I would think you was on some bullshit too. Until you can get him to talk, fuck him. Get under some new dick and stop playing those sad-ass songs that I'm tired of hearing."

Dreux laughed, and it made me smile. My baby had been moping around this house like she lost her best friend or some shit.

"I hear you. Okay, I'm done crying over him. After today, it's Kamron who?"

"Good. Now, get up. Your godmama and Auntie Tiba are on their way over here. We got grown folks' business to handle."

"Dear God. I can only imagine. Thanks for the talk, Mama." She kissed my cheek and left.

"Knock, knock! It's us!" Tiba yelled as they walked through the front door. I should have kept Ahdia from around her because that's where she got that loud shit from.

"I'm in here."

They walked into the white room.

"I know y'all hoes fucking lying. Yall know daaamn well."

"Aww, shit, here you go. Come on, Tiba. I forgot this bitch plays that no shoes on the carpet shit." Sommer rolled her eyes, but I bet she went and took them shoes off.

"Damn, you ain't cooked?"

"Tiba, don't start that shit. Go in the kitchen and see."

We all got up and moved to the kitchen because everybody knew how Tiba's attitude got when she was hungry. I whipped up some barbecue wings and fries while running down the stuff that Kam hit me with. Neither of them said anything until the food was done, so I guess they needed a minute to think on it.

"So which team we on? Do we get to pick?"

Leave it to Tiba.

"No, crazy. It's automatic that we run in the traps. We don't know shit about dealing no drugs, fool, and whose husband ain't finna kill me is yours."

"He'll be all right. Mr. McKnight knew what it was when he put a ring on it."

"Okay, Griselda Blanco. Don't call me and Lo to ride on his ass after he pulls you out the trenches." Sommer bent over, laughing at her damn self. Clearly, she was the goofball of the bunch.

"You hoes in or not?"

"First of all, I stopped hoeing a long time ago, but yeah I'm down."

"Me too."

For Tiba to be the hungry one, Sommer was taking them wings back.

"Okay, when I know everything, I'll let y'all know. We gon' go to the gun range next week. I'm sure y'all don't remember how to bust a gun," I teased.

As we finished eating, I couldn't contain my excitement. After meeting Drew, I had to hang up my guns. I was going to enjoy coming out of retirement.

Yeah, Lolo from the block was back.

Chapter Thirty-four

Ahdia

Turks and Caicos was beautiful. We'd been there for four days, and I honestly never wanted to return home. The way the waves crashed against the sand while I rolled my blunt was everything. Since the first time Dash let me smoke with him, ganja had become a part of my daily routine. Premium Kush brought me peace, but my mind still drifted to the things Dash said to me back home. So far, I'd kept my mouth shut, but it was getting harder to ignore the elephant in the room.

"Damn, bae, fire me up. Shiiid!"

I glanced over my shoulder to see Dash walking toward me in all his naked glory. Licking my lips, I couldn't deny how fine my man was. From the way the muscles in his thighs flexed with each stride to how his dick swung side to side. When he wrapped me in his strong-ass arms, I melted.

"Nigga, no. You don't share your blunts with me, so I'm not sharing my shit with you."

"That is my shit. You rolled that fatty outta my stash. You know damn well you ain't bring no weed here."

I giggled because he really had his face twisted up. Now, if I would have found some weed from these islanders, his ass would have stroked out. I passed the blunt to Dash and stepped out of his embrace.

Sitting on the chaise with my legs tucked under my butt, I scrolled down Facebook and saw Dreux was on a date. The little ho finally decided to move on from Kamron. The chaise shifted as Dash sat down, pulling my feet onto his lap. He massaged them in a circular motion, and a moan escaped my lips.

"Ight, don't start that shit, or we'll be fucking them sheets up again."

"Boy, whatever. Come on. I wanna go to the Humpback Dive Shack."

"What the fuck is that, bae?"

Lord, guide me over because he was about to act a fool.

"It's a place where we can snorkel and swim with humpback whales. The pictures online look fun as hell."

Three, two, one, explode.

"Maaan, hell naw. What the fuck you lace this weed with? It got you tripping. I ain't swimming with shit. Hell, I barely wanna swim with yo' ass."

"You know what? Okay. Remember that shit when you tryna swim in this pussy tonight."

I got up and went inside to change. He was already on thin ice with me, but my ass was trying to cut him some slack. If Dash thought I was about to lay up in this room and fuck all night, he was sadly mistaken.

Reaching into the dresser, I pulled out a peach thong bikini set that would have my cheeks clapping like thunder. I jumped in for a quick shower, then threw the bikini on. Grabbing my wraparound and waterproof phone case, my ass was on my way out the door.

"You got me fucked up."

I turned around to see Dash standing there, chest heaving up and down.

"Where the fuck you going with that bullshit on?"

"I told you where I was going. You don't wanna do shit but fuck on me, and as good as it is, I'm over sitting in this room."

Every day that we'd been there, Dash had his dick in me ninety percent of the time. The kitchen, Jacuzzi, pool, everywhere was blessed with my juices. We had three more days left, and I'd be damned if I spent it looking at these walls.

"Square bidniz? That's how you going out in public?"

"Oh my God. Dashir, I have a fucking coverup."

"That wash rag ain't finna cover up shit."

I couldn't believe he was really cutting up like this.

"Just wait. I'm coming wit' you."

After Dash threw his temper tantrum, we finally made it to the Humpback Dive Shack. I was bouncing with excitement, and he was standing there stale-faced. At this point, I didn't give a damn. My ass was going to enjoy this with or without Mr. Grouchy Pants.

"Three hundred and twenty dollars for some fucking whales. You putting them jaws to work tonight."

Not bothering to respond, I grabbed his hand and led him to the tour boat. Dash's palms were sweaty, and he was trembling a little bit.

"Aww, my baby. You scared? It's okay. Mama got you." I pinched his cheeks, and he nudged me away.

"Man, back up, ain't nobody scared of shit. You know who I am."

I heard what his mouth said, but his body language told the truth. As we climbed on the boat, Dash's hands found their way to my hips. This nigga was possessive in the cutest way. He did just enough to let a muthafucka know I was his, but not too much that would make me uncomfortable.

After we took our seats, the tour guide began. Dash began to loosen up, but when it was time to dive in, he clammed up. I turned his face to me and planted a passionate kiss on his lips.

"If you go under with me, I'll make sure the head is real sloppy tonight."

He reared his head back to look in my eyes. "I better see a puddle of slob on the floor by the time you done, man. Got me out here doing this unnatural-ass shit. Come on. Damn."

Once we had our gear on and my phone inside the waterproof case, Dash and I tipped over the edge of the boat. The water was more beautiful up close. The view from the room did it no justice. As we waited for the tour guide to give us further instructions, Dash pulled me to him and placed a kiss on my temple. Once we were given the go-ahead, my baby and I sank underwater, and my ass was in pure bliss.

"See, baby? That was so much fun. The way the whales swam around us like we weren't even there. God, I could stay here forever."

"Yeah, it was straight. Don't think I forgot what you said, either." Dash winked at me, and if we weren't getting dressed to go eat, I'd have laid all my shit bare.

For our dinner date, I decided on an olive green bodycon dress with a split up the side, paired with nude sandals that wrapped up my legs. When Dash walked into the room, the panties I wasn't wearing hit the floor. He matched my fly in a quarter-length olive green button-down, cream pants, and a pair of olive green Ferragamos on his feet. The diamond earrings he wore had him looking extra daddyish, and he knew it. I couldn't help but smile at the chain with my initials on it that he refused to take off.

Biting down on his lip, Dash held his hand out and pulled me from the bed. "Bring yo' pretty ass on before we miss out on our reservations and you end up feeding me that pussy." His words made it from my ears to my clit, and it took everything in me to leave.

Sitting across from Dash, I was doing my best not to bring up the fight we had, but my mind wouldn't let me. The waitress brought our food back to the table, and while Dash was fucking it up, I was pushing mine around the plate.

"What's wrong, mama? Why you not eating?" He dropped his fork and looked up at me.

"Did you mean everything you said before we came here?" I asked.

He raked his hand down his face as he blew out a breath. I could see him trying to get his words together before he answered. Unbeknownst to him, the answer was already in his eyes. Dash grabbed my hand and held it between both of his.

"Baby."

"Did you?"

"I did, but not in the way that you took it. I know it's not your fault, but damn."

I snatched my hand away from him. "What the fuck does 'but damn' mean?"

"Babyyy, can we not do this here? Come on, mama."

I threw the napkin from my lap onto the table and left his dumb ass sitting there. Thankful that the restaurant was in walking distance to the hotel, my ass took off. I heard rustling from behind me before hearing his voice.

"No. You don't get to do that shit, either. You don't get to run when shit doesn't go how you want it. Ain't that what you told me?"

The strain in his voice stopped me dead in my tracks. He was right. We didn't walk away from each other, but I was scared as fuck to hear what Dash had to say. I turned around.

His hands were tucked in his pockets with furrowed eyebrows. “You asked me a question, and I owe it to you to answer.”

I didn’t respond, so he continued to talk.

“Before this shit happened to you, I knew that you were it for me. Even when you were acting like you didn’t want me, I knew. My ass had a whole future mapped out for us. I was going to romance you, fuck you into marrying me, and then load your ass up with all the kids that my bank account could support.”

I laughed because knowing him now, I knew he was serious.

“When that fucking doctor came and told me you were already pregnant, everything in me shut down. I real-life felt my heart falling out of my chest. It wasn’t enough knowing he’d already taken you from me, but shit, now I had to live with the fact that a piece of him was growing inside of you. As a man, that shit fucked me up. My wife was housing another nigga’s baby, and I couldn’t do shit about it.

“It was easy to ignore for a while because you didn’t know, so it wasn’t talked about. Your body was the same. Hell, you were still you. That day at the cabin, when you remembered, it brought everything back to the forefront. Here I am trying to love *you* while hating that.” He pointed at my stomach.

“Since we’ve been here, I’ve racked my mind trying to figure out how I was going to do that. I realized that there’s no way I can love you and not love it too. So, if you want to keep it, then okay, that’s what we’ll do. If you choose the alternate route, then I’m here for that too. I’m here for you.”

Dash walked over and wrapped me in his arms. I silently vowed to myself that this was the last conversation about it.

"I ain't no sap-ass nigga, but for you, I'll lay all my feelings out on the table. Shit, this is the third time you done got me in my bag in less than a month."

Standing on my tiptoes, I wrapped my arms around his waist and pulled him closer to me. On instinct, his hands gravitated to my ass and squeezed. I bit down on my baby's neck then sucked on the same spot to soothe the sting. Placing kisses up to his earlobe, I captured it between my teeth.

Dash let out a low groan, and I felt his dick grow against my stomach. With my lips on his, I began to massage his piece. He bit down on my lip, and I knew what time it was.

"Fuck this shit. Come on. You finna put that mouth to work." Dash bent his knees enough for me to hop on his back. You think I didn't hike this dress up?

His big ass ran all the way to the hotel and maxed me out all night long.

"Baeeee, get up. Your phone keeps going off. Who the fuck is calling you at four in the morning?" I nudged Dash to wake up. My mood was on one hundred.

"Mamaaa, what's up, baby? I know you see yo' man tryna sleep."

"Get your fucking phone then. It keeps ringing."

"Answer it, then. Shit." He pulled my leg back around his waist and nestled his head into my neck.

Groaning, I rolled my body over his and grabbed the phone. As soon as the phone stopped ringing, it started again. Kam's name flashed across the screen.

"Hello?" My voice was laced with attitude.

"Dia, where ya nigga at?"

"Sleep. Where the fuck else, Kam? It's four in the morning here."

"My fault, but aye, tell that nigga to check his burner."

"Bye." I hung up before he could say anything else.

Reaching over to grab Dash's work phone, I rolled my eyes because I knew our "baecation" was over.

"Dashir, your work phone is dinging."

As if somebody lit a fire under his ass, Dash hopped up, causing me to fall back on the bed. He read the message and rolled out of the bed. Tapping on his phone, Dash moved around the room, gathering our stuff. I sat with my arms folded across my chest, pouting.

"Let's go, boo. It's showtime."

Great. Just fucking great.

Chapter Thirty-five

Choppa

This shit with Trell was going off smooth as fuck. I hit Dash to let him know the time was now. Tonight, that snake-ass nigga was gon' feel me in the worst way. His shipment came in at ten this morning, so by noon, that bullshit was flooding the streets. My dude Bones was at my warehouse with the real product to keep shit moving the way it was supposed to be. Once Trell got his ass handed to him, everything was Bones's.

Walking into Santino's, one of the sports bars I'd opened in my dad's honor, I wasn't surprised to see it jumping at one in the afternoon. Snooty was behind the bar, mixing up a drink for this bad-ass bitch. He was one of Santino's closest friends, so it was only right that when he hit hard times, I put him on.

"Nephew, what's up wit'cha, youngin'?" He reached over the bar and dapped me up.

"Same shit, Unc. Getting this money and fucking these hoes."

"Aww, neph, what happened to that li'l beauty you brought to the house? Y'all done already? If so, pass her number to me. Let a real OG show her what's good."

"Stop playing wit' me. Even when that ain't me, it's me. I'm cool on her right now, though. Can't say what the future holds for me and her." When I said that, the cutie at the bar looked over at me. I winked at her before going upstairs to my office.

As I sorted through the month's finances, there was a knock on the door.

"Come on."

When I glanced up, the chick from downstairs was standing in the doorway. She was about five foot six with a honey complexion. Freckles covered her face, but it was the amber-colored eyes that drew me in. My eyes scanned down her body, and shit, baby girl was dragging that wagon.

"How can I help you, sweetheart?"

When she turned around and locked the door, I already knew what was up.

"The better question is how can I help you?" She seductively walked toward my desk, and I slid my chair back.

"Shiiid, bust down, Thotiana."

Shorty stood between my legs and freed my mans. Her soft-ass hands stroked my dick until it reached its full potential. She looked at me, and I hit her with a smirk. Baby girl's eyes let me know that she bit off more than she could chew. It didn't stop her from getting on those knees, though.

Circling her tongue around the head of my shit, Thotiana licked up the precum that oozed out before taking the dick halfway down the throat. Tears pooled in her eyes, but that's what her ass got for trying to be greedy.

"Be easy, li'l mama. That dick ain't going nowhere. You ain't gotta eat it like yo' ass is starving."

Pulling back, she inched my piece slowly down her throat until she hit the base. As shorty bobbed up and down, I wrapped her ponytail around my hand.

"Yeaaaah, straight like that. Do that shit, baby girl."

Thotty popped the dick out her mouth and swallowed it back in one motion. Oh, shorty was trying to show out now. Not one to be outdone, I started thrusting my hips forward, making my shit play tetherball with her tonsils. Slob was falling from the corners of her lips, running down my balls. When she started massaging my nut sack, I could feel my stomach tightening.

"Say, if you ain't tryna swallow this nut, get the fuck up."

Baby girl kept sucking like her life depended on it, so I gave her what she was looking for. My kids blessed the back of her throat, and she held her tongue out to show me the shit was gone.

"'Preciate it."

She turned her nose up. "That's it? 'Preciate it?"

"What else you think you was gon' get?"

"Some dick. Hell.

"Nah, I'm straight. You can see your way out."

Thotiana rolled her eyes and left without saying shit else. Oh, well. You act like a ho, you get treated like a ho.

Sitting in my blacked-out Dodge Hemi, I watched as Dreux smiled in some nigga's face inside of Denny's. My ass felt disrespected as fuck because she knew this was our shit only. She had some fucking nerve to bring this Poindexter-ass bitch here. After that bullshit with her at Lolita's place, I had a tracking device placed in her car. Today I happened to be stalking her social media accounts and saw that she was on a date.

Fuck it. If Dreux was on a date, then I was too.

I dumped my blunt, slid my phone in my pocket, and got out of the car. My mind couldn't figure out why we were headed inside, but my heart already knew what was up. Her back was to the door, making it easy for me to slide into the booth beside her.

Dreux's eyes damn near rolled out of the sockets, and Dexter's Laboratory didn't say shit. That was his best bet. Leaning over, I kissed Dreux on the corner of her mouth and draped my arm over her shoulders.

"Damn, baby boo, you didn't wait on me before you ordered? Lemme get some of yours." I reached over and grabbed a piece of bacon off her plate.

I was smacking on the bacon like my ass hadn't ate in days, while Dreux burned a hole in the side of my face. Picking up the knife and fork, I cut a piece of French toast and put it to her mouth. Dreux's stubborn ass didn't open her mouth, so I delivered her a deadly stare, and she made way for the food.

"Umm, Dreux. Who's this?" Norbit finally found his balls and spoke up.

Extending my hand, I introduced myself. "Kamron, the boyfriend."

"I wasn't speaking to you. Dreux?"

Oh, this nigga had me fucked up.

"Naw, but I was speaking to you, my nigga. You heard what the fuck I said, and if you didn't, I'm sure this will open your ears." I pulled my gun out my waist and set it on the table.

Norbit's eyes widened at the sight of it, and I knew then that he didn't have shit for me. Muthafucka better sit the fuck back and eat them dry-ass pancakes.

"Kamron, outside, now." Dreux was looking at me with eyes the same size as this weak-ass nigga.

I stood up and held my hand out for her, which she ignored. Shrugging, I followed that round ass out the door. She was ready to light into my ass, but I pointed to her car. My ass wasn't with that arguing in public shit, and Dreux knew it.

"What the fuck is wrong with you? How did you even know I was here?"

"It don't matter. What I tell yo' ass at Lolita's? You my bitch until I say you ain't. I'm not with that disrespectful shit."

"I'm not your girlfriend anymore. Did you forget that conversation at Chipotle? You told me to stay away from you, but somehow your ass keeps showing up in my space. If you gon' kill me, do it, my nigga."

I wrapped my hand around her throat, pushing her head into the window. This was the third time Dreux had gotten me out of character like this, so I knew it was best to stay away after today. She dug them claw-ass nails into my wrist, fighting for me to let her go. I squeezed a little tighter before speaking through gritted teeth.

"Don't worry. Yo' ass is living on borrowed time. I want you looking over your shoulder every time you move."

"Ain't nobody fucking scared of you. Either kill me or leave me the hell alone."

I knew she was done when she stopped fighting me, but I wasn't. I wanted to love her, but there was no room left for that. I removed my hand from her neck. Dreux eased out of her car with me following.

"Kam, just stop, okay? It's done." She disappeared back into the restaurant, leaving me to walk back to my truck alone.

"Yeah, okay."

Later that night, I watched Dreux pull up behind Norbit in a quiet neighborhood of decent houses. As I screwed the silencer on my gun, this nigga leaned into Dreux's window. I let them talk since this was going to be his last conversation with her—or anybody else, for that matter. Seeing him lift her chin and kiss her lips like I used to had me hotter than fish grease. Norbit pulled back as my finger squeezed the trigger, and blood splattered over Dreux. She started screaming.

Jogging toward her, I yanked the car door open and pulled her out. “Shut the fuck up. You wasn’t crying when his lips were on yours. Every nigga you try to fuck with will die by your hands involuntarily. Get yo’ ass in the car. We gon’ take a little ride.”

Pulling up to the Inferno, I jumped out of the truck and walked around to the passenger side. I opened the door, and Dreux sat there with her arms folded across her chest. I didn’t know why she thought I gave a fuck about her attitude. It wasn’t going to change a damn thing.

“Dreux, get the fuck out, man.”

“For what? Bro, if you gon’ kill me, what the fuck am I getting out for? Do that shit now. On Ghost, I ain’t going out like no bitch.” The way her neck was rolling had me ready to put my dick down the motherfucker.

“I ain’t gon’ say that shit again. Let’s go.”

Huffing and puffing, Dreux hopped out of the truck, slamming the door, and I damn near slammed her head behind it. She stopped at the door and waited for me to open it. I pushed her inside, making her stumble.

“Muthafucka, if I woulda fell, I was gon’ beat yo’ ass. Stop fucking playing wit’ me.”

“Sit the fuck down and shut up.”

When she sat down, I pulled the gun from my waistband and placed it on the table. Knowing the kind of female Dreux was, this conversation wasn’t going to go well. My mind was ready to blow her shit back, but my dumb-ass heart said wait. Staring at her beautiful ass I wondered, if she said the wrong thing, how the fuck could I bring myself to kill her?

“Are we gon’ play who blinks first, or are you gon’ do whatever it is that you brought me here for?”

Still, I stared. I fucking loved this girl.

“Choppa!”

“Damn, chill. I hear you. I’m tryna keep myself from splitting yo’ shit before I hear what you gotta say.”

She rolled her eyes like always. "I didn't have shit to do with you getting shot. I keep telling you that."

"And I don't fucking believe you. How was you conveniently at the same place at the same time? You think I believe you was really kidnapped? You was talking to that nigga for weeks."

Her eyes widened before turning into slits.

"Yeah, you didn't think I fucking knew that, did you? So, you still trying to play me like I'm some ho-ass nigga? Nah, you got me fucked up. You better start talking. Quick."

"Kam, I've never seen you with him. How the hell would I know what he was planning?"

"You still ain't explaining how you ended up at the shop." I picked the gun up from the table and chambered a bullet.

"I was meeting him there to break things off with him. I swear."

"Some shit ain't adding up, so let me help you remember."

I placed the Magnum to her head, and her eyes grew big as saucers before I felt cold steel on the back of mine.

"That ain't what you wanna do, young blood."

Chapter Thirty-six

Drew "Ghost" McCoy

"Daddy?"

Hearing my baby girl's voice brought tears to my eyes. Almost six months with no contact, and I was filled with emotion.

"How are you here? We buried you."

Choppa stood by with a stunned look on his face while Baby Dreux shot off question after question.

"We'll talk later. Right now, I need to speak with Choppa. Go home, but don't tell anybody I'm back yet. In due time."

I handed my keys off to let Dreux leave because it was time for me to have a man-to-man talk with Choppa. What they didn't know was that I'd been following them for the past two months. I'd seen the way he had been moving regarding my daughter and my empire. My ass was genuinely impressed with the way business was thriving, but the treatment of my junie was in question.

"We can do this here, or we can take it elsewhere. Either way, this conversation is well overdue." I jumped right into it.

"With all due respect, how the hell are you even standing here talking to me? You was shot the fuck up. There's no way you should have made it."

"That will be addressed with my family later. Sit down."

Before I fell off the grid, shit between Choppa and Dreux was rocky, but not enough for him to want to kill her. Even after she lit his trap up, he was still all about Dreux. They reminded me a lot of Lo and myself when we were younger, so to see them like this had me disappointed.

"Wassup, Pops? Go ahead and get it off your chest." Choppa cut right to the chase.

"Aye, put some respect on my shit. I'm the same muthafucka you met eleven years ago. Now, why the fuck you have a gun to my baby's head? When I said take care of her, that ain't what I meant." Yeah, Choppa was *like* my son, but Dreux was my daughter, so she came first.

"On some real shit, ya daughter is flaw as fuck. I let her slide when she shot up my trap, but setting me up? Nah, that ain't some shit I can just let go. My ass could be standing here dead cuz of Dreux."

"Standing here dead? Boy, what the hell kinda sense that make? You know for a fact that she set you up?" I knew my baby girl, and that shit wasn't in her. I made thoroughbreds only.

Choppa blew out a heavy breath, and I knew then that he didn't know shit. Whatever it was had happened during my downtime, so unless he told me, my ass didn't know shit either.

"Long story, she was fucking with a nigga that was supposed to be my right hand. I kept her from around my people, so I knew that she didn't know. That part I'm not holding against her. After I broke Dreux's back in—"

I cut my eyes at him.

"My bad. Anyway, I run down to his barbershop, and before I can get inside, I see her getting pulled into the same van that was sending shots at me. If that ain't a setup, I don't know what is."

Nothing about this situation made sense to me. Choppa was too damn smart to be so fucking dumb. Li'l nigga didn't even know he was standing in his own way of happiness. His ass was too stubborn to sit down and listen. Instead, he was running around here, pulling guns and wilding out. Choppa was so much like me when I was younger.

"Let me tell you something. It may look suspect, but you need to sit down and talk that shit out. You love her. I see it. I get it. What I'm not getting is why it's so hard for you to hear Dreux out. You're too stubborn for your own good, Chop." I spoke with much sincerity.

"I do love her, and that's the reason she's still breathing. Every time I get close enough to knock her off, my ass freezes."

"Go get your girl. That's all I can advise you to do. Think before you react, son. Come on so you can take me past my hotel room. I need to shower before going to see Lo." I reached out to dap him up, and we left.

As we rode back to the hotel, I sat in silence, reflecting on the last few months. It was a miracle that I was still alive. I'd never been a nigga that was scared to die, but better believe my ass was thanking God that He wasn't ready for me yet.

We pulled up to the hotel.

"All right, youngblood, I'ma run up and shower real quick. Shouldn't take me too long because I'm ready to get back to my wife."

Nodding his head, Choppa let me know that he was cool chilling in the car while I handled my business.

Thirty minutes later, I jogged to the car in a pair of sweatpants and a white T-shirt. My old ass felt weird as fuck dressed down, but all that was about to change. Tonight, I was getting back to my woman and the life I left behind.

Chapter Thirty-seven

Lolita

"Yeah, call Tiba and let her know we moving in tonight. Y'all come by my house. We gon' take Ghost's old dump."

"Chris said don't have me out fucking around all night." Sommer started laughing because she knew how Chris and I argued.

"Tell Chris this is our going away party, so don't start no shit, won't be no shit."

"Y'all make me sick. Anyway, let me call her and grab my bag. I'll be there."

After we hung up, I jogged down to the basement to get shit popping. I placed my hand on the touchpad, and the steel door opened. My eyes lit up because Big Drew didn't play when it came to his guns. His custom Desert Eagles, Ghost and Lo, hung in a case at the back of the room. Those babies were coming to the party tonight. Grabbing the noisemakers, I loaded the AR-15s in the black duffle bag. Sommer and Tiba could choose their shit when they showed up. I took the bag upstairs, leaving it by the cellar door, and went to make a small lunch for Tiba's hungry ass. Shit, I needed to call and make sure her nigga was feeding my girl.

"Damn, bitch! Drew was giving it up like this?" Sommer's eyes lit up in fascination with my husband's gun collection.

I brought her to the cellar to pick a gun or two while Tiba stuffed her face. Li'l bitch barely made it in the door without asking if I cooked.

"Girl. That man and his guns. Grab whatever you want."

"Ho, you wrong as fuck for these sandwiches with the crust cut off. Who you thought was coming over here? Susie homemaker?" This bitch came down the stairs talking shit like always.

"Atiba, you was up there with a fully stocked refrigerator. Yo' ass could have made anything in there. Matter fact, call yo' husband so I can ask him if he been feeding you."

"Hell, I can answer that. The muthafucka don't feed me shit but dick. If I don't cook, I don't eat."

I started laughing because for Ike to be a well-known chef, when he was off the clock, his ass didn't touch shit in the kitchen. Glancing around the gun room, Tiba's eyes landed on the Glock 19, and I knew then my girl was ready to make bodies drop.

After I cooked a small breakfast for my hitters, they left to tend to their men, and I went upstairs to catch a nap. A while later, stepping into my closet, I pulled out an all-black ensemble which consisted of tights, a hoodie, and my signature Timberlands. Adrenaline was surging through my body as I got dressed. My girls and I had been waiting on this shit like food stamps on the fifteenth.

"Siri, call Sommer Rain." I waited for the phone to pick up.

"Ooooh, shaaat! Yesss!"

"Hello? Helloooo! Sommer!" I know this nasty bitch didn't answer the phone while she was getting her ass dug out.

"Wait wait wait, Chris. Hold on. Shit! Hello?"

"Bitch, don't nobody wanna hear that shit. Don't bring yo' ass over here smelling like budussi."

"Girl, fuck you. I'll be over there as soon as I put his ass to sleep." Pulling the phone from my ear, I realized this disrespectful bitch hung up on me.

I shot Tiba a text, letting her know to be at the house by seven. I'd be damned if my ass listened to another muthafucka getting her shit blown out too. I checked in on my babies. Ahdia was chilling at the house, and Dreux was on a date. Knowing that they were squared away, I turned my motherly instincts off and got into savage mode.

"Okay, bitches, no bullshit. We going in guns blazing, hitting everything moving, and getting the fuck out. Tiba, toss that gahdamn grenade, and we on to the next." I pointed at Tiba 'cause this bitch was known for doing some extra shit.

"Listen. I got this. You just get ready to A-Town stomp these muthafuckin' doors in, big foot bitch." Sommer started laughing like Tiba had said the funniest shit in the world.

"Ha ha ha, Kevin Hart–ass ho. Let's go."

We loaded up in Ghost's hooptie and rode out. The drive was filled with us reminiscing on the shit we used to get into before meeting our husbands. Tiba brought up the time when Sommer hit two brothers in the same week. When Twan ran into her and Dre at Oasis, the look on her face was priceless. Later that night, we ran into Twan's crib and cleared that bitch out while Som took care of his brother. That was her last lick before Chris came through and changed her life.

The car was filled with silence as we approached the house on Birdsong. I looked in the back seat to see Tiba chambering her twin Glocks. Sommer had the Sig Sauer locked and loaded, so I parked across the street and grabbed Ghost and Lo.

"Y'all hoes ready?"

"Hell yeah." they replied at the same time.

"All right, let's do this shit."

Tiba screwed a silencer on her gun, and in less than fifteen seconds, she cleared out the niggas hanging in the front yard. Pulling our masks down, we jumped out of the car and hauled ass to the front door. Raising my foot, I kicked the door down.

Boom!

Wasting no time, I sent a dome shot to the muthafucka getting head on the couch. Niggas came running from the back of the house, and I lit their asses up like the Fourth of July.

"Sommer, make sure it ain't nobody left in this bitch. Tiba, cover her ass." I threw out orders while covering the front.

Once they came back with an all clear, we jetted out the front door, and Tiba let off the grenade. As soon as we pulled off, the trap was up in flames. One down, three to go. We hit trap after trap, and my old-ass knees were starting to feel the burn from kicking doors down like G.I. Jane.

We'd finally made it to the main trap, and I knew this one was going to be a problem. Unlike the ones before, this house had a slew of niggas hanging around outside. There was no way we could roll up like the jump out boys without getting laid down in the process.

"Tiba, pull the big bodies out the bag. We finna make some noise around this bitch. Sommer, grab one. It's showtime." All the waiting we did for this moment right now was going to be worth it.

Parking a few houses down, we jumped out of the car and did a quick scan of the area. The best part of living in Texas is the trees and bushes that are everywhere.

"All right, so look. We need to cross the street and cut through the trees. We gon' have to light their asses up from the bushes. Ain't no way we can run directly up on them. Y'all ready?"

"Bitch, we too old for this shit. Come on. Hell." Tiba and her funky-ass attitude was gon' get our shit blew back.

We shuffled coolly across the street and crept low through the rubble of tree limbs and leaves. Once we were in front of the trap, I unscrewed the silencers on my guns. They might not see me, but they were going to hear and feel my ass tonight.

"Aye, take them silencers off. It's a party tonight." I watched as Tiba and Sommer began untwisting the tips.

"All right, let's get it popping."

We sat back for a minute, scoping the scene out, and when I locked eyes with Sommer, she nodded her head.

Tat-tat tat-tat-tat! Tat-tat tat-tat-tat!

"Bodies start to drop, hit the flo'." Tiba's goofy ass started singing Drake's song, "Nonstop."

"Come on. Shit! The muthafuckas inside should be on the way out. Hit any and everything moving." I stood up, climbed through the bushes, and took off. My old ass was going to feel this in the morning.

Like I suspected, niggas came running out the front door. With no hesitation, I let Ghost and Lo sing my favorite song.

Pew! Pew! Pew!

Sommer and Tiba were beside me, making those things clap the only way that they knew how. Tiba took the lead and entered the house, and we were close behind. Lord knows I was thankful that the door was open. My knees couldn't take having to kick down another one.

Pop!

"Fuckkkkk! Tiba!"

Her body hit the floor, and Sommer lit up the nigga who let off the shot. As she took off through the house, killing any nigga that was left, I dropped to the floor to check on Tiba. There was no blood in sight, making me shake my head at her dramatic ass.

"Bitch, get the fuck up. You got hit in the vest. Hell."

"Oh. Okay, and? That shit still knocked the wind outta me." She pulled herself off the floor.

"What you say outside? Bodies start to drop, hit the flo'." I started doing the Milly Rock.

"You's a dumb-ass bitch. That shit ain't funny."

"While y'all out here kicking it, we need to go. I cleared out the house." Sommer came from the back with her piece by her side.

As we made our way outside, Tiba grabbed the last grenade from her pocket and pulled the pin. When she tossed it inside the house, I saw a figure coming around the back. He raised his gun and let off a shot before I sent a bullet through his head.

"Sommerrrrr! Nooooo!" My knees hit the ground as I pulled her body into my lap.

How the fuck was I going to explain this to Chris?

"Family of Sommer Watts?" the doctor called out.

It had been two hours since we made it to the hospital after the shooting. On the way, I made the dreadful call to Chris, and his painful sobs tore my heart to shreds. Seemed like just yesterday that they were comforting me through the death of Drew.

Chris stepped forward. "I'm her husband."

"The bullet that pierced Mrs. Watts in the back is dangerously close to her spine. If we leave it in, we run the risk of paralysis. However, if we operate, we run that same risk. At this point, it's up to you, Mr. Watts."

Chris dragged his hand down his face and took a deep breath. "Do it. Do the surgery, Doc."

After the doctor agreed, I stood and pulled Chris into a hug. When he pushed me off, I knew it was about to get ugly.

"This is all your fucking fault. If you didn't want one last gahdamn hoorah, my wife wouldn't be laid up in this shit with the possibility of being paralyzed. I fucking knew better, but I let you talk me into this dumb-ass shit."

"Aye, now hold on. We all knew the possibilities when we agreed to this. This shit ain't just on Lo. We all grown, and we all said yes, so you need to calm the fuck down, Chris." Tiba jumped to my defense, and even though I was thankful, it didn't stop the guilt that was building inside of me.

"Thanks, Tib, but I'm gonna go. It's clear that I'm not wanted here. Just let me know how Sommer is when she wakes up. Chris, I'm sorry you feel that way, but it's still love on my end, and I'm praying for my girl."

Without waiting for a response, I left the hospital. Tears spilled from my eyes as I drove through the streets of Dallas. I cried for my dead husband and my lifelong friend. Heartache was real in my life nowadays.

Once in my driveway, I killed the engine and made my way inside. Upon entering my bedroom, I saw a figure sitting on the bed. I pulled my piece from my waistband and turned on the light.

"Drew?"

"It's me, baby."

I was paralyzed by the presence of his voice. For months, this home was drained of the love we created in these walls, and with just three words, Drew refilled it. His steps were heavy as they made their way to me. Drew's eyes bore into mine, and I couldn't break his gaze even if I wanted to.

My husband wrapped my body into his, and my dam broke. All this time, I'd been holding it together, but in this moment, I couldn't. My body shook as the tears cascaded down my face so rapidly, I couldn't catch them if I tried.

After standing in his arms, bawling for what felt like forever, I finally reared my head back to take him in. He looked the same. Shit, he even smelled the same. My eyes trailed from his broad chest up to those brown eyes he blessed our baby girl with. I gripped the sides of his shirt and just stared.

"Drew."

"I'm here." He stroked my cheek so softly.

"How?"

"We'll talk. I just wanna love on you tonight."

"Please do." I grabbed his hand and led us to the bathroom.

I adjusted the water to the perfect temperature, and as I stripped out of my clothes, Drew sat on the toilet with his bottom lip tucked between his teeth. Damn, this man was just as fine as the day I met him, maybe even finer. I placed one leg in the shower and then turned to look at my man.

"Come on."

His clothes came flying off as he joined me. I stood under the shower, letting the water run down my body, when I felt Drew's lips on my neck and arms around my waist. As he licked and sucked, his hands found their way to my ass and squeezed.

"Babyyyy." A breathy moan escaped my lips as Drew lifted me against the wall and my legs wrapped around his neck.

With my ass resting in his hands, he blew on my clit, and it came peeking out. Drew grabbed it between his teeth while gliding his tongue up, down, and in circles. My hands gripped onto the back of his head for support because baby, Mr. McCoy didn't need any guidance.

"Mmm, gahdamn, I missed this shit." He moaned into my sweet spot. "You been giving my pussy away, Lo?"

"Oooh no, baby. Oh, shiiit, Drew. Suck this pussy." And boy, did he! Drew ate my cat like it was the last supper.

My orgasm was building, and as soon as I reached my peak, he slammed me down on his dick. My fucking legs trembled as I came undone. Drew put my feet on the ground, and I was shaking like Bambi. He turned me around, pushing my back down, and slid back inside.

"Throw that shit back, baby. Gahdamn!"

With my hands resting on the shower bench, I gave him exactly what he asked for. Drew massaged my nub as I made my ass clap on the dick. Good lord, I missed this shit.

After thirty minutes of my man putting the pound game to me, we finally washed up and climbed in the bed, asshole naked. I threw my leg over his body and caressed the hairs on his chest. His hands were in my hair, massaging my scalp, and before I knew it, sleep overcame me.

Chapter Thirty-eight

Dash

Touching down on American soil, I looked over at Ahdia, who was knocked out, and smiled. This little vacation we took was critical to the status of our relationship. We were finally on the same page, but even if we weren't, there was no way I would let her get away. This beautiful being had slowly become my whole heart, and I wasn't trying to live without that.

Reaching over, I stroked her cheek, and she slowly came to. Ahdia stretched, letting out the sexiest moan that sent a blood rush straight to my groin. As much as I wanted to bear her back in, business needed to be handled first.

"Baby, come on. It's time to get off the plane."

"Mmm, already? Did I really sleep the whole way?" Dia stood up with her ass eating her shorts.

Pulling her shorts out her butt, I slapped that fatty then grabbed her hand. "Yeah, you did. Now, let's go so I can get you home."

As we stepped off the plane, the four-day vacation I was coming from slowly slipped to the back of my mind, and murder replaced it. This wasn't necessarily my beef, but anything that fucked with Chop was my problem too.

Cruising the streets with the windows down, I tucked my hand between Ahdia's thighs and admired her beauty.

She bobbed her head to Li'l Wayne's *Carter V* album as she stared out the window.

"What's on your mind, beautiful?"

She looked over at me and smiled. "Nothing, really. Just about the trip. Despite our little spat, we had a good-ass time, and now you have to leave me."

"It's business, baby, and it's only for a few hours tonight. I got the rest of my life to devote to you." I lifted her hand and kissed it.

Ahdia blushed, showing all thirty-two teeth with that beautiful smile I'd fallen for.

Intergalactical love. The sky is fallin', fallin' down,
but I'll be waiting for you,
for you, for you on the dark side of the moon.

The way my baby vibed to "Dark Side of the Moon" had me feeling like she'd follow my ass anywhere. I hoped so, because once this shit was over, I planned on locking her beautiful ass down legally.

When we pulled up to the house, I noticed the way Ahdia's shoulders dropped. That shit had me ready to say fuck this mission. Gripping her chin, I turned her face to me before placing light kisses on those plush-ass lips.

"Talk to me, sweets. What's up?"

"I want some dick, and you finna leeeave." Her pout was so serious it drew a hearty-ass laugh from the pit of my stomach.

"I know damn well that ain't why you got an attitude. It's daylight. I ain't shaking shit till later. Come on, so daddy can tune you up."

Ahdia started digging around in her purse, and once she found her keys, she took off toward the front door. Shaking my head, I turned the car off and followed behind her. By the time my black ass made it in the house, this crazy-ass girl was laid out on the couch, playing in my good stuff. I wasted no time slapping her hand away and digging into her sugar bowl.

After sliding my pointer finger up and down her slit, I lifted it to her mouth. “Suck it.”

Ahdia wrapped her tongue around my finger as mine wrapped around her clit. The warmth of her mouth had my dick hard as fuck. I ran my tongue from her nub to the opening of her wet-ass pussy for a drink of the freshest water I’d ever tasted. Fiji doesn’t have shit on my baby.

“Oooh, shit! Mmm,” Ahdia moaned, enticing me even more.

“Put your ankles by your ears and keep ’em there. If they fall, that’s your ass. Literally.”

As she grabbed her ankles, I pulled my finger from her mouth and slid it into her round ass. One of Ahdia’s legs started to fall, but when I looked up at her, she caught it. Baby wasn’t about that ass play yet. Slurping my way back up to her clit, I finger-fucked her asshole until Ahdia’s juices rained down on me.

“Baeeee.” As she ran her fingers over my waves, Ahdia cried out to me.

Pulling myself away from her sweet-ass pussy, I inched my way up to look into those beautiful grey eyes. I stuck my tongue out, and Dia’s freaky ass licked it from the middle to the tip before sucking it into her mouth. As we kissed and sucked on each other’s lips, my dick stabbed her clit, and that pussy got wetter.

I pulled back, and lust was written all over Ahdia’s face.

“Put it in.” She snaked her arm between our bodies and reintroduced me to the softest place on earth.

“Fuuuuckk!”

“Shiiiiit!”

We moaned simultaneously from the feel of her walls around my piece. As I slow-stroked her pussy, Ahdia’s eyes rolled to the back of her head. Looking down at the connection between us, I saw shorty was creaming down my dick.

"Shit, ma, this pussy is the fucking truth."

Her legs wrapped tighter around my waist, and my hand went to her throat, squeezing as my pace increased. Ahdia's body began to shake as I pounded her pussy into her back. I was doing my best to hold on to my nut, but as soon as she came, my ass was right behind her.

"Ohhh, fuck!" I groaned and laid my forehead on Ahdia's.

"Wheeeew, shit! That was the best eight minutes of my life, baby."

I pulled out and muffed her in the head because she had me fucked up.

"Girl, don't play wit' me. That was eleven minutes of long dick. Now, get up and come shower with me."

After we showered, I stared at Ahdia as she rested peacefully beside me. I placed my hand on her small protruding belly and sighed. When my hand touched her stomach, Ahdia flinched.

"You good, mama?"

"No. It's been heavy on my mind, and I don't wanna have this baby. For days, my mind has been battling with my heart. So, for the sake of my peace, I'm going through with the abortion."

Damn. I wasn't expecting that.

"Whatever you want to do, baby. I'm here for anything you need." I kissed the back of her head, and shortly after, I heard light snores.

Around two a.m., I eased out of bed once my baby was asleep. I stepped in the closet and exchanged my balling shorts for some black track pants and a matching hoodie. I grabbed my keys, wallet, and Tech Nine before kissing Dia, and jogged out the door.

I jumped in my Dodge Ram and pulled out of the driveway while dialing Choppa.

"Yerrrr." This nigga here.

"Man, how many times I gotta tell yo' dumb ass you ain't from New York? Quit yo' shit." I replied, shaking my head.

"Fuck you, nigga. What's yo' twenty?"

"Just left the crib, headed to the spot. You there?"

"Not yet. I'm handling something, but I'm right behind you."

"One hunnid." I disconnected the call and hit shuffle in the music app.

Welcome to the mind of a maniac, street nigga, street nigga.

When Boosie started blaring through the car, I caught the vibe. It was time to show Trell why my brother and I were *unfuckwit'able*. There was not a nigga that had ran down on us and lived to tell about it.

I pulled up to the Inferno, and Choppa was pulling in behind me. We got out and dapped up.

"You ready to handle this shit?"

Choppa hit the Birdman hand rub. "Hell yeah. The only way I know how."

"Aww, shit. Why you can't just shoot the muthafucka like normal people, dawg?"

"'Cause, bitch, my name is Choppa for a reason."

Not bothering to respond to his ass, I followed as he entered the warehouse. The first thing I saw was Trell hanging from the cuffs on the ceiling, knocked clean the fuck out. A sinister smile was plastered on Choppa's face, and I knew his ass was about to have a field day. He walked over to Trell's body and slapped him like the bitch he was.

"Aht aht! Wake that ass up. Nap time is over."

The look on playboy's face was priceless, and I couldn't help but laugh. Grabbing a chair from the table, Choppa sat in front of Trell, and I followed suit. Chop pulled out a blunt and sparked it up. We sat silently passing the blunt back and forth, and his eyes never left Trell's. I could feel the heat radiating from my brother's body, so I knew it wouldn't be too much longer before he snapped.

"You bitches gon' stare, or y'all gon' make sum' shake?" Trell started talking shit like he wasn't right seconds from being maggot food.

Choppa let out a low chuckle that low-key shook the fuck outta me. He stood in front of Trell and blew smoke in his face. Before we knew it, a glob of saliva came flying from Trell's mouth, hitting Choppa's forehead. That was the most disrespectful shit I'd ever seen, but before my ass could do anything, Chop was raining blows on him.

"Bitch-ass nigga, you musta forgot who the fuck I was." For every word Choppa spoke, he delivered a punch. "That's ight. You caught me slipping, and that's cool, but I got something better for yo' ass."

Aww, fuck.

"You know you done fucked up, right?" I said that shit like Bill Duke from *Menace II Society*.

"Fuck you, bitch. You ain't shit but a follow-the-leader-ass nigga anyway."

"Yep, and I'ma follow up wit' these bullets to yo' dome." My ass hit the Kayne shrug.

Choppa came from the back with a long-ass sword and a switchblade. Scooting my chair back, I kicked my legs up on the table to prepare for the show. He set the switchblade on the table, then pulled some alcohol and a Bic grill lighter from his pocket.

As Choppa walked over to Trell, his face read nothing. There was no hatred, no anger, nothing, and Trell wore the same expression. Choppa began to slice deep cuts into Trell's skin, and I watched as Trell gritted his teeth, but he refused to break. I guess he called himself trying to die a G. Shit, I don't know.

"Whistle while you work. Aye, bro, slide me that alcohol."

I shook my head at this nigga. I didn't understand why he couldn't just shoot like regular niggas. "Don't ask me for shit else unless it's to dead this bitch."

"Ahh, shut the fuck up and enjoy this shit 'cause I know I am." The way Choppa was grinning had me ready to tell his mama to get him evaluated. Nobody should get this fucking excited over torturing someone.

Choppa started dousing Trell with the alcohol, and he finally broke. Homie was flopping around like a fish out of water.

"Arghhhh, fuck, my nigga, just kill me."

"Say please." Choppa taunted Trell in the calmest tone I'd ever heard him use when offing somebody.

"Fuck you!"

"Nah. I'll pass on the faggot-ass shit. I got something better for you, though."

Choppa swung that big-ass Katana sword and took Trell's arm clean off his shoulder. Blood was sprouting everywhere, and if I was a weak-ass nigga with a weak-ass stomach, that shit would have fucked me up. Trell looked down at his shit on the ground and passed smooth out.

Dropping the sword and picking up the switchblade, Choppa started carving the letter "C" into this nigga's cheek. "Aht aht! Wake up, li'l nigga. You're about to miss my grand finale."

Trell's eyes popped open as blood ran down his face. Choppa started doing that dumb-ass whistling shit again, and I shook my head. This mufucka was too excited for me.

"Man, bring yo' ass on so I can get back to my woman."

"Quit acting like a bitch. I'm at the end of my show," he said.

About fucking time.

He did that dumb-ass Birdman hand rub like always before he picked up the grill lighter. Walking toward Trell again, Choppa made the lighter flicker near his foot. Trell attempted to snatch it back, but the flame caught his pants leg.

"Up, gotta be quicker than that. Now look what you've done. I planned to torture you a little longer, but looks like you've set yourself ablaze." Choppa took the lighter and set his other leg on fire.

Trell started screaming, crying, and begging for somebody to put the flame out. I grabbed my gun from my waist and pointed it at his head.

"Who's the bitch now?" With one single shot, I ended the bullshit.

"Damn, nigga, you always fucking up my shit. If I didn't know any better, I'd think you ran this shit."

"Choppa, shut the fuck up, man. I'll call the clean-up crew, then I'm out. You good?"

"Yeah, I'm straight. I'm headed out right behind you." I dapped my brother up before calling our people. Once that was handled, I jumped back in my truck and made my way to the house.

Chapter Thirty-nine

Ahdia

Every morning, the clock and I met at the same time—four a.m. I rolled over to find Dash sleeping peacefully beside me. Caressing his face, I placed a soft kiss on his lips as my mind began to wander. My hand went instinctively to my stomach, bringing the reality of pain to the forefront. Dash wanted to talk about it, but my mind was already made up. Before this went any further, I needed to get a handle on it.

Gently rolling out of bed, I tiptoed to the kitchen and started a cup of tea in my Keurig. I added a spoonful of honey, lemon, and sugar, then plopped on the couch with my iPad. Opening my Kindle app, I started on a new book since the last series had ended. Reading had slowly become my escape.

Before I knew it, three hours passed by, and I heard footsteps coming down the hall. Dash walked up and wrapped his arms around my neck, placing a kiss on my temple.

"Good morning, beautiful." No matter how many times he'd called me beautiful, I still got butterflies.

"Good morning, baby. I'm surprised you're awake since you got home late."

"I rolled over to hold my wife and she wasn't there. That's enough to awaken any man. You okay?"

Why would he ask that? Now I had to smile and lie to avoid this dreadful talk.

"I'm fine, babe. I had to pee and couldn't go back to sleep, that's all." My ass gave him the fakest smile known to man.

Dash came around and sat beside me. His hands went to my stomach, causing me to cringe. I slid toward the edge of the couch, attempting to run from the conversation that was sure to come.

"Ahdia, we can't keep avoiding this and acting like the baby doesn't exist."

Halting my steps, I turned around and hit Dash with the deadliest look. "Listen, Dashir. I *know* this baby exists. I'm reminded every fucking day when I look in the mirror, so don't. I'll talk about it on my time, not yours." I hated being rude to Dash, but between him and this baby, my emotions were all over the place.

"I'm sorry, babe. This has to be hard as fuck on you, but I don't want you carrying this weight alone. You know I'm here, right?" Dash said.

I climbed into his lap and laid my head on his shoulder. "Yes. I know, and I'm sorry too. I don't mean to take my frustrations out on you. This shit just has me stressed beyond belief."

"I get it, love. Gimme a kiss."

Lifting my lips to his, Dash kissed me so deeply I could have sworn he exchanged his soul for mine. His hands started to crawl up my thighs, and I put a stop to that real quick.

"Nope. Get your little nasty hands off me. I have to meet Mom for breakfast."

He groaned and released me. "Fine."

I hated lying to him, but the thing I loved the most about Dash was that he didn't pry. He always said if I wanted him to know, then I would tell him. With this termination, it wasn't that I didn't want to tell him, it was just something I had to do by myself. Leaving Dash on the couch, I went upstairs and got ready.

As I pulled up to the abortion clinic, women of all colors, shapes, and sizes stood outside the building. They held signs that read things like BABY KILLER and MONSTER. I was already struggling internally, and these bald-headed bitches wasn't making it any easier. Putting my car in park, I stepped out and locked the doors. With my purse clutched tightly to my chest, I briskly walked through the crowd of women. I was a few feet away from the door when a big, burly bitch jumped in my way. My nerves were already going crazy, so my patience for this bullshit was as thin as the hair on my ass.

"Move." It was taking everything in my body to keep me from snapping out on this lady.

"What would Jesus do? He's given you one of his children, and you have the audacity to kill it. How dare you?" She stood in front of me, shouting obscenities, and my blood began to boil.

"Moooove. Get your big, manly ass out of my way, bitch."

"Move me." This woman was really testing me.

Before I could stop myself, I reared back and punched the shit out of her. Blood was spewing everywhere, and as she held her nose, I used that as my chance to run into the building. As soon as I stepped foot inside, the cold air sent chills down my spine. The farther I walked, the heavier my steps became. My heart was beating so hard, and my palms were sweaty.

I made it to the counter, and the receptionist was too damn chipper to be working here. "Welcome to Planned Parenthood. How are you?" I'm pretty positive this bitch ate rainbows and shitted sunshine.

"Ahdia McCoy. I have an appointment for a termination."

"Oh, umm, well, okay. Let's get you checked in."

My revelation must have put a cloud over her sun rays because her smile dropped almost instantly.

"Look, I'm already having a hard enough time with this, so I'd appreciate it if you kept your judgment to yourself. Thanks."

"Yes, ma'am, I apologize. You're checked in, so you can have a seat until they call you back."

Without another word, I grabbed my purse and sat down. A woman that looked to be a few years older than me was seated in the chair beside mine. I scrolled through my social media accounts, trying to keep my mind occupied, when I felt her hand on my knee. I turning in her direction. There was a soft smile on her face.

"You're shaking. You might not feel like it, but it's going to be fine. God is with you regardless. Now, I'm not a Bible beater like those women outside, so don't you go side-eyeing me. I just want you to know that you aren't alone."

I placed my hand on top of hers and squeezed. "Thank you." This lady had no idea how comforting her words were. The internal struggle I'd had these past few weeks was draining, but after she spoke, peace settled over my heart.

"Ahdia McCoy."

I glanced up to see a nurse standing in the door, waiting for me. I checked the time on my phone. Fifteen minutes had passed by without my knowledge because I was so wrapped up in my thoughts. Standing, I adjusted my shirt and followed the nurse to the back. Once again, my palms were dripping wet, and my heart was thumping. I contemplated turning around and running the fuck out of there.

"Step up here. Let's get your height and weight."

In complete silence, I did as the nurse asked. She led me to a cold-ass room, and I was mad as hell for not having a jacket or something. The nurse instructed me to undress from the waist down, handed me a sheet to drape over my legs, and left the room. Once everything was off, I called for the nurse to come back in. She checked my vitals and informed me that there would be an ultrasound done. Immediately, my nerves kicked it up a notch. I'd been dreading this moment since I found out there was a baby growing inside of me. I'd been ignoring the fluttering in my stomach and going on about my day as if nothing was happening. Anything to keep this baby from being real.

"This is going to be a tad bit cold." The nurse lifted my shirt as she squirted the gel on my belly.

I turned my head as she moved the transducer around my stomach. The sounds of the baby's heartbeat filled the room, and my eyes welled with tears. How could something so small and innocent cause so much pain? Why wasn't I strong enough to see this baby come unto life through me? Why?

"Turn it off, please."

The nurse was so busy clicking keys on the machine that she didn't hear me, or her motherfucking ass was ignoring me.

"Turn it off, please!" I yelled louder than intended as the tears fell from my eyes.

"Yes, ma'am, I'm so sorry. I wasn't trying to upset you." She turned the machine off before letting me know that the doctor would be in shortly.

I waited, fiddling my thumbs, until the doctor finally entered the room.

"Hello, I'm Dr. Tusan, and I'll be performing your procedure today." She could have avoided the pleasantries, but apparently, I was raised better than that, so I spoke back.

"Before we start, I wanted to let you know what to expect during and afterward. During the process, you'll experience some pain, tugging, and it will be extremely uncomfortable. The procedure doesn't take very long; however, after we're done, we'll keep you here for a few hours to monitor you. Once you're discharged, over the next few days, you'll have cramping and heavy bleeding, which is normal. If you begin to feel faint or anything outside of the things I've listed, go immediately to the emergency room. Any questions?"

I shook my head. The nurse wheeled in a tray of instruments and a bucket covered with a sheet and a tube attached.

Dr. Tusan pulled the stirrups out, and I stuck my feet inside, letting my knees fall to the side. She grabbed the speculum and placed it inside of my vagina. Next, she picked up a tool, which she explained was called a cannula, from the tray, and attached it to the end of the tube.

"Are you sure you want to do this?"

Once again, with no words, I nodded my head.

She pulled a mask over her mouth and glasses over her eyes before flipping a switch on the machine. It sounded as if someone had turned on a vacuum, and my eyes widened. Without saying a thing, Dr. Tusan inserted the cannula, and sure enough, a sharp pain ripped through me. Despite the pain, nothing hurt worse than seeing bits and pieces of my baby floating in a pool of blood that they tried to cover up.

Tears flooded my face, racing to see which one could hit my chin the fastest. I placed my hand over my mouth to stifle my cries as my body shook violently. I felt horrible, like I was the worst human being to walk this earth. This was the hardest decision I'd ever had to make, but how could I love a being that came from the most horrific thing to ever happen to me? My heart and my mind battled for weeks, and now here I was, hurting and relieved at the same time. What kind of monster was I? I wouldn't wish this kind of pain on my worst enemy. I cried and shook and cried and shook until the procedure was over.

Once she was finished, Dr. Tusan had the nurse move me to a recovery room. While I lay on the bed, still crying, I heard commotion coming from the hallway. I listened closely. The voice I heard belonged to the last person I needed here. Dash.

"Where is she? Huh? Where is my wife?"

"Sir, you can't be back here."

"You think I give a fuck? You can either tell me, or I'll open every fucking door until I find her. Ahdia!"

I was so scared, but at this point, there was nothing left to do but face him. The door opened, and there he stood, with the meanest look. Dash walked slowly inside, and once he noticed the tears on my face, his softened. He stroked my hair and wiped the tears from my eyes.

"Baby." His head dropped. "Why didn't you tell me? I would have been here for you. We could have done this together."

"I had to this for me, Dash, and I need you to understand that." I placed my hand on his cheek and stroked it with my thumb. He nodded his head and kissed my forehead. I was relieved that he didn't put up a fight because I didn't have the energy to go back and forth.

"How long you gotta stay?"

"Two hours for monitoring, but I want to go now. I can do this at home."

"Say less." Dash gently scooped me into his arms and carried me out of the clinic. He sat me down in the passenger seat and gave me a quick kiss.

"I love you, beautiful."

"I love you so much more."

Chapter Forty

Dreux

Mind fucking blown. How the hell my daddy was alive was beyond me. I had so many questions, but they would have to wait until he was ready to explain. As confused as I was, the one thing that kept playing in my mind was Kam holding me at gunpoint. All these months dealing with his bullshit, and he still refused to listen to me. How many fucking times could I say my ass didn't set him up until he believed me? I loved this man with everything in me, and as hard as I tried to act, this situation fucked my ass up.

As I stepped into my house, memories of Kam started flooding my mind. I'd been staying with my mama to avoid this very moment. I closed my eyes, and his boisterous laugh filled the living room. Walking further inside, my hand glided across the couch, and images of back shots to the sounds of "The Love Scene" by Joe were on a mental replay.

Pulling off my shoes, I ran to the bathroom to relieve my heavy bladder. I reached under the sink to grab a roll of tissue and realization was looking back at me. A box of unopened tampons sat in the middle of the cabinet. Fuck! All this bullshit with Kam, Trell, and the kidnapping had me so stressed out that I hadn't noticed how my cycle never came. I finished my business and took my ass to Walmart.

"Shit!"

Staring back at me were two pink-ass lines, confirming my suspicion. Kamron trapped the shit out of me. Tears began to fall down my face, and I was so pissed off because my ass was tired of crying. Shit, crying had become such a daily routine for me that half the time I didn't even know it was happening.

"I gotta get the fuck away from here. This shit is too much."

Jumping from the toilet into the shower, I stood and cried until the water ran cold. Wasting no more time, I bathed and got out. I began pulling clothes from hangers and out of drawers, throwing them into my luggage that was open on the floor. There wasn't a clue in my mind as to where I would end up, so I packed regular shit, swimsuits, heels, sandals, all that shit. By the time I finished, there were two big suitcases, a duffle bag, and my purse. It took me two trips to get everything loaded in the car, then I headed to the airport.

Hooking up my phone to the Bluetooth, I hit play. "Consequences" by Camila Cabello filled the car, and sure enough, the tears came again. Damn, I was tired of being an emotional-ass bitch.

Lovin' you was sunshine, and then it poured,
and I lost so much more than my senses.
Lovin' you had consequences.

Shit. That verse read my whole life. Loving Choppa damn sure came with consequences. Heartbreak, sadness, and pregnancy were only a few of them. I rode and vibed to the music until my ass was finally pulling into the airport.

"Welcome to Delta Airlines. Where to tonight, ma'am?"

"Honestly, as far away from here as possible. What do you have open?"

The attendant began tapping on his keyboard before he read off the options. "Let's see. We have a flight to Dubai, the Dominican, Japan, and Jamaica. All of those leave within the next hour."

Contemplating my options, I decided on the Dominican Republic.

"Okay, great. One last-minute round-trip ticket to the Dominican Republic. That's going to be seven—"

"The price doesn't matter." I slid my personal card across the counter, waited as he finalized all of my flight information, and checked my bags.

"All right, here's your boarding pass, ma'am. Enjoy your trip."

I walked toward the gate, leaving all my problems at the ticket booth. This mini vacation was going to be everything I needed and none of what I didn't. Sitting down, I slid my right AirPod in and zoned out until I heard them call for boarding.

Stepping off of the plane, I shuffled through the crowd of people to get to baggage claim. While I was in the air, I had found a nice resort and made reservations to stay for two weeks.

Once my belongings were gathered, I made my way to the car service that was waiting to take me to the El Carmen Resort. I walked out of the airport, and the weather was warm and welcoming. The climate was a great change from the smoldering Texas heat, and the palm trees were beautiful. I spotted the driver holding the sign with my last name on it. As I strolled toward him, the trunk to the car opened, and he placed my luggage inside.

The ride over to the resort was short and sweet, which I was thankful for because a bitch was tired. The concierge escorted me to my room, where I dropped my bags at the door and took a much-needed nap.

Later that night, my stomach started to growl, bringing me from the deep slumber that I was in. Grabbing my phone, I saw that it was a little past nine o'clock, and I hadn't eaten. Changing out of my jeans, I threw on a pair of Pink leggings, the matching sports bra, and slides. Instead of leaving, I decided to eat at the resort restaurant.

"Welcome to El Carmen. Will it be just you?" The hostess greeted me with a pleasant smile.

"It's just me, and I prefer to sit at the bar."

"Okay, right this way." She led me to the bar, and to my surprise, it was kind of jumping.

I opened the menu and began scanning the contents. The bartender came over and asked for my drink order, and for a brief second, I forgot I was pregnant.

"I'll take a Coke with light ice, please, and can I order ten of your boneless barbecue wings with spicy fries?"

"Sure, coming right up."

I pulled my phone from my bra and scrolled through Facebook. It was the same shit as any other day. Dumbass memes, couples arguing, and the usual bitter bitch who still wanted her baby's daddy. Rolling my eyes, I turned off my location after I posted a status about peace. The bartender brought my food back, and I ate that shit like Ike made Anna Mae eat the cake.

"Whoa, slow down, mama. It ain't going nowhere."

Dropping the wing, I looked up into the eyes of a Boris Kodjoe lookalike.

"Shit! I probably look like a damn fool stuffing my face like this."

"Nah, don't sweat it. I think you look beautiful as fuck. There's nothing more attractive than a woman who can eat."

I lowered my head as my cheeks burned from blushing. Boris Kodjoe lifted my chin and caressed my cheek, causing me to smile. It had been a while since a man had genuinely put a smile on my face.

"What's your name, handsome?"

"Channing. Yours?"

"Dreux. It's a pleasure to meet you. What brings you here?" I was curious to know if he was here alone or with somebody.

"My best friend is getting married in a week, so I'm here for that."

"Interesting. I'm here for the next two weeks, so hopefully we'll run into each other again." Shit, a bitch had her fingers crossed that he would accept how forward I was and not run.

"I'd love that. How about we exchange numbers and agree to meet up tomorrow?"

"Or, how about you meet me down here at ten a.m., and we can find something to get into."

He laughed a little, and I joined him.

"Okay, Dreux, we'll play this your way. I'll be in the lobby at nine forty-five, waiting on you to show at ten. Don't dip on me, either." Channing squeezed my hand, and then he was gone.

Four days later . . .

For the past few days, Channing and I had been kicking it real heavy. He was the perfect distraction from the problems I was having back home, and I appreciated it. The first day we went jet-skiing and had dinner at this cute little café a few miles from the resort. Yesterday, Channing took me kayaking, and when I say this man rocked the boat, I mean it. We ended up in the river upside down with tears in our eyes from laughing so hard. Today, we were set to explore everything the resort had to offer, but I woke up feeling like shit. My head was pounding, and I'd been hugging the toilet like it was my long-lost friend.

You don't hit my line no more, oh ohhh. You don't make it ri—

"Hello?"

"What's up, li'l bit?" Channing's voice came booming through the speaker. Yeah, I broke down and gave him my number.

"Hey, Chan, what's up?"

"Not shit. Just checking to make sure we were still on for today."

"Ugh! I really hate to cancel, but I'm not feeling well at all. Can I have a rain check?" I felt awful for flaking our plans, but there was no way I could go out like this.

"Aww, I'm sorry to hear that. You need me to bring you anything?"

"No, it's okay. I'm gonna lie down and try to sleep it off. If that doesn't work, then I'll definitely give you a call to come nurse me back to health."

"Cool. Don't hesitate, love. I'll talk to you later."

"Bye."

Pulling myself from the toilet bowl, I lay down and read before drifting off to sleep.

***

The moonlight was beautiful as it reflected off the ocean while I strolled down the beach. Since waking up from my mid-day nap, Kamron and this baby had been on my mind something heavy. As unexpected as this pregnancy was, the shock had worn off, and I was excited to bring life into the world.

I laid the blanket out on the sand and sat with my knees tucked under my chin, admiring the night in this beautiful country. Then it happened. I felt him before I could see him. He was here for me. He came for me. I'd run a million miles away, and Kamron ran after. There was only one explanation for it.

Love.

Chapter Forty-one

Ghost

Rolling over, I was greeted by the smell of breakfast being cooked. It felt good waking up to home-cooked meals by my wife instead of the help. I climbed out of the bed and threw on some boxers and a pair of sweatpants. Lolita had been wearing my ass out, talking about she was making up for lost time. Shit, she had me ready to disappear again to get her ass off of me. My balls were so damn empty, I was sure she'd given me an involuntary vasectomy.

I took the stairs two at a time, ready to smash on whatever Lo had sitting on this table. When I stepped into the kitchen, my wife was laid out on the table with some grapes hanging from her mouth. Hell no, she had me fucked up.

"Lo, get yo' ass up. I have no more dick to give you. Shit! Look, my dick won't even get hard. That's how tired he is."

"Ghost, stop playing and give me some." She had the nerve to be pouting, and I didn't give a damn.

"Lolita McCoy, get yo' naked ass off my table so I can eat. You too old to be fucking like this. My dick is broken."

"Ugh!"

I bet she got her ass off that damn table like I said, though. Grabbing a plate from the cabinet, I threw some bacon and shit on it. If Lo couldn't do shit else, she could cook her ass off, and I appreciated it. She was walking around the kitchen, slamming pans and cups in the sink. Her little attitude was cute, but I knew she was only throwing a fit, thinking I would fold on giving her some of this premium beef.

"Aye, bring yo' ass over here. Now."

She kept throwing shit around like she didn't hear what the fuck I said. Putting my fork down, I eased over to where she was standing and yoked her up by the T-shirt.

"When I said come here, that's what the fuck I mean. What the fuck is your problem?"

"I'm horny, and you holding out on me."

"Woman, you've been fucking on me since I came back home. Give me a day to rest. Shit. One damn day. I need to talk to my kids and explain where I've been. We can fuck tomorrow." I released her shirt and cupped her ass.

"Okay, baby. Can I have a kiss?" Lolita looked into my eyes, and hers were filled with lust. She thought she was slick.

I gave her a quick peck and went back to finish my breakfast. Lo fixed her plate and sat beside me. We ate in silence, stealing glances at each other every now and then like we were kids all over again.

Once we finished, my baby cleaned the kitchen while I washed my ass. I contemplated how this would go, considering I hadn't seen Ahdia since I'd been back. The last time I laid eyes on my baby girl, she was borderline dead, and I was dying. The heaviness of that realization had my chest tight as fuck. Seeing my daughter like that was enough to bring the strongest man to his knees.

"Drew, you okay? You've been in here for almost an hour. I'm surprised the water hasn't ran cold yet."

I didn't notice I'd zoned out for that long, and sure enough, the water was fucking freezing.

"Yeah, mama, I'm getting out now."

I grabbed the soap and washed up quick as hell to keep the cold water from shrinking my dick. Stepping into the room, I saw that Lo had my clothes laid out on the bed already. As I dried off, I scanned the room for my phone to call Choppa. Picking it up from the dresser, I dialed his number and put the phone on speaker.

"Yerrr." Choppa answered the phone with that same dumb-ass greeting like he was from New York.

"I was really hoping you would stop doing that shit when I died. That was my request to God as I walked into the light."

"Aye, Ghost, don't play like that, man. I'm answering the phone like that until my ass dies, and that's how I'm greeting God when I get to the pearly gates. What's good, though?"

"I sure hope not. Anyway, get ahold of Dash. I'm holding a family meeting at my house in a few hours. I need to talk to y'all about what happened."

"Yeah, you right about that, since you appeared outta nowhere like yo' name Patrick Swayze or some shit."

"Muhfucka, my name is Ghost, and this ain't no muhfuckin' movie." What the hell didn't his young ass know about that damn movie anyway?

"Yea ight, we'll be there around three so make sure you put your balls up." Choppa hung up in my face, because he knew I was about to talk my shit.

Slipping on my clothes, I sat on the bed with my hands clasped under my chin, my eyes closed, and I prayed. I prayed for guidance and clarity during this meeting. I prayed for the Lord to give me the right words to explain why I stayed away from my family even after I was well, and I prayed for their understanding. The look of disappointment on Dreux's face made me feel like complete shit, so I hoped, if anything, she understood.

***

While I was sitting in Lolita's white room, the doorbell rang. Before I could get up to answer it, Lo was already greeting the first guest. Choppa came through the door, and I stood to dap him up.

"Boy, I know you fucking lying. Get them raggedy-ass Jordans off my white-ass carpet before you be paying to have it cleaned." Lolita came in swatting Choppa with a dish towel.

"Damn, ma. I'm good for it, but I'll take 'em off for you. Shit!"

"Cuss a-damn-gain in my house, and I'm gonna make you eat your teeth." Lo slapped him with the towel again, but I guarantee his ass didn't say shit else.

We made small talk while we waited for Dreux, Ahdia, and Dash to show up. He filled me in on how the business was running since I hadn't stepped back in yet. Even though I'd been watching, I still gave Choppa the respect he deserved for stepping up and keeping things running.

The doorbell rang again, and my heart rate quickened. One of my babies was on the other side of the door. Holding my breath, I stood and waited to see which one would be walking in.

"Hey, Mama, you look cute." My baby girl complimented her mother, and still, I held my breath.

Dash appeared first, and he stopped, causing Ahdia to run into him.

"Dash, what the hell? Walk." She still had that fiery attitude, just like her mama.

Instead of walking in, Dash stepped to the side and allowed her to walk in first. When Ahdia laid eyes on me, tears filled her eyes and mine.

"Daddy." It came out in a whisper, but I heard her.

She ran into my arms, and I released the tears and the breath I was holding. Ahdia squeezed me tight, body shaking from crying, and I returned the love. I lifted her head and wiped the tears from her cheeks. Placing a kiss on her forehead, I held my baby girl to my chest and let my own tears continue to run down my face.

"I thought I'd never see you again. I thou–thought you were—"

"Shh, I'm right here, baby. Nothing, not even death, can separate me from you. Okay?"

Ahdia nodded her head, and I let her go. She stepped back, allowing me to greet Dash, who also looked like he'd seen a ghost.

"Well, damn. I guess you're trying to live up to your name, huh?" He laughed as I dapped him up.

"Sit yo' ass down, and when Dreux gets here, I'll explain."

I sat down on the couch, and Ahdia's overgrown ass sat on my lap, laying her head on my shoulder.

"Baby girl, you too damn big to sit on my lap. Hell."

"Daddyyyy." She pouted, and I gave in.

"Fine."

We sat another thirty minutes, waiting for Dreux to show up, before Lo came in and said she wasn't answering her phone calls. This was my fault, and I knew it. Dreux was me made over, but once she was upset, baby girl was as stubborn as her crazy-ass mama.

"She'll come around, so I'll go ahead and start this little meeting. All of you have questions that you want answers to. Mainly, how the hell I'm sitting here right now."

"Yeah, that would be a great place to start," Choppa said.

"Don't say shit else until I'm done. Anyway, years ago, I ran across a young man that didn't belong in the streets. He was selling to take care of his family and to put himself through medical school. After a few conversations about his situation, I made the decision to make his life easier from that day forward. I footed his tuition and gave him a legal job. We'd never crossed paths again, but I kept up with him from a distance.

"When my ass finally came to, I woke up in a homemade hospital room. I was confused as hell until he came into the room. He explained to me that I'd been in a coma for almost two months, suffering from gunshots to the chest and stomach."

I looked up to see everybody staring at me the same way I had stared at Adrian when I came to.

"Oh, Daddy, I'm so sorry. I feel like this is all my fault. I brought Jabari into our lives, and he almost killed us."

I could only imagine how much guilt Ahdia was carrying around because of this.

"Baby girl, this isn't your fault. You didn't know that he would come back years later on some revenge tip. We're both alive and well. That's all that matters."

She hugged my neck and planted a kiss on my forehead. "I love you, Dad, and I'm glad you're back."

Lolita came in from the kitchen and announced that she cooked lunch for everybody. Choppa's big ass was the first one out of the white room with no question. As we sat around the table eating, Dash finally spoke up.

"Aye, Ghost, you ever thought about putting that doctor on our payroll? I mean, shit, if he's bringing people back from the dead, then we need him."

"Nah, this is Choppa's operation for the time being, so unless he wants me to ask Adrian, I'm not saying anything." I looked over at Choppa, who was still stuffing his face.

"Oh. Well, shit, Chop, what you think?"

He picked up his cup and washed down his food before speaking. "I don't see why not. I mean honestly, since you're back, I'm ready to step down completely. Dash can have my part of the business like he's been doing, and you can have your shit back. I'm done."

"You sure? You've been doing this for a while now."

"Yeah, man, I'm good. I just wanna focus on my legal businesses and getting Dreux back. Everything else is null and void to me."

He spoke so confidently that I had no choice but to believe him. We mulled over it a little while longer before my kids decided that it was time to leave.

Once they were gone, Lo came and sat on my lap, running her hands across my waves. I grabbed her other hand and kissed it.

"I love you, mama."

"I love you too, baby, and I'm so glad you came back to me." She kissed me with everything she had in her body. I palmed the back of her head and deepened the kiss. My piece began to rise, and Lo broke the kiss, hitting me with that cute-ass smirk. She stood up, and I followed.

I guess she was getting some of this wood after all.

Chapter Forty-two

Choppa

It had been five days since anybody had heard from Dreux. Lolita and Ahdia both called me yesterday, wondering if she'd contacted me. Why they thought Dreux would call me was puzzling. Normally, if she was upset, she'd take a day and regroup. This wasn't like her. I took a leap of faith and called her, but my shit went straight to voicemail. After the way I treated her, I was not surprised that she had me blocked.

Leaving my auto body shop, I decided to go by her house. A real talk was well overdue, and I refused to let another day pass. I hit play and let "Victory Lap" by Nipsey Hussle bang through the car. Driving from the city to her house gave me the time I needed to sort out my thoughts. I didn't want to go in there and argue because we would never get anywhere that way.

Forty-five minutes later, I was pulling up to Dreux's house. Her car wasn't in the driveway, so I assumed it was in the garage. I put the car in park and knocked on her door. My ass waited for five minutes before I decided that she was ignoring me. Shifting through her bushes, I found the extra house key she had hidden there. I entered her home, thankful that she had not changed the alarm code. Slowly walking inside, I saw that everything looked just as it had the last time I was there. It was oddly quiet, so Dreux must have been asleep. Walking upstairs, I tiptoed to her bedroom, only to find it empty.

"Shit!"

There were clothes and shoes strewn all over the place, so I knew Dreux hadn't been taken again. A wave of relief washed over me. Stepping farther inside, I started going through her shit to see if there was any indication as to where she might have gone. I flipped through the papers on her dresser, but all of it was work-related. Going into her bathroom, I got the shock of my fucking life. I stepped closer to make sure my eyes weren't deceiving me. Sure enough, there was a positive pregnancy on the sink , so not only was she missing, but my baby was too. Even though I was pissed, a nigga was happy as fuck that those soldiers marched. Picking up the test, I stuck it in my back pocket for safekeeping.

Finding nothing upstairs, I damn near gave up until some shit said to check the mail. I ran down the stairs fast as hell to her mailbox. Sorting through it, I came across her bank statement. This shit had me feeling like a stalker, but I was determined to find my baby. Ripping the envelope open, I scanned the contents until I saw a charge from Delta Airlines. Pulling out my phone, I called my guy to see if he could trace her location while I raced to the airport. I don't know why the fuck I didn't think of that before, but shit, it was all good.

Tech hit me up as soon as I pulled into the airport. "She's in the Dominican. By the time you get there, I'll have a direct location sent to your phone."

"Good looking out. I'm walking in now, so I'll be out of touch for a few hours."

"One hunnid."

She was beauty. Everything about her was even more beautiful tonight than it was the day we first met. The way the wind blew through her hair as the moonlight illuminated her skin made me fall deeper in love with her. Dreux was everything. My entire world rested inside of this woman.

The closer I walked to her, the heavier my steps became. I was coming undone at the thought of being in her presence. Her body shuddered once I was only a few feet away from her. The weather was warm, so I knew that Dreux felt me. After all this time, we were still in sync. She turned around as I stepped up behind her, and knocked my breath clean out my fucking body.

"Kam." My name fell from her lips, so soft and sweet.

I lifted Dreux from the blanket into my arms. She bounced on her toes, waiting for me to pick her up, and I did just that. Her legs instantly wrapped around my waist, and I was home.

"Kam."

I grabbed the back of her head and pressed my lips to hers. For a second, Dreux didn't return my kiss, but I wouldn't let up. I missed this. Shit, I missed her. As she kissed me with the same passion I was giving her, I laid her ass back down in the sand. Fuck that blanket. Pulling back from the kiss, I stared into her eyes, searching for the answer to the question I'd been asking myself for months. She shook her head side to side, and I believed her.

Bringing my head down to hers, Dreux's hands roamed my body as mine did the same to hers. They stopped on her stomach, causing her breath to hitch.

"I told you," I spoke against her lips, and she laughed.

"You trapped me."

"I know."

Lifting her back, I pulled the strings of her bikini top, and her breasts spilled out. Baby girl was stacked, and I appreciated every inch of her. Trailing kisses down to her chest, I sucked her left titty into my mouth and feasted. As my tongue swirled around Dreux's big brown nipple, I rolled her other one in between my fingers. She was gripping the sand like the grains would relieve the pressure that my tongue was giving her. I slipped my hand into her bikini bottoms, and a puddle of water was waiting for me. I dipped my fingers into her ocean. Dreux moaned my name, and I almost busted.

"Kammm, eat it, baby."

She didn't have to say shit else. Slowly, I licked and sucked on every part of her body as she bucked against me. Pulling her shit completely off, I ran my tongue from Dreux's opening to her clit, drinking up the juices flowing from between her thighs.

"Ohhh, fuck!" Her hands went to my head, guiding my mouth where she wanted it. I didn't need any help, but I let Dreux have her way. It didn't take long before she was coming in my mouth and down my chin. I ate her pussy like Thanksgiving dinner, sucking and slurping until I was full.

"Baby, I can't take anymore. Pleaseee!" Her hips were meeting my tongue, thrust for thrust, so I gave it one last lick, and she was done.

Picking her up, I walked us into the ocean until we were up to our waist in water. Holding her in place with one arm, I positioned my piece at her opening, and she slid down slowly.

"Ahhh."

"Ssss."

We moaned simultaneously as our heads fell back. Gripping her ass cheeks, I lifted Dreux up and down, creating a slow rhythm. She caught on, and I held on for the ride. As she drove me, the waves were rocking us back and forth, heightening the feeling of her wrapped around my dick. Everything about this moment felt so right, and there was no way I was leaving this country without her as my wife.

"Kaaaam, fuck me," She moaned in my ear before taking my lobe into her mouth. Her nasty ass knew that was my spot.

Squeezing her ass again, I pulled Dreux down on my piece, planting him as deep in her pussy as he would go. Repeatedly, I slammed her up and down, tapping on her G-spot with every stroke.

"Gahdamn, Dreux, I missed this shit. Fuck me back, baby."

With every wave that crashed against us, Dreux would come down at the same time. Our bodies were rocking with the ocean, and when I hit the bottom of her pussy, we came. That nut was so backed up, her body shook, and my legs damn near gave out.

"Shit! Come on, boo. We going back to your room." I let her down and followed back to her room, where we made love all night.

The next morning, I woke up to a mouthful of hair and smiled. My baby was back in my arms, and I couldn't have been any happier. Three months without her was long enough, so today, I was locking her ass down for life.

Dreux's phone started ringing. I picked it up to see somebody named Channing calling. I nudged her. Her head popped up, and I put the phone in her face.

"Answer it and tell the nigga not to call you no more. Daddy's home." I kissed her before getting up to go take a leak.

While I was using the bathroom, I could hear her explaining to whoever was on the other end of the phone. That shit irritated the fuck out of me, but I let it slide since I did just pop up on her. Washing my hands, I came out of the bathroom, letting Dreux know that I had to run to my room.

Running down the hallway and up to the third floor, I rummaged through the shit I picked up yesterday when I got there. Feeling the black box, I opened it up and admired the seven-carat princess-cut diamond ring. It was all I could find, but it would have to work for now.

Making my way back to Dreux's room, I took a deep breath before entering. She was standing at the window, staring out into the morning. Dropping down to one knee, I called her name.

"Dreux."

She turned around, and her hand instantly went to her mouth.

"Oh my God, Kam. Get up, get up."

I shook my head and nodded for her to come to me. She slowly made her way over to me, and I grabbed her hand.

"Dreux, baby girl, I ain't ever did no shit like this, so bear with me. You are everything to me. I know these past few months have been shaky, and it's partly my fault. Shit, it is my fault, but I don't wanna live there. I want to move past that and spend the rest of my life proving how much my life revolves around you." I placed my hands on her stomach.

"I know we did shit a little backwards with this little one that's growing in here, but I don't give a damn. I'd take a chance on doing this just like this all over again if the end result is always you and me. My heart doesn't beat without you, baby. I don't breathe when you're not around. Nothing in me functions right when we're left. So, do me a solid, my baby. Marry me. Give me a chance to love you the right way, and I swear on Jesus, I won't disappoint you again. Say it, Dreux. Say you'll marry me." I pulled the ring from my pocket and opened the box.

Tears were streaming down her face, but she was still the most beautiful girl in the world to me. I held my breath, waiting for her answer.

"Yes! Yes, baby, I'll marry you."

I scooped her up and kissed my baby with everything inside of me. This was it for me. Dreux was it for me.

"I'm not going back to the States without you as my wife."

"Why wait?"

"Say less, mama. Say less."

Epilogue

Two years later . . .

Kamron

"Roman Kiari Vega, get your little ass down! When you fall, don't come over here looking for me to coddle you." Dreux reprimanded our daughter while waddling around nine months pregnant with our son, Kamden.

"Aye, watch how you talk to my daughter. Her daddy got her."

Dreux rolled her eyes because she already knew how I was coming behind my seed. "You and your daughter make me sick."

"We don't give a fuck either. Gimme some lips."

She leaned over and pressed her juicy-ass lips on me.

Today was Ro's second birthday, and her little ass was driving her mama up the wall. The whole family, plus the kids from her daycare, were gathered in our backyard for the carnival-themed party. There was a Ferris wheel, a carousel, and different games set up everywhere. All of this, and baby girl decided that climbing the tree was a better idea. I don't know who that child belonged to.

After Dreux and I were back on good terms, I'd found out that she was a little over two months pregnant. When I hemmed that ass up in Chipotle, all my soldiers marched in that pussy like the choir on Sunday morning.

I told Dreux that she was gon' carry my seed, and now look. I got her ass twice.

Ghost had returned to his place in the business, and I stepped down, leaving the streets to Dash. My businesses were making money for me, while I enjoyed the fruits of my labor at the crib.

"Babeee, get your daughter. I'm too fucking hot and big to keep pulling her from that damn tree. What two-year-old tree climbs? Yours. Ugh! It's ninety-five degrees, and we live in Texas. I'm not playing with Ro's ass."

"Come here, fat mama. Lemme talk to you."

With her arms folded across her chest and the cutest pout on her lips, Dreux sat down on my lap.

"Daddy needs you to relax before you stress out my son. You know I don't play about my babies, mama, so chill. She's fine. If Ro falls, then it'll be her first life lesson."

Dreux laid her head against my shoulder and let out a deep breath. I caressed her stomach, and her body relaxed.

"Ooooh, shit!"

"Baby, did you just fucking piss on me?" I looked down at the wet spot on her ass and my pants.

"Nooo. My water just broke."

"Today? Right now? Fuck. Okay." I don't know why I was nervous like this was my first kid. Hell, I wasn't this nervous when Ro was born. That was my baby girl, but this was my son, my heir, and it was solely my responsibility to make sure he grew into an upstanding man one day.

Well, here we go.

Dreux

Why me? How in the hell did I let this crazy nigga knock me up a second time? We were doing good with just Ro, and boom, another one. I didn't regret my babies, and I loved my husband, but this was it. He got one of each, and that's all I could do.

The past two years for us had been interesting, to say the least. My two-week vacation to the Dominican turned into a secret marriage and honeymoon with the love of my life. The excitement wore off as soon as we made it home, since I had to face my dad. We sat down for a few hours, with him explaining and me filling him in on the stuff he missed.

Ahdia slipped into a small depression again from the secret abortion she had. The guilt was eating her up, and poor Dash was doing everything he could to pull her from it. Eventually, she got her shit together, and Dash wasted no time dropping a load off in her. Last year, she gave birth to my nephew, Denver. He was the cutest, fattest little boy I'd ever laid eyes on, and we had him spoiled rotten.

"Shiiiiit! I don't remember this shit hurting as bad with Ro. I swear to you, Kamron, that little-ass dick of yours ain't touching me again."

"Yeah, okay, we'll see."

I glared at his dumb ass as we walked to the door.

"Pee, I go with you." Ro was running behind her grandpa with her arms stretched for him to pick her up. He had her just as spoiled as me and Ahdia were.

"Come on, sweets. You can go with Grand P." My dad grabbed Roman and buckled her into the car seat he kept in his car. The guests filed out of the backyard, and we apologized for having to cut the party short. I had a feeling Kamden was going to be a problem. He was already forcing himself to be the center of attention. Of all days, his stubborn ass decided to come on his sister's birthday.

"Kammm, stop talking and get in the damn car. My vagina is throbbing, and you wanna run your mouth.

Shiiiit!" Another contraction rippled through my body, and it felt like this baby was coming.

Kamron finally got his ugly, light-skinned ass in the car, and we were on our way. Contraction after contraction hit me as we headed to the hospital. We were literally ten minutes away when we got stuck in standstill traffic. Fucking Dallas traffic.

"Babyyy, I'm not gonna make it. I feel like I have to push."

"Nahhh, baby, close your pussy up. Hold that li'l nigga in there as long as you can. We right around the corner."

I punched him in the chest for being an asshole. "I can't. Pull this fucking car over and come deliver this fucking baby."

"Ohhhh, fuck! Shit. Okay, baby. Hold on."

He eased over to the shoulder and put the car in park. Jumping out, Kam rushed over to the passenger side and swung the door open. He pushed the seat back and reclined the back.

"Okay, baby, I'ono what the fuck to do, but prop one leg up by the gear shift, and put the other one on the dashboard. Open that fat cat up." He was really pushing my buttons, but I followed his lead.

"Gahdamn, baby! Aww, shit! It's some shit coming out your pussy."

I swear I was married to the dumbest nigga on the planet. "If your ass was in the room when I had Ro instead of roaming the fucking streets, then you wouldn't be so fucking shocked. Get the blankets out of the backseat and put one under my ass, one on the floor, and keep one to wrap Kamden in. I think there's a few Walmart bags back there too."

"Why you gotta bring up old shit, Pooh?"

"Kamron, focus damnit."

He grabbed the blankets from the backseat and did exactly what I told him to. I looked into the mirror and saw my parents pulling over behind us. Thank God. My mama climbed out of the passenger seat and walked over to our car.

"What's wrong? Y'all okay?" she asked.

"Hell naw, we ain't okay, Mama. Dreux finna have the baby on side of the road." Kam was panicking, and the shit was working my nerves.

"Kam, shut the fuck up and come on. Mama, please stay here and make sure I don't kill him."

Lo laughed like I was joking, but little did she or Kam know, I was dead-ass serious. A contraction hit me, so I bore down and pushed.

"What the fuck? Baby, gahdamn! Yo' shit is wide as hell. That's craaaazy."

Ignoring him, I pushed again.

"Aww, I see him, bae. Do that shit again and he gon' be out." Kam was bouncing around, excited as hell, and it brought a smile to my face.

The most painful contraction shot through my body, and I gave it one big-ass push.

"Oh, shit, Mama. What I do?" Kam looked over at Lo.

"Rest his head on your forearms and use your hands to gently pull his body from the birth canal."

Relief came over me, so I knew he was out, but if that wasn't enough, the tears on Kamron's face as he held our baby boy was. He cried when he held Ro, but this was different. He was proud.

"Baby, traffic is starting to move. Grab the Walmart bags so I can push out the afterbirth."

He kissed Kamden on top of his head before handing him to me. I looked down into the eyes of the second most perfect person in the world. After I pushed out the placenta, Kam tied the bag and got back in the car. He leaned over the console and kissed me so deeply.

"I love you so much, mama. Thank you."

"I love you too, baby."

He looked down at Kamden and kissed him again. "You know you're paying to get my car detailed, li'l boy. I'm taking that shit out your college fund."

I slapped his arm and laughed.

As he drove us to the hospital, I could feel the love radiating through the car, and I smiled. Shit, I guess that's what happens when a good girl falls for a boss.

The End